ANDREA,
Princess of Ziv

ANDREA,
Princess of Ziv

Jean Schoenmaker

iUniverse®

ANDREA, PRINCESS OF ZIV

iUniverse books may be ordered through booksellers or by contacting:

iUniverse
1663 Liberty Drive
Bloomington, IN 47403
www.iuniverse.com
1-800-Authors (1-800-288-4677)

ISBN: 978-1-4917-8431-0 (sc)
ISBN: 978-1-4917-8432-7 (e)

Library of Congress Control Number: 2015921119

Print information available on the last page.

iUniverse rev. date: 01/06/2016

DEDICATION PAGE

In Memory of My Late Husband
Jantinus Schoenmaker
1927 – 2013

Thanks to
Marian Nash
for her assistance and encouragement.

"Andrea, Andrea Lyn. Where are you?" a cheerful voice called. Andrea pulled her pink sheet up until her pink sleep-set was hidden. She tugged further until her hair slid under the sheet.

I am in bed. It is a rainy day and I am in bed pouting. Anyone can see that, Andrea thought. There had been no money under her pillow this morning in place of the tooth she had shed just yesterday. Even the tooth was gone.

"I can't see you. I am looking out the window. Come! I have something to show you," the cheerful voice said.

Very carefully Andrea pulled the sheet down. She peeked out with one eye and looked around. She could see no one. Her other eye couldn't see anything either. The room was as empty as her morning cereal bowl had been after her baby brother had knocked it onto the floor. She pulled the sheet over her straight dark hair again.

"Don't do that! Come quickly or else you will miss it," the voice said.

"Miss what?" Andrea said to whoever might be there. She threw off her covers and sat on the edge of the bed. She still could see no one. Snowpink, her beautiful pink-and-white teddy bear, sat on the high chest of drawers as usual. If Snowpink had been able to stand up and walk around, she would have been as big as Andrea when she was a little girl. Snowpink couldn't move or talk, but Snowpink was talking.

"Do hurry! It is such a beautiful sight!" she said.

Andrea raced to the window and looked out. A double rainbow, its colors dancing with life, played across the sky. The air all around Andrea hummed a happy song: Tum-tum-tiddley-tee. Tee-tee-tiddley-tum. "It is beautiful! It is special! But why?" she said.

"It is yours. Everyone, at least once, sees her or his own special rainbow. Nothing is ever the same again," the teddy bear said.

"You mean my dreams will come true? Can I be a princess?" Andrea said. Her big brown eyes flashed with excitement. She jumped up and down and clapped her hands.

"Yes. But you have to work at it. It isn't easy being a princess," Snowpink said. She still hadn't moved one fuzzy pink hair. She always smiled, and now she was talking, too.

Andrea imagined as a princess she would live in a grand palace and travel in a fast coach. Her silk gowns would be embroidered with pearls. Her golden crown would be set with diamonds and emeralds, and she would wear a ruby ring. She knew, however, there was no way a plain little girl could be a princess. Never! Not ever!

"What you dream is what you shall be. You are a princess, and you have a princessdom," Snowpink said.

"I don't believe it," Andrea said. She sat on the floor and crossed her legs. She swung her bangs back and forth across her forehead.

"Shall I summon your royal coach, My Lady?" Snowpink said.

This Andrea had to see. "Surely! Summon my royal coach!" she said. Andrea looked out the window at the rainbow again. It was fading. If there were any magic in it something had to happen very fast.

The street below had a few mud puddles in it, but no black coach trimmed with gold was coming down the street. No matching white fillies were prancing around the corner either. Andrea would have been surprised to see even one old farm horse.

A red sports car cruised down the street. *Maybe that is my coach. I would like a nice red sports car,* thought Andrea. The sleek car raced down the street hit a puddle and sprayed water all over before rounding the corner.

"See! I knew there wouldn't be any coach," Andrea said. She stuck out her lip.

"Open the window!" Snowpink said.

"What for?" Andrea said. She got up and opened the window. The air smelled damp and fresh after the rain.

Clunk! Rattle! A big car was turning slowly into the street. The rusty fenders shook over the ruts of the road. The hood had no paint, and the horn sounded like a sick frog. The sagging shaking car stopped in front of the house.

"Some coach you got for me," Andrea said. She sat cross-legged on the floor again. Something flew in the open window and started to buzz around the room. She covered her mouth so she wouldn't scream. She hated bees.

She tried to hide in the window curtain and closed her eyes. The buzzing turned into a faint hum then silence. "Is it safe?" Andrea said. She was still wrapped in the curtain.

"Of course, it's safe. You really do have a lot to learn about princessing don't you?" Snowpink said.

Andrea let go of the curtain and opened her eyes. Both hands flew over her mouth, and she closed her eyes again. When she opened them a shimmering conch shell quivered in the middle of the room, and one edge rested on the floor. As she watched it glowed and pulsated. When it grew as large as her dresser, it became still.

"Get in, Your Highness. Your royal coach is ready to take you anywhere," Snowpink said and smiled.

Andrea stared at the creamy-colored conch. Its inner flare was pearly pink shading to a deep pink inside. She climbed in and sat down. "How do I steer?" she said. She looked for a wheel, or handle-bars, or a control panel. She bumped her head on a solid wall of air that had closed behind her. "I want out," she said.

The room around her grew bigger and bigger. *No. I am growing smaller,* thought Andrea. Suddenly she was flying by the curtain and out the window. Her shell-coach flew over the house next door and down the street on the other side. Soon she was buzzing around over the cars at the supermarket. The conch swooped so low she was sure it could crash.

"Higher! Go higher!" Andrea said.

The shell turned and dove upward straight into the gray clouds. Now they were in the sunshine dancing through piles of fluffy white clouds that looked like white cotton candy. Music started playing all around her which sounded like dryads dancing in a waterfall. Soon they were in the sunshine again. Below them the clouds were piled thick like dopples of whipped cream, while puffs of gray clouds drifted over them.

Andrea looked out through the glassy wall. Her conch shell started to slowly circle downward in a spiral. Below them a large building towered over a huge expanse of grass dotted with all kinds of green trees. The walls of the building were covered with huge mirrors set in white panels with gold trim. A garden on the roof swirled in a rainbow of colors.

Her coach dove down past the walls of mirrors and made a three-point landing on the parking lot. It tipped and Andrea put her hand against the wall of air holding her in. She fell into a deep puddle. Muddy water dripped from her sleep set, and the young princess-to-be wiped her tears away with a muddy hand.

"Fine thing! The princess is crying," someone said. It sounded like her teddy bear.

Surely Snowpink is here, Andrea thought. She began to look everywhere. A big white conch shell stood on the far side of the puddle, but Snowpink wasn't in it. The big building looked like an apartment building. *Maybe Snowpink is in there,* she thought.

She climbed a flight of wide stairs to the huge doors at the top. She put her hands on one and pushed. She reached for the handle and pulled, but the doors stayed shut. No one was coming who might want to go into the big building, and no one came out. Andrea was sure Snowpink had to be somewhere playing hide-and-seek. A gleaming brass plaque on the wall beside her caught her eye. On it in bold letters was her name, ANDREA LYN.

Andrea wondered if this were her palace. Snowpink had said there was a princessdom. *Surely a princessdom has a palace,* she thought. She stood directly in front of the big brass door. "I am Princess Andrea. Let me in!" she said. A potted palm threw her through the opening doors and inside a huge foyer.

Curiously carved doors on both sides of the foyer reached from the floor to the ceiling. Lights hung from the mirrored ceiling like crystal teardrops. Andrea got up and pushed on one door, but it didn't budge. "Snowpink, where are you?" Andrea said. A long hall echoed, "Where are you? You? You?"

On looking around she saw an escalator on the other side of the hall. She stepped on the escalator which immediately speeded up. In one Ziv breath she stepped off on the next floor and knocked on the bright red door in front of her.

"Yes," a lively voice said.

"I am Princess Andrea, and I would like to come in," Andrea said most pleasantly.

When the door opened, a giant-sized red salamander was standing in front of her. "I am Zander. Do come in, Your Highness," he said and bowed.

Andrea screamed. She hated lizards and toads. This monster was as long as a yard stick, and his tail was at least half that long.

Beside her another set of moving stairs led to the next floor. Andrea ran up them and knocked on a door that was painted gold. The golden velvet drape on the window beside it was pulled back. Inside two large chipmunks were playing ring-around-a-rosy with eight small chipmunks. It was just like in the nursery school where her brother went. Plunk! They all fell down.

Andrea knocked on the door. "I am Princess Andrea. May I come in?" she said. The nursery school went on as if no one heard.

She took the elevator to the next floor where yellow curtains hung by a yellow door. Through a crack in the curtains, she saw bowls of yellow lilies on the table. Giant yellow dragonflies hovered over the flowers. "Never shall I want to go in there. Never! Not ever!" Andrea said.

Behind the violet curtains on the fourth floor, a mother seal played with her baby. The mother gazed at her pup with eyes that were pools of love. The baby gazed back with eyes full of trust and love.

From up the next flight came the sounds of a party. There a plush cat-like creature holding back an orange curtain grinned through the glass and waved an orange balloon.

The sound of tiny hammers tapping, and busy scissors snipping came from behind a dark-blue door. The princess could hear machines humming, but the curtains were drawn tightly. She could see nothing.

Andrea stepped off the escalator again and walked smack into a very dark door. Beside it pink curtains were pulled back. Butterflies flitted through the room. They danced through the air and rested on pretty flowers. They were too happy to notice a poor little princess.

It was fun seeing the things in each window but Andrea was getting farther and farther up. Down was a long way away. She couldn't run down the up escalator without getting hurt so she hopped onto the steps and went up.

She sat a few moments in front of the next window watching the birds nesting there. Not one of them moved a scarlet feather. A painting of a lone bird hung in the next window. The blue of the bird blended with the sky as the bird flew over a stormy sea.

On the floor above she knocked softly on the green door. "I am Princess Andrea. How do I get out of here?" she said.

A voice chattered. "Climb higher! Climb higher!" the voice said.

As the next stairs moved up, Andrea could hear a dreadful buzzing. She ran right past the crimson door and up the last flight of the escalator. From behind a glass window, sunfish glided through calm sea-green water. *I am trapped,* Andrea thought. Then she noticed three narrow steps that led to a little door. Andrea climbed the steps and timidly opened the door.

Behind the little door were some steep steps. Andrea climbed them to a dark room at the top. "Snowpink, are you here?" she said loudly. Only the walls answered. "Are you here? Here? Here?" they said.

She felt on the wall for a light switch. Her fingers touched a row of flat push buttons. When Andrea got brave enough to push one, beautiful music filled the room.

The young princess pushed a second button. A soft glow grew brighter and brighter in the middle of the room. A girl who looked just like Andrea was standing on a low stool. Another little girl, who looked exactly like the first, stood beside her. In fact a dozen girls were standing on stools in a half-circle each wearing different outfits.

"Who are you?" Andrea said. No one spoke or moved. *They must be life-sized dolls,* Andrea thought.

"I am Princess Andrea, I order you to talk to me!" Andrea said. She stamped her foot and clapped her hands. A switch on the wall clicked. Brightly colored lights played around the room. Very slowly the dolls began to move.

"I am Andrea, Princess of Ziv," a doll said. She was wearing a red-print dress trimmed with lace. A doll in a silver-colored crown strode to the center of the circle. Her yellow princess-styled dress nearly reached the floor. She turned and Andrea noticed a row of pearl buttons down the back of her gown. She looked exactly as Andrea had dreamed of looking even down to the ruby-and-pearl necklace. "I think we should dance. Music!" the doll said just as if she was Princess Andrea.

A polka started playing and a doll wearing purple velvet knickerbockers caught Andrea's hand. "I know you would love to join us," she said. The rhythm of the music started moving Andrea's feet. As they danced a doll whirled past in a light-blue skirt and blouse. Whirling around with her was great fun. Everyone clapped while the doll in a scarlet dress with a tiered skirt danced a Spanish flamenco.

When another melody started to play, a doll in a sailor dress took Andrea's hand. Everyone marched up to the doll with the jeweled crown. One by one they curtsied and danced away. Andrea tried to curtsy, but she lost her balance and fell face forward on the floor. All the dolls stopped dancing looked at Andrea and laughed.

"She calls herself a princess but she can't even make a curtsy," a doll said. She was wearing a dotted orange jumper.

"A princess should have some manners even if she has no good clothes," a doll said who was dressed in gold.

A doll in a green coatdress sniffed. "She probably wouldn't wear them properly anyway," she said.

"She looks rather muddy to me," another doll said and smoothed down her neat navy skirt.

Andrea started to cry. Snowpink had tricked her. She wasn't a princess at all. This was no dream. It was a horrible nightmare. A real princess would never have come to a party in a sleep set streaked with mud.

A doll put her arms around Andrea. "Please don't cry," she said. She lifted the hem of her pretty print dress to wipe away Andrea's tears. The flowers on the skirt smelled like fresh violets.

"We are dancing dolls waiting for our true princess. We are modeling the dresses our princess will wear when she visits the spheres of Ziv," a doll in a pink slacks-suit said.

The music stopped and the lights went out. Andrea went up some steps. She opened a door and stepped out onto a flat roof of the palace. Tired she sat down so she wouldn't fall and shut her eyes because she couldn't see in the dark anyway.

When Andrea woke up it was still dark. She didn't know where she was anymore. A soft quilt had been put over her. The still air smelled fresh. It was slightly damp and carried the heady scent of roses, violets, and lily-of-the-valley.

As the day lightened a bird chirped from somewhere that seemed to be overhead. Another bird's morning call woke up a whole choir of songsters. Andrea sat up to listen. She shivered and pulled the cuddly quilt around her shoulders.

Rosy fingers reached across the deep-blue sky. Streaks of yellow joined them as the sun's golden rays warmed the air around Andrea. Soon she could see the beautiful garden where a fountain was throwing drops of water into the air. They scattered everywhere and sparkled like diamonds on green shrubs and fresh flowers. Andrea clapped her hands in delight.

Immediately everything became absolutely still. Birds stopped singing. Flashy hummingbirds stopped searching for honeysuckle flowers. Bright butterflies lit on twigs and folded their pretty wings while tawny crickets on the castle wall quit chirping their happy song.

"Good morning! Who are you?" a gaily colored bird-of-paradise said.

Andrea thought a minute. Being a princess had not been much fun, so she decided not to be a princess anymore. "I am Miss Nobody from Nowhere," she said.

"I know who she is. She is Andrea Lyn our Princess!" a bird said. "Our Princess!" dozens and dozens of bird voices said together. "Quick! Our welcome song!" said a sunny voice.

Multi-colored budgies flew into position in the bushes in front of her. One in red feathers raised his right wing. They all began to sing.

"Princess, dear Princess,
We hope you will stay.
We are happy to sing
For you each day.
Tum, tum, tiddley-tee.
Tee, tee, tiddley-tum," they sang.

The bird of paradise shook out his red, yellow, and deep-blue plumage. "Welcome, dear Princess. Any wish we can grant is yours," he said.

The humming birds started humming and the crickets started chirping. Bright butterflies flit to pretty flowers. Andrea felt like a real princess. "You are all wonderful!" she said. Glad the blue quilt hid her sleep set she pulled it closer.

"We put it over you last night," a pink budgie said.

"You snore," a bright-blue budgie said.

"That is no proper way to speak to our Princess," a green budgie said and flicked her wing.

"Perhaps your Highness would fancy a tasty treat," said a golden budgie. She plucked a berry by the stem and placed it in Andrea's hand. The happy princess ran to the fountain to wash.

A weary pigeon lit on the wire dome over the garden and dropped a gray feather into the fountain.

"I think there is trouble!" a yellow budgie said.

"Your princessdom needs you! Come this way!" a red budgie said and led Andrea to a very narrow a door.

She slipped through the door and ran down a long flight of stairs. When she came to an escalator again, it was going down. Andrea raced down the first escalator then rounded the corner and ran down the next flight. She was out of breath when she reached the main foyer again.

"This way, Princess!" a boy's voice said. A door of carved oak stood open to her right. From inside a faint whirring reached her ears. Andrea tiptoed over and peeked around the corner into a room that smelled like the office where her daddy worked.

A boy about her own age took her hand and let her into the well-lit room. "I am Donald, Adjutant of the Three Moons of the Land of Fyrh in the Princessdom of Ziv. I am here to help you, Your Highness," he said and placing his right hand over his heart bowed low.

A little taller than Andrea, the boy wore a western shirt, Levis, and boots that shone like copper foil. A silver buckle held his belt. Both were studded with blue lapis lazuli stones. He waved his hand toward the middle of the room. A huge organ sat there waiting just for Andrea.

"It is a computer-organ. I am here to show you--" Donald said.

Andrea didn't let him finish. She ran over and jumped up on the stool. The organ was too big and the stool was too high to reach the pedals, so she pushed the stool away. The young princess stepped on two of the pedals and pressed down hard on four keys.

Colored lights started flashing red and black. The noise of a thousand lions roaring after a million thundering buffalo filled the room. A dark shape circled near the ceiling like a vulture. From its wings and talons dripped dark-red blood.

Bats who were pale as death flew after the drops of blood. Each drop they sucked up turned their veins redder and redder. Soon they became haunting red-black shapes and black veins stood out in their still pale wings. One swooped low at Andrea. She screamed, ducked under the organ stool, and banged her head.

The next thing she knew Donald was bending over her. The orange headband had slipped down on his fiery-red hair and she was dripping wet.

"It took two buckets of ice water to bring you to," he said and helped his princess to her feet.

Andrea looked around the room. The monsters were gone. "I want to do this myself," Andrea said. She wiped her face on the hem of her sleep-set.

"You need to learn how. I am here to help," Donald said. He set Andrea on the stool. Slowly she circled down until her toes touched the pedals. She could barely see the keys which were in a row of colors like a rainbow.

"Now push the key behind the color red," her adjutant said.

Andrea obeyed. A clear note filled the room making everything a soft red.

"Next, push the orange key," Donald said.

A happy note, just a tone higher than the first, sounded. Everything in the room looked as if the sun were shining on it.

"This is fun," Andrea said. She started to smile and pushed another note.

"You are learning the scale. Next you will learn a tune," her adjutant said.

"How will this help the princessdom?" Andrea said. She pushed a note and watched a sky-blue light appear.

"You will see," Donald said quietly and smiled.

Click! Andrea could hear someone coming. She turned away from the computer-organ. A black girl wearing a shiny gold jumpsuit and a green headband came into the room. In her navy tap shoes she danced across the floor. She placed her right hand over her heart and bowed low. Gold hoop earrings swung loosely from her ears. "I am Gabrielle, Adjutant of the Three Globes of the Land of the Folke de Terre in the Princessdom of Ziv. Please come with me, Your Highness," she said.

Andrea's eyes opened wide. "Are you the angel Gabriel?" she said and got off the stool by the computer-organ.

"Hardly, Your Highness. Please call me Gabi," she said. Her tinkley laugh spilled over her bright teeth.

In her bare feet Andrea followed her helper's shoes down a long hall. They stopped in front of an elevator which opened with a wave of Gabi's hand. They got off on floor thirteen and walked down another long hall to a room of mirrors.

The fun of playing the computer-organ had made Andrea forget how mud spattered she was. She stuck out her tongue at her image. "I am not a real princess at all, am I?" she said and with a sigh allowed her shoulders to droop.

"Of course, you are a real princess, Your Highness," Gabi said. She opened a door which revealed colored bubbles dancing over a sunken tub. Andrea could smell lavender-scented bath salts. She raced across the floor and slid into the sunken tub sleep-set and all.

"Your dress, Your Highness," Gabi said and hung a red-print dress on a revolving clothes stand. Andrea began to sing a happy tune. "Tum, tum, tiddley-tee. Tee, tee, tiddley-tum," she sang.

When she was dressed and her hair brushed, Andrea turned in front of every mirror. "Now I look like a princess," she said and clapped her hands.

"Come, Your Highness. You must see your princessdom," Gabi said and led Andrea to a huge sliding door that opened to a dimly lit room.

One wall was a single sheet of glass. Andrea tip-toed over to a silver chair in front of it and very carefully sat on the red velvet seat. She pushed button number one in a panel of buttons inlaid in one arm. A video screen lit up just as a red salamander scampered across a red-tiled courtyard. He climbed into a bright-red conch shell and flew off.

"When may I visit the Red Moon?" Andrea said to Gabi as she pushed another button.

"After you are given your tiara," Gabi said and danced out of the room.

"I am Ming, Adjutant of the Three Orbs of the Land of Eau de Phyn in the Princessdom of Ziv," a voice beside Andrea said.

Jumping up Andrea turned around and saw a smiling girl with almond-shaped eyes standing there. Her violet kimono swished as the girl placed her right hand over her heart and bowed low.

"Your Highness, the tea ceremony is ready in the Green Room," Ming said. Her bright navy slippers slid across the floor as softly as a satin pillow. She led Andrea to a low ebony table in the tea room. Pulling her sea-green sash tight, Ming motioned for Andrea to kneel.

An emerald green teapot sat on the shiny table and a cup with no handle sat in front of Andrea. A large golden dragon wound its way around the pot while a smaller golden dragon wound around the cup.

Ming poured tea into their cups. As the steam rose the tang of unsweetened peppermint wafted through the room. When the tea was cool enough, each girl curled her hands around her cup and held it up.

"To Ziv, the Land of Be Alive," Ming said.

"To Ziv, the Land of Be Alive," Andrea said.

They sipped their tea in silence. When both girls set their cups on the ebony table, Ming got to her feet. "You must choose your coronation dress, Your Highness," she said.

When Andrea clapped her hands, the dancing dolls waltzed into the room. One by one they curtsied to Andrea. "I think the yellow dress is best," the princess-to-be-crowned said.

Ming led Andrea into a small change room. The princess-style dress nearly brushed the floor. Rubies and pearls glowed in the platinum necklace Ming fastened around her neck. Andrea's eyes sparkled as she whispered in wonderment. "I am Andrea, Princess of Ziv," she said.

Ta-taw--ta-tay! A bugle sounded over the intercom. "Donald is summoning everyone to the throne room. We all want to see you receive your tiara. Follow me!" Ming said. She led the way down a long hall and across a courtyard.

Gabi stood guard in front of twin solid-oak doors. They swung open and Andrea entered a room bigger than a supermarket. When she saw that it was crowded with creatures like those she had seen on her trip up the escalators, she held her breath.

Gabi's heels clicked down the marble-tiled aisle toward a dais in the middle of the room. Ming slippered toward the crystal-clear throne on the dais. Andrea followed her helpers toward the rainbow which bowed over the throne. Donald took her hand and they climbed the steps of the dais.

When she was finally sitting on the throne, she took a deep breath. Milling around for a better look at their princess were dozens and dozens of various creatures who were smiling and waving at her. Tiny wings whirred as four hummingbirds flew in carrying Andrea's tiara by silken threads. Of platinum the tiara was set with twelve clusters of diamonds and precious stones. Their colors lent sparkle to the rainbow that hovered over the throne.

"Viva Andrea! Health to Her Highness!" the crowd said and cheered.

Andrea couldn't help it. She started to cry. The crowd cheered and cheered for their princess. Never had Andrea dreamed of anything this splendid. She smiled and held out her hands.

A boy, in fringed yellow buckskin, touched the newly crowned princesses' hand. "I am Drake, Adjutant of the Three Satellites of the Land of Vligan in the Princessdom of Ziv. May I have the honor of going with you to the gala," he said. He placed his right hand over his heart and bowed low. The flamingo feathers hanging from his pink headband brushed his dark face, and the toes of his beaded moccasins were already dancing.

Andrea loved parties. She smiled and took Drake's hand.

Double doors opened to the great ballroom. The glass floor shone like gold. Bubble-like lights orbited around the top of crystal pillars that towered to the ceiling. "Let's dance to the Ziva," Drake said, as a gay tune started to play. As they whirled around the room, everyone caught a partner's hand and followed.

A salamander in a red-velour jogging suit came up to the Andrea. "Your Highness, I am Zander," he said and bowed. She took his velvety hand and jigged with him. When she bumped into an aqua-gowned sunfish who was floating merrily around the room in a plastic bubble, she danced through the ball room with her.

"May I have this dance, Princess," a butterfly said, and fluttering her indigo wings she bowed to Andrea. As they flit through the steps of the Ziva, the butterflies' feet barely touched the floor.

A chipmunk in golden leotards held out a silver tray of unsalted nuts. Andrea had a crystal goblet of fruit punch offered her by a sky-blue gannet.

Gabi's shoes clicked as she strode toward Andrea. "Donald has assembled the budgies in the palace garden. They wish to sing to you," she said.

"How can I leave everyone here, when everyone is having such a good time?" Andrea said.

Suddenly Drake appeared at her elbow. "Call the dancing dolls. They will take your place," he said.

When Andrea entered the garden, everything was very still. Donald raised his right hand. Two birds-of-paradise shook their red, gold, and royal blue feathers. They bowed to each other and started to dance for their princess.

The budgies from the roof garden began to sing.

> "Princess, dear Princess,
> We hope you will stay.
> We are happy to sing
> For you each day.
> Tum, tum, tiddley-tee.
> Tee, tee, tiddley-tum," they sang.

While the budgies sang, the princess tossed the white rose into the fountain in the center of the garden. Each drop of spray became a tiny white rosebud. The hummingbirds caught them and presented each guest with a sweet-smelling nosegay.

A striped golden chipmunk raced up to Andrea and held out a microphone. "Will your Highness be making a statement? It's for the spheres above us that we call Zivoids," he said.

Andrea looked at her adjutants. Gabi nodded. Ming smiled a sweet shy smile. Donald saluted. Drake reached for the microphone. He held it steady for Andrea who was shaking with excitement. "I am Andrea, Princess of Ziv. I want everyone to feel happy. We will choose to live in peace. I know we are going to have a good time together," she said.

"Andrea, Andrea Lyn. Where are you?" a voice said.

Andrea looked all around. She could see no one, but she knew it was Snowpink talking. "I am in the palace in Ziv. We are having a wonderful time," the newly crowned princess said.

"It is time to change and ride the conch back home," Snowpink said.

"Must I? We are having a party," Andrea said.

"I'll get your conch ready," Donald said.

"Drake will clear the airways and I will see to the ground crew," Gabi said.

Quickly Andrea changed into her freshly washed sleep set. In racing for her coach, she almost tripped again. Donald took her hand and raced with her. When she climbed into the shimmering conch, a solid wall of air closed behind her.

"I want to go home," Andrea said. She waved goodbye to her helpers. The conch circled upward and paused over the palace garden.

She waved goodbye to everyone. "I will come back," she said. Her words echoed from a hundred tiny speakers amid the flowers. The yellow daffodils nodded their heads and roses wafted perfume into the air. Red tulips swayed back and forth, as they waved goodbye to their princess.

When she saw the parking lot at the supermarket, it was raining again. Big puddles were still in the street and a rainbow played across the sky. The conch grew smaller and smaller until she was no bigger than a bumblebee. It flew through the window and settled on the floor. As soon as they were the right size, Andrea got out and slipped into bed.

"Can I ever go to Ziv again?" she said to her teddy bear.

"Naturally you are their beloved princess. Remember the twelve doors you saw as you went up the elevators? Behind each door is an adventure you will share with one of twelve cousins each of whom will aspire to become a princess in her own sphere or Zivoid," Snowpink said.

As the newly crowned princess of Ziv, Andrea happily dreamed herself to sleep.

Love, Grandma Schoe

Andrea Explores the Red Moon

SPIT! SPLAT! RAINDROPS! ANDREA RAN to look out her bedroom window. If there was a rainbow, she didn't see one. She sat in the middle of the floor and crossing her legs pulled the skirt of her red-print dress down over her red leotards.

Andrea had been looking for a rainbow every day. That is every day since she had been in Ziv the Land of Be Alive. In Ziv she had been a real princess with a crown, beautiful dresses, jewels, and a pearly-pink conch shell to be her coach. Everyone loved her in Ziv.

The bedroom door screaked as it opened. Her brother, with a large orange bath towel over his head, crept in. "Grr, grr, grr," Nicky said.

"Go away!" Andrea said. She was as cross as a bear. If her royal coach came for her Nicky would be a nuisance. She slid off the bed and ran to the window. Still there was no rainbow. She tugged on the window until she got it open.

"Grr," Nicky said. He grinned and pulling the towel off his blond hair sat on the floor wriggling his bare toes. Just then the conch shell Andrea was looking for flew in the window. The shell shimmered and glowed as it settled down beside Nicky.

When he stared at the pearly pink conch, which pulsated and grew larger his eyes grew wide. The shell became just his size, so he crawled inside and sat down on his orange towel.

Andrea ran across the room. "Nicky, get out of there," she said. She reached for his arm to pull him out. Smack! A solid wall of air had closed the open shell and hurt her hand.

"Take him with you," a voice said.

Andrea knew that Snowpink, her big pink-and-white teddy bear, was talking to her again. "No! He is too little. He will be in the way,"

Andrea said. She shook her dark bangs back and forth across her forehead.

"In Ziv he will be as big as you are," Snowpink said.

"I don't care. He will be a pest. I want to explore my Zivoids all by myself," Andrea said and stamped her foot. Quickly she put on her red running-Kekks.

"Take him with you!" Snowpink said.

"How? I can't get him out. I can't get in, and there isn't enough room for two," Andrea said.

"Surely you have heard of piggyback trucking. I will order another unit, and you can go piggyback conching," Snowpink said.

Immediately another conch shell flew in the window. It shimmered and pulsated to size right in front of the first conch. Andrea got in. "Take me home to Ziv!" she said. Andrea and her shell were getting smaller and smaller. With a bump the shell Nicky had climbed into attached itself to hers.

Together they flew out of the window into a puffy white cloud. Andrea's head hit the side of the shell. Her coach had made a rough landing.

"You should watch where you are, Your Highness," a voice said. A boy in copper Levis and western shirt stood beside her. The turquoise in his bolo tie shone in the light.

"Donald! Am I glad to see you! How is everyone? Is someone taking care of the palace? Are the birds-of-paradise still in the garden? Is the fountain as pretty? I can't wait to see everything," Andrea said. She climbed down out of her coach and looked around.

"Whoopee!" Nicky said. He threw his towel to the ground and jumped down beside them.

Donald placed his right hand on his left shoulder. "Nicky, General of the Moon of Fyrh, I am Donald. I am Adjutant of the three Zivoids of the Land of Fyrh in the Princessdom of Ziv," he said. He clicked his heels together.

"Wow!" Nicky said. He grinned and picked up his towel.

Donald turned to Andrea. "Your Highness, we must take the shuttle service to Red Moon right now," he said. Grabbing Andrea's hand he raced across the parking lot with her. They stopped in front of a huge door.

"Please open it, Your Highness," her adjutant said.

Andrea crossed her fingers. "I am Andrea, Princess of Ziv. Please open," she said.

Slowly the door slid upward until Andrea could see a gigantic conch shell that was as red as an old-fashioned fire engine. The three children ran to its side and stepped into a saucer-shaped shell which floated up and into the great conch.

Silently as a falling snowflake, the conch lifted off of the ground and drifted gently out of the parking garage. Suddenly they were soaring up like a rocket. Andrea took a deep breath and looked out. The palace was already a tiny speck far below. The land of Ziv was getting smaller and smaller.

"You do remember Zander, don't you? You know, of course, that Red Moon is the first Zivoid of the Princessdom of Fyrh." Donald said. He went on to explain that Zander was exploring new hectares of Red Moon.

"Fire," Nicky said and pointed ahead of them. The nose of the conch pointed straight towards a ball of flames. Nicky clapped his hands and grinned.

Andrea hid her face in her dress. *Stupid brother,* she thought.

The shell was changing direction and began to slow down. In minutes they stopped on a strip of red sand. "You should have seen the moon as we came in. It glowed like a barbecue fire," Nicky said.

"The conch keeps us from being burned as we go through the Great Barrier of Fyrh," Donald said. He held out his hand to help Andrea out of the conch. Ignoring him she jumped to the ground and landed awkwardly in a red fire-bush.

"This isn't quite like the palace. It is new, primitive," Donald said. His copper-colored suit shone in the light.

"Is there no landing strip?" Andrea said.

"There is one on the other side of the moon. We have a colony there, but Zander is exploring here. He was supposed to meet us. He has discovered something very exciting," Donald said.

Andrea looked around. Red sand was everywhere. The hills were piles of sand. The valleys between them were reddish sand. Right where the rocket conch had landed a garden oasis grew.

Nicky picked a shiny leaf from a red alder. A spray of water soaked everyone. A huge drop of water fell on a red stone nearby. It sizzled and was gone.

"You do have to watch the cinnabar rocks here. You can fry an egg on them," Donald said.

"If the rocks are so hot how are plants able to live here?" Andrea said.

"Only the cinnabar rocks are hot. This moon is really rather swampy," Donald said.

"I guess Zander likes it better where it is hot and dry. After all he is a salamander," Andrea said.

"Of course not salamanders are quite terrified of fire. They prefer the swamp," Donald said.

A growl came from a cloud of red dust that was coming close. It looked like a monster roaring across the sands. Andrea ran for shelter in the conch.

An oversized three-wheeler sped out of the cloud of dust. The rider pulled a wheelie and stopped. A salamander who was slightly smaller than Andrea slid to the ground and brushed the dust from her red velvet warm-up suit.

"What is it?" Nicky said. He ran his hand over the white letter M on the machine.

"It's a terrier. They can go absolutely anywhere in Ziv. So far they are great here on Red Moon. This is Melody, she is Zander's sister. They are exploring the uncharted lands of Red Moon together," Donald said.

Melody's warm-up suit revealed her smooth moist tail. Her soft face was yellow with black spots. Andrea forced herself to smile at Melody. She held out her hand.

Touching Andrea's hand with her velvet glove Melody bowed. "I am most pleased to meet Your High - Your Highness," she said.

"I am always pleased to meet members of the Princessdom of Ziv. Where is Zander? I want to see him again. I thought we were meeting him here," the princess said.

Melody began to shake all over. "May we be excused, Your Highness. I must talk to Donald," she said.

"Surely," Andrea said. She turned and walked toward the terrier. Nicky was sitting on it pushing and pulling everything in sight.

"Nicky! Stop it!" Andrea said. She ran to the now purring machine. The terrier sprang into action, and Nicky raced away across the red moon dust.

"Princess, I think Melody should tell you about Zander," Donald said.

Melody's words tumbled out. "He was riding his terrier. He was just ahead of me going over a dune. It's quite safe you know. Really it is and it's lots of fun. The crest of the hill gave way just as Zander hit it. His bike flew into the air, and he fell off." Melody said. She wiped a tear from her spotted face with her red velvet glove.

"And--," Andrea said. She put her arm around Melody.

"I am a good rider. Really I am. I pulled for a swerve, but—" Melody said, and shook her head.

"Melody went over the edge, too. She was nearly buried in the sand," Donald said.

"I don't think we will see Zander alive again. I dug everywhere," Melody said and rubbed her glove over her face.

"Let's not give up yet. After all you didn't find anything, did you?" the Princess of Red Moon said.

"Not even his terrier," Melody said. She brushed away another tear.

"Will the saucer shell take us to the dunes?" Andrea said.

"No. There are no charts for this side of Red Moon. The computers have no data. There are, however, three terriers in the rocket conch," Donald said.

In the ship Donald found a scarlet jogging suit for Andrea. She pulled it on along with a red helmet and dark goggles. Racing out to the machine, which Donald had started for her, she climbed on.

"The tracks go toward the dunes," Melody said. Climbing aboard her terrier she raced away across the dry sand.

Andrea followed Melody up a little hill. Down the other side the three of them flew. The wind picked up great mounds of red sand. The sand whirled into the air and danced with the wind. Spent of its energy the wind dumped the dry grains of sand all around the young princess stinging her face. She tried to brush it from her goggles with her right hand. Her machine swerved and landed in a large fire bush.

When she picked herself up, she saw that the forks of the terrier were bent. A stick poked out of the front tire which hissed and started to go flat. *Whatever can I do now?* Andrea wondered.

She sat down on a knoll to think. The knoll moved under her, and a small voice beside her began chanting. "I am Mini Padme, I am. I am Mini Padme, I am. Who are you?" the voice said.

Andrea stared at the earth mound. It was quite still. She looked over the field. It was empty. She stood on the mound to see better. It crumpled and Andrea fell to her knees. She saw a pair of very dark goggles peering out of a tunnel beside her. The creature wearing them looked like a large mole in a brown warm-up suit.

"Do come in out of the light. It is bad for your eyes," Mini said and backed into the tunnel. The dark tunnel smelled of the red earth. There was just enough room for Andrea to creep in on her hands and knees.

"Just wait a minute. Things are always better in a minute. These diamonds get in our way when we dig," Mini said. She handed Andrea a tiny bright object.

"Diamonds!" Andrea said. She would love a beautiful diamond necklace. She could wear it at the next festival.

"Throw it away and follow me. It is nearly lunch time. We can dig some sweet potatoes," Mini said.

Andrea crawled after Mini. "But I have to find Nicky and Zander," she said. The tunnel was so dark she could hardly see.

"Why are you looking for Cousin Zander?" Mini said. She took a sharp turn in the tunnel. Andrea nearly got stuck following her.

"Melody said he disappeared in the dunes," Andrea said. With a tug she pulled herself free.

Mini sat down crossed her short stubby legs. "Start at the beginning. I don't even know who you are yet," she said.

Sitting down on the bare ground Andrea leaned forward. "I am Andrea," she said.

Mini clapped her gopher paws. "Andrea! You are the Princess Andrea, Ruler of the Princessdom of Ziv, Koa of the Three Moons of Fyrh?" she said.

When Andrea sat up straight her helmet touched the ceiling. "You could say so," she said. Taking off her helmet Andrea shook out her dark hair.

She could hear someone chanting. "I am Mani Padme, I am. I am Mani Padme, I am," another voice said. Mani stopped just outside the room. He wore a brown warm-up suit and goggles. He looked exactly like Mini.

"Who is our guest?" Mani said politely.

"Just wait until I tell you. It will fry your potatoes," Mini said. She slapped the dust off of her suit.

"You are our Princess, Koa of the first Zivoid of Fyrh! Quickly my Princess, you must hide," Mani said.

Mani and Mini sat with their short backs against the wall. They crossed their feet and put their paws on their knees.

Mani said, "Where can we hide our princess?"

"Why do we have to hide our dear Koa?" Mini said.

Andrea looked from one mole to the other. "I can't hide! I have to find Nicky, and Zander, and the others," she said.

"Wait until I tell you what I know. It will fry your potatoes golden brown," Mani said. He slapped the dust off of his jacket and adjusted his cuffs. He cleared his throat and began. "It is the diamonds. They are useless to us, of course. We can't eat them, but I hear they have value in Ziv," he said.

"Diamonds! Whoever would want such things?" Mini said. She wiped furiously on her goggles.

"Belial," Mani said.

"Belial!" Mini said. She shook all over and covered her face with her sleeve.

"I have never heard of Belial. Who is he?" the young princess said and looked from one mole to the other.

Mani and Mini cried out together. "Belial is the lying lizard. Belial shines like copper. He hurts our eyes. He throws cinnabar rocks. He makes us dig for diamonds. We have no time to dig for potatoes. Dear Koa, you must hide. Take the Y tunnel," they said. They took Andrea's hands and started toward a nearby tunnel.

"Wait. I have to find Nicky," Andrea said and forgetting where she was stood up. The earth started coming down around them. Andrea climbed on the falling sand until she could crawl out of the tunnel. It collapsed behind her.

The fresh air smelled like ripe crabapples. *So Red Moon isn't just sand and hot rocks after all,* Andrea thought. "Tiddley-tee," she said and wiped her goggles.

The dunes were far, far away. There was no sign of her terrier. She had no idea how to find her way back to the rocket conch, and Donald wouldn't know where to look for her.

The crabapple orchard was close by, and the tantalizing odor of ripe juicy apples made Andrea realize she was hungry and thirsty. She walked through the red orchard grass to a nearby tree and picked a ripe red crabapple. She took a bite and found it was tart but delicious.

"Tiddley-tum," Andrea said. She would just have to find Nicky and Zander herself. Perhaps this Belial creature knew where they were. She tried to remember what Mani and Mini had said before the tunnel collapsed. "I do hope they are all right," she said. The second bite of crabapple tasted even better than the first.

"Cheer-rup. Cheer-rup," a voice said from high in the crabapple tree. A bird flew to the grass in front of Andrea. He wore a suit of brown feathers with a red vest. "Robbi Robin, Your Highness," the bird said and bowed.

"How do you do. And how did you know?" Andrea said.

Robbi hopped across the grass. He turned one ear to the ground. "I listen a lot," he said.

"Can you help me find Nicky? Have you heard where he and Zander are?" Andrea said. She started brushing the sand out of her dark hair.

Robbi flew into the crabapple tree and chirped. "Nicky and Zander are together," he said.

"Are they safe?" Andrea said.

"Hardly! Cheer-rup," Robbie said. He started to sing.

"What do you mean by hardly? And why should I cheer up?" the princess of Ziv said.

"Cheer-rup. Things could be worse," Robbi said. He flew to the fallen mound and listened.

"Tiddley-tee! What are you trying to tell me? And are Mani and Mini all right?" Andrea said and stamped her foot.

Robbie flew into a nearby tree. "They are now. They won't be. Belial is back. Cheer-rup. Let's go," he said.

"Where? And how? I have no wings," Andrea said.

Robbie bowed. "Pardon me, dear Koa. You have feet," he said and flew to the edge of the orchard.

"Wait! You said something about Belial," Andrea said. She started running toward Robbi. He flew out of the orchard. A branch switched

Andrea's face. It was loaded with ripe crabapples. She snatched a few to put in her helmet.

Robbi was calling from a meadow. He had his head on one side listening at a mound of red sand. "Cheer-rup. Let's go," Robbie said. He flew toward a forest of the tallest trees Andrea had ever seen.

Next time Robbi put his ear to the ground Andrea tried it. She listened carefully but heard nothing. She looked at Robbi. He put his left ear to the ground. When Andrea tried her left ear, she heard a strange rumbling sound. *So that was what Robbi was listening to,* she thought. She had no idea what it meant.

"This way, dear Koa, my princess," Robbi said. He flew toward a path that led right into the dark trees. Andrea followed. Far ahead of her Robbie disappeared into the redwoods.

Andrea wished she were back at home. This strange moon frightened her, but she couldn't go home without her brother. She started down the dark path that led through the thick trees.

Big tree branches touched over her head. They shut out the light of the Great Barrier of Fyrh and made the path pleasant and cool. The air was so still Andrea started to sing. "I am Andrea a happy princess. I am singing along the way. I am Andrea a happy princess. I am glad for each new day," she sang.

A growl in the distance sounded like Nicky playing doggie again, or perhaps it was Nicky on Melody's terrier. A cloud of dust was coming into the tunnel of trees, and two red terriers were speeding down the narrow path. Andrea saw a flash of copper. *That must be Donald,* Andrea thought.

The first terrier roared past. The tall slim rider wore a copper colored suit. In a cloud of dust and the roar of a motor a second terrier stopped beside Andrea. Though much bigger this rider looked much like the first. His copper-plated armor covered his long slender tail.

Andrea was very frightened. *This lizard, the largest I've ever seen, must be Belial,* she thought. She wondered why ever Robbi had led her here since he must have known who she would meet. No doubt Belial had been warned she was on Red Moon and was looking for her.

"And who might you be?" the lizard said. Even in the dull light the horns of his helmet shone.

"I am just a young girl who is lost in a forest," Andrea said. She most certainly didn't feel much like a princess with Belial's beady eyes staring at her. If there had been anywhere for her to run she would have.

"I am Fyrh. I am Prince of the Princedom of Fyrh. I am High Ruler of Red Moon," the lizard said. He patted his chest with his red velvet glove.

"My pleasure, Your Princeship. May I offer you an apple?" Andrea said politely and held out her helmet.

"Delightful! They're my favorites but no thanks. My diet you know," he said. Sliding forward on the saddle of the terrier, he patted the seat behind him and smiled. His teeth looked sharp, very sharp. A letter Z was painted in white on the side of the red terrier. Andrea was sure it had been Zander's.

"Throw the apples away and come with me," Fyrh said.

"No. Thank you. I prefer to walk," Andrea said and shook her head.

Belial pulled out a diamond necklace. "Come on. I can give you pretty things," he said.

The diamonds sparkled and shone brilliantly in the light of the Great Barrier of Fyrh. Andrea did want the necklace very much. If she had a diamond necklace that shone with rainbow colors, she could visit Ziv whenever she chose.

"No. Thank you," she said and shook her head again. She wished there were someone who could help her get away from him.

The other rider came back down the trail and did a wheelie. A white letter M stood out on the side of the red terrier. "Hurry it up, Bug Breath. This kid is no Koa. You're wasting our time," the rider said over the roar of the engines.

Cool your motor, Belila. I'm coming," the larger lizard said and sped off.

"Climb on behind me, Princess," a voice said beside Andrea.

"I am very glad to see you, Donald!" Andrea said and quickly climbed onto Donald's terrier.

As he wheeled to race away, Melody dropped from a tree. "There is room for you, too, Melody. Jump on," Donald said.

Soon they were racing down a grassy knoll far from the tall dark trees. As they splashed through a swamp of elder bushes deep-black berries fell from the branches and became crushed by the tires of the terrier. At the top of the next hill Donald stopped. When he turned off the motor of his bike, Andrea could hear someone singing.

"That's my brother! He's singing to let me know he's okay," Melody said. She slid off the terrier onto the dry red sand.

"They're off to the right somewhere," Donald said as he wheeled his terrier under a nearby fire bush.

"Nicky may be with him," Andrea said. She raced on foot into the thicket of ferns that stood in the direction her adjutant indicated.

Donald yelled after her. "Princess, be careful! Belial could have a trap set for us," he said.

Andrea slid to a stop at the edge of a deep pit. The tall ferns had hidden it from view. She tottered on the edge of the pit, and her foot slipped in the soft sand. Grabbing for a fern she caught Melody's arm instead. Both nearly fell headlong, but Andrea reached out with her other hand and caught a branch of a fire bush. The bush was hot, but she was able to pull herself and Melody to safety.

As they lay there panting, Donald came up and pointed to one side of the pit. Far below Nicky and Zander huddled under Nicky's orange towel. Nicky was beating on a log with two sticks.

Zander was singing. "I am Zander, the salamander. I am singing this happy song. I am Zander, the salamander. I am happy the whole day long," he sang.

Andrea started to cry. "How can Zander be happy when he is in a pit? They can't get out, and we can't get them out," she said.

"Zander is always happy. He is glad he's alive," Melody said. Her voice was filled with pride in her brother.

A noise like a kaboom drew Andrea's attention to the other side of the pit. Belial had just rolled a large cinnabar rock over the opposite edge. Belila tossed two small cinnabar rocks into the pit which landed beside the larger rock.

"Whatever are they doing?" Andrea said in a whisper.

Donald whispered back. "Sacrifice. Belial believes he will find more diamonds if he makes sacrifice," he said.

"How silly! All he has to do is dig. Mini told me there are lots of diamonds," Andrea said.

"Belial and Belila make Cousin Mani and Cousin Mini do the work. All the mole people are divided into digging teams," Melody said. She crept back from the edge of the pit.

The copped-clad lizards were throwing more red rocks into the pit. Andrea was sure her brother and Zander were intended victims. The young princess sat down and thought, *it's a tough job, this princessing bit*. She could think of nothing else.

Andrea put her elbow on one knee and rested her chin in her hand. She picked up a crabapple that had spilled from her helmet when she fell. "If only we had--. No, we must use what we do have," she said. She rubbed the crabapple until it was shiny.

Across the pit Belial had been tossing more cinnabar rocks to Belila who had been dropping them into the pit. They glowed red hot like coals. Andrea was glad she and her friends were hidden in the thicket of ferns. She hardly dared move for fear the lizards would see them. Suddenly the lizards climbed onto the terriers. They raced away toward a thick hazelnut grove.

"What do you think they are up to?" Andrea said.

"Wood. They need wood for a fire," Melody said and shivered.

Andrea moved toward the edge. "Isn't there any way we can get down the side of the pit? We could slide down couldn't we?" she said.

"If we went down we couldn't get back up," Melody said sadly.

Andrea groaned. "If only Mani and Mini were here, they could show us how to dig a tunnel into the side of the pit," she said.

"I am Mani Padme, I am," a voice said behind them. A brown mole in a dusty suit was sitting on a mound of earth in the ferns. He squinted as he polished his goggles. "Dear Koa, we have dug. The old L tunnel starts near the alder swamp, but fry my potatoes it is hard digging. We ended out only part way down the pit," he said.

Belial and Belila roared back from the hazelnut grove with a load of sticks on their terriers. They tossed the sticks onto the rocks in the pit.

Andrea shouted to her brother. "Nicky, the sticks will catch fire. Pull them away from the rocks! Hurry!" she said.

Melody grabbed Andrea's arm. "Koa, run! They have seen you," she said.

Belila shrieked. "You," she said. She and Belial scurried down the side of the pit and raced across the bottom toward them.

Andrea clutched her helmet full of crabapples. Her feet wouldn't move. As Belial ran she shouted at him. "I am Princess of Red Moon," she said. She threw an apple which hit Belial's copper helmet.

Belial screamed. "Stop! You are ruining my flashy armour," he said. He was shaking with anger.

Andrea shouted back at him. "Fake," she said. She took a step closer to the edge of the pit.

The lizards slithered back to the heap of cinnabar rocks. They threw the hot rocks at the pile of sticks Nicky had pulled away from the fire pit. Suddenly Andrea saw that Nicky and Zander were hiding behind a log under the sticks.

A very red rock landed on the bottom of the pile. Smoke began curling up, and bright forked tongues of flame followed. As the flames licked at the dry sticks, they glowed a bright red. More and more smoke rose from the pit. Nicky and Zander had no place to hide.

Andrea shouted to her brother. "The orange towel! Beat out the fire with the orange towel!" she said.

Nicky beat at the flames as fast as he could. The fire just spread.

Tiddley-tee, Andrea thought. "Tea. We need water," she said.

"There is lots of water in the alder swamp right here. Zander and I often swim in a pond near there," Melody said.

That's where Mani said he and Mini had started the tunnel, thought Andrea. She clapped her hands. "Melody! Donald! Start the water flowing through the tunnel the Padmes dug!" she said.

Quickly Donald raced for his terrier. Melody followed and jumped on behind him. Soon water began to trickle into the pit and form a puddle by the log in the center of the pit.

Andrea shouted to her brother. "Nicky, soak the towel!" she said.

Suddenly water gushed out of the tunnel, and the pit started to fill. Nicky climbed onto the log that was floating on the rising water. Zander swam to the log, but when he tried to climb up beside Nicky the log rolled.

"Yahoo! This is fun," Nicky said. He climbed back aboard the log while Zander clung to its side.

Belial scrambled up the far side of the pit. Belila slithered up behind him. Their suits had become a dirty gray. They disappeared into the gaping door of a rocket ship and launched toward the Great Barrier of Fyrh.

Nicky and Zander swam from the log to the edge of the pit and pulled themselves onto the grass. "Dear Koa, you were wonderful! Thank you," Zander said. He kissed her hand.

"We have to hurry, Princess. The Great Barrier of Fyrh is setting. It will soon be dark," Donald said, as he waved his hand toward the flaming sky. Gradually as the fiery light began to stream onto Red Moon, it looked like a reverse run volcano.

"I forgot to ask Zander what he discovered. Everything was so exciting!" Andrea said. As they flew back to the palace, she wondered how exploring the next zivoid could be any better.

Love, Grandma Schoe

Andrea on Golden Globe

OH BOTHER, MY BATH IS cold. Nicky, the pest, must have used all the hot water, Andrea thought. She slipped her left wrist into the tub to see just how waterproof her watch was.

Busily she splashed the suds into rainbow bubbles. "I wish I were in Ziv, it's been at least seven weeks since I was crowned princess," she said and reached for her bar of soap. It slid off the tub and across the floor.

When Andrea tried to grab it, she caught something hard with pointy feet. She opened her hand and saw a shimmering pink conch shell, which she quickly set on the floor. While she watched it grow larger, she wrapped herself in her oversize golden bath towel.

As fast as her digital watch flashed one second, she was flying out the bathroom window. She sat back and began dreaming of her marvelous bathroom with its sunken tub, and all the hot water she could want.

Soon Andrea saw the tall building covered with mirrors. The conch circled lower and lower. It hovered over the palace garden and swooped to a glass capsule on the side of the building. The glass capsule whisked Andrea up to the thirteenth floor, where she stepped into a huge hall.

A click outside the door warned her that someone was coming. *No one should see the Princess of Ziv in a bath towel. I must hide,* Andrea thought. She opened a door and tripped into a darkened room. With a crash Andrea fell against something hard. She rubbed her elbow.

"Excuse us, Princess, but this is our closet," a staccato voice said.

A black girl peered around the door. "Whatever is Your Highness doing in the cleaning closet?" she said.

"Gabi! Do help me find the bathroom and some clothes. Surely you can call the dancing dolls. I want a dress," Andrea said.

Gabi's white teeth shone through her smile. "Relax, Princess. You are just in time for your Fiftieth-day Jubilee. Everyone has been gathering golden leaves to decorate the table where your loving cup will be displayed," she said and led Andrea down another long hall.

In a big bedroom a robot was dusting the furniture. "Go to the closet, Thith!" Gabi said. Tucking her duster under her arm, the robot rolled out of the room.

Andrea ran to her bathroom and stepped into her sunken tub. Warm water gushed around her feet, and lavender fragrance filled the room. Bubbles piled up to her chin, and she blew a handful into the air. The tiny globes of rainbows danced through the room. She started humming to the song on the intercom: Tum, tum, tiddley-tee. Tee, tee, tiddley-tum.

An announcer cut in cleared her throat and began. "We have a special bulletin. Today is the golden jubilee of our Princess Andrea. The hostess for our festival is here from Golden Globe. Chippy, our roving reporter, is in the palace garden with her right now," she said.

In the video screen beside her tub Andrea could see the garden. A chipmunk was arranging marigolds in a bowl. Beside it a gleam of gold shone through some golden leaves.

"Butter on your golden kernels this is a good day. Our hostess is nearly hidden by marigolds," Chippy said and held out his microphone. "Mrs. Butterball, tell us about today's festival," he said.

Mrs. Butterball smoothed down her golden mantle and chattered. "Frost on the pumpkin! Am I on? Is everyone looking at me? Do I sound all right?" she said.

"Right as pecan pie," Chippy said. He smoothed down his striped golden coat.

"The Folke de Terre has planned carefully. The Golden Jubilee Festival is very down-to-earth. We have pretty flowers, butter pecan ice cream, and good music." Mrs. Butterball said.

"Isn't there a special surprise for her highness?" Chippy said.

"There will be no surprise at all if you chatter on about it," Mrs. Butterball said. She whisked her tail and stuck another marigold into the bowl. The golden loving-cup gleamed in the sunlight.

The video went dead. Something flashed past Andrea's bathroom window that looked like a conch coach coming in to land.

"The dancing dolls, Princess," Gabi said from the bedroom doorway.

Twelve dolls with bright brown eyes danced across the golden carpet to the bathroom. Their rich brown hair floated as they twirled in a rainbow of fashions. A gold silk dress caught Andrea's eye. The waist dropped to a full skirt and sequins finished the neckline. "The gold silk is perfect," Andrea said and clapped her hands. The dolls waltzed out of the room.

The video picture turned on again. Chippy was fanning Mrs. Butterball with a marigold. "Can you tell us what happened?" the announcer said.

An outward-bound golden rocket flashed across the screen. The sound from the palace garden went dead again. "That's it folks. That's all I can tell you for now," the DJ said when the sound came on.

Andrea grabbed her towel to dry herself. She just had to find out what was happening. She slipped into a golden jump suit like Gabi's and tugged at a tangle in her dark brown hair.

From the doorway Gabi said, "Your brother is here. Shall I have him wait in the blue room?"

Andrea put her brush down. "No. I don't want him here. Send him home! He is a pest," she said.

Gabi turned toward the door. She put her right hand over her heart and bowed low. "General Nicky, I am Gabriel, Adjutant of the Three Globes of the Folke de Terre. Our Princess, your sister Andrea, wishes you to return home," Gabi said.

"No. She wanted Cousin Amber but she's got me. Another conch came so I suppose she's coming when she is ready," Nicky said. He patted the medals on the chest of his kaki warm-up suit.

"A garden party is no place for a boy. Please go home. You will spoil everything," Andrea said and started down the hall. She had to get to the garden to find out what was so exciting.

"It's missing," Nicky said. He was just one step behind Andrea. They walked to the glass capsule on the side of the building.

"What's missing?" Andrea said. It was annoying to have her baby brother know something she didn't. The moment they stepped inside the capsule, they swooshed down to the lower garden.

Chipmunks were dashing from shrub to shrub poking their noses under every bush. A small chipmunk scampered up to Nicky. "Oh please, General Sir. Don't tell our princess about our secret surprise," he said.

"What secret? What surprise?" Andrea said to Gabi who was already in the garden.

"Princess, may I introduce Buttercup Butterball. Her mother is hostess for the festival," Gabi said.

Buttercup curtsied. "My pleasure, Princess. May I suggest we all take a rocket to Golden Globe? I'm sure Mrs. Pennyweight has taken the surprise there," she said.

"And just who is Mrs. Pennyweight?" Andrea said.

"She's mean. She hides all our nuts and won't let us hunt for them," Buttercup said.

"Mrs. Pennyweight didn't receive her invitation to the festival. I think she stole the surprise to get even," Gabi said.

"Just wait until I see Mrs. Pennyweight," Andrea said.

The golden rocket left the parking garage quietly and slowly lifted off for Golden Globe. Soon Andrea could see a soft golden glow that grew larger every second. She barely heard Gabi. "This globe is the first Zivoid of the Folke de Terre," her adjutant said.

They landed in a field of bright yellow buttercups. Beyond the green grass in the next pasture a field of clover shone in the dappled sunlight. As green trees swayed in a gentle breeze, their leaves turned their golden undersides to the light.

Buttercup puffed out her cheeks proudly. Flipping her tail over her back, she began to sing.

"Buttercups dance in a meadow wide.
Buttercup is my name. In them I hide.
Buttercups play in golden gowns.
Buttercup dresses in shades of browns.
Chipmunk's cheeks are what I wear.
Striped is my coat so fair.
Buttercup is my name so never fear.
Nuts I'm storing for winter near," she sang.

"Beautiful! You have a lovely home, but where are we to look for the stolen surprise?" Andrea said.

"Frost on the butternuts! I am so excited about being back in my buttercup field I almost forgot. It could be anywhere, anywhere at all," Buttercup said.

A dozen chipmunks scampered up. "We will help search. Mrs. Pennyweight gives us lots of practice. We have to look for our nuts every day. She hides them everywhere," they all said.

Andrea started searching. It was almost as much fun as a treasure hunt. She looked in a pile of leaves. Nothing special was there. Nothing special was by the roots of the pecan tree. All she found were some nuts.

"The nuts are for the butter-pecan ice cream. The chipmunks have been hiding them from Mrs. Pennyweight," Gabi said.

Buttercup scampered into a hollow log. She came out the other end and danced away into the buttercups.

When Andrea tried to follow, she tripped over the log and fell into a clump of goldenrod which made her sneeze. A shrill whistle made Andrea put her hands over her ears. She parted the goldenrod and looked over the meadow. She hoped the big black cow there wasn't Mrs. Pennyweight. The whistle sounded close by. Andrea looked down and saw dark eyes peering out of a furry face in a burrow at her feet.

"Hi, I'm Chucka Woodchuck. Do come in," the furry creature said. Her long front teeth clicked together.

"I would prefer to stay here. Your home is awfully dark," Andrea said.

"You will get used to it," another voice said. Andrea jumped. She looked down and saw another furry creature sitting on his haunches beside her.

"Please hurry in while no one is looking. My brother will watch to see that it's safe," Chucka said.

Slowly Andrea crawled behind Chucka down the long passage to a large room. She sat against the dirt wall. A ray of sunshine lit up a square of golden paper on the floor.

"My brother has a riddle for you. I'll bet you can't guess the answer," the first woodchuck said.

Chucky sat up and took a deep breath. "How much wood would a woodchuck chuck if a woodchuck could chuck wood?" he said.

Andrea laughed. "My goodness! That's a wonderful riddle, but I have a riddle for you. Where is the surprise for the festival hidden?" she said.

Chucka's brown eyes widened. She looked at her brother. Chucky looked at his sister. "What festival? What surprise?" Chucky said.

"The Golden Jubilee Festival for Princess Andrea Lyn is being held this afternoon, and someone stole the surprise. We think Mrs. Pennyweight has hidden it here on Golden Globe," Andrea said.

"No one told us about the festival. We don't know anything about a surprise," Chucka and Chucky said together.

"Oh! But you have to come to the festival. All the chipmunks will be there," Andrea said.

"Mrs. Pennyweight didn't get an invitation, and if she can't go we can't go. Besides we're too poor and too clumsy. We have no gift for the princess, and we can't dance the Ziva. We don't even know how to read, and we really don't want to go anyway," Chucka said.

Andrea decided she would never find the surprise if she didn't start looking somewhere else. She said goodbye to the woodchucks and crawled out of their burrow into the goldenrod again. The young princess sneezed. She knew she had to get out of it as fast as she could, but the goldenrod was so tall she couldn't see where she was.

"Moo. Moo. Over here," a voice crooned.

Andrea pushed her way through the golden rod. The tall stalks were hard to break, so she pulled them apart and wriggled between them.

The big black cow was standing up to her knees in golden clover. Her tail switched at some flies. "Welcome to my pasture. Have some lunch," she said.

"Just a little bite," Andrea said. She didn't want to offend her hostess. After all she had dropped in at lunchtime. She nibbled daintily at a white and gold clover blossom.

"Do have moo-re. This is the best clover I have ever tasted, or my name isn't Angie McPail," the cow said.

Andrea swallowed. "Perhaps you can help me. I am Princess Andrea and I am looking for a lost surprise," she said.

"Do help yourself, Andrea. We will stop and think after lunch. I have to make milk and cream for the Golden Jubilee Festival," Angie said. She meandered to the edge of the field. Her hoofs kicked up golden dust on the winding trail that led to a cottonwood by a clear stream. As Angie bent her head to take a deep drink, a dragonfly flit over the water.

"Where are we going?" Andrea said.

"To meditate in the shade," Angie said. She lay down under the cottonwood.

"I thought you were going to make milk and cream," Andrea said.

Angie swallowed her cud. "I wouldn't be able to make any milk at all if I ran around all day," she said. She flicked a fly off her ear. Her gentle brown eyes looked dreamy and far away.

The shade of the cottonwood was cool and pleasant. Andrea climbed a rock by the trail. "About that lost surprise are you ready to think about it now?" she said.

Angie flicked a fly off her back with her tail. She started chewing again and gazed at something away off in the distance.

The princess flopped down on the grass like her new friend Angie McPail. Andrea had to do something herself if all Angie would do was lie in the shade. *But whatever could a little girl do*, she wondered. She looked across the field.

Away on the other side something orange that was big and round stood in a grassy field. *Maybe that is my surprise*, she thought. "Excuse me please, Angie. I really have to go. Thanks for lunch," Andrea said. Slipping off the rock she skipped down the dusty trail and through the field. She wondered where her brother and her helper were. When Andrea tripped over a pumpkin vine at the edge of the field, mice scattered everywhere.

The breeze coming from an orchard off to the right smelled like apricot nectar. Paths between neat rows of apricot trees led in every direction. While following the path she chose, she was tempted to stop and pick, but she was looking for Mrs. Pennyweight. Something sounded like the swing on Grandma's porch. The old swing skrawked just like this.

"Where do you think you are going little girl? I have had enough trespassers for one day, quite enough," someone said.

Andrea looked around the trunk of the last tree by her path. At the edge of the apricot orchard, two trees of delicious looking golden apples stood in warm sunshine. Their branches dipped low to the ground. On a swing hung between the two apple trees, a golden goose was swaying back and forth. A huge hollow log lay at her feet.

The goose honked. "Don't come any further. I have learned magic. I will put you into my gerbil cage," she said. The goose flew down and beat against the log with a powerful wing. "Keep moving! Keep moving!" she said.

"Do you know where I might find Mrs. Pennyweight?" Andrea said. She wiped her sweaty palm on her golden jumpsuit.

The goose stood up on the log and flapped her wings. "You have found Mrs. Pennyweight. Now get out before I turn you into a gerbil like the others," she said. She pounded on the log with her wing.

A gerbil! The others! Stupid goose, Andrea thought. She wondered if Mrs. Pennyweight had actually turned Nicky and Gabi into gerbils and put them in the hollow log.

Andrea would have to forget all about her surprise and her Golden Jubilee Festival. Nicky and Gabi were more important.

The goose flapped her wings again. "Whatever are you doing? I told you to go away," she said.

"Why did you steal my surprise?" Andrea said.

"Your surprise? So you think you're Princess Andrea! Honk. Honk," the goose said.

"What's so funny?" Andrea said.

"Look at me! My feathers are pure gold. They are fine as eider down. I am no princess, and I don't believe you are either. Not in that cheap outfit. You wouldn't even be invited to the Golden Jubilee Festival. I wasn't," the goose said.

"But everyone got invited to the Festival. The woodchucks were given the invitations to deliver," Andrea said.

"Well, I didn't get an invitation, nor did the McPails. The Chucky Woodchuck family didn't get one either for that matter," the goose said. She straightened her feathers and hopped up onto the swing.

Andrea stood up and smoothed out her jumpsuit. She wanted to look as much like a princess as possible. *After all Golden Globe is part of my princessdom,* she thought.

The noise she had heard was coming from within the hollow log. If Gabi and Nicky were in there they were the ones powering the swing. It sounded as if they were getting tired.

Andrea knew she had to get Mrs. Pennyweight to release them and soon. *But how,* she wondered. Perhaps the golden square of paper in the woodchuck's home had been the invitation. They couldn't read. Perhaps they didn't even know it was an invitation.

Putting one her hand on her heart Andrea bowed low. "I am Andrea Lyn, Princess of the Land of Ziv, and of all the globes of the Folke de Terre. I would be very pleased to have you at my festival," she said.

Mrs. Pennyweight honked. "I wouldn't go even if you were the Princess, and you're not. So there! Get into the log, Scum!" she said and shook her golden wings at Andrea.

A golden feather floated to the ground at Andrea's feet. She picked it up.

"Give me my feather! It's worth its weight in gold. I can't afford to let you have even one," the goose said. She flew down off the swing and beat at Andrea with her huge wings.

Andrea dropped the feather and ran. She hid behind a nearby tree whose branches drooped with golden apples. She reached up to pick one.

"Don't touch my apples with your sticky fingers! I have none to spare," Mrs. Pennyweight said. She raced at Andrea with her huge wings flapping.

In backing away from the furious goose, Andrea fell over one end of the hollow log.

Mrs. Pennyweight touched Andrea with one feather at the tip of her golden wing and chanted.

> "Princess you say?
> No way. No way.
> My servant you stay
> From today to today," she said.

The golden jumpsuit grew tight to Andrea's skin. She became smaller and smaller, and her fingernails became claws. She could feel pouches forming in her cheeks.

"Get into the cage gerbil!" the angry goose said. She picked Andrea up in her beak and dropped her through a small opening in the end of the drab brown log.

Andrea fell into a myriad of tiny golden bubbles surrounded by a little golden globe. She fell through the cloud of bubbles all the way to the bottom of the log.

"Welcome, Princess," said a black gerbil.

"Hi, Sis," said a white gerbil.

A loud knocking jarred the log. The black gerbil jumped back onto a big wheel. "Come on, Princess, the faster we turn, the faster we will get out of here with your surprise," she said.

"But it's so tiny! I thought we were looking for something bigger," Andrea said.

"Mrs. Pennyweight made it small, too," Gabi said. She ran faster and faster turning the wheel.

"Whatever happened to make Mrs. Pennyweight so selfish?" Andrea said. She was nearly out of breath from running around the squeaky wheel.

"Her cousin laid a golden egg once, and the owner killed her. He wanted more golden eggs all at once." Gabi said. She panted as she ran.

"You mean the poor goose is hoarding everything gold to protect her precious feathers?" Andrea said.

"Yes. She's even hoarding pecans and butternuts," Gabi said and jumped off of the wheel for a rest.

"If I offered her my golden loving cup, she might let us go then," Andrea said.

"Stupid Sis, we can't get the loving cup from the garden at the palace. We're just gerbils running around in a log," Nicky said.

A loud knocking on the log started them all running again. Clearly they would never get off the wheel. They would never get out of the log unless Andrea did something. "I'm still a princess," she said. She panted as she ran.

"In a cage," Nicky said.

"But I have helpers," the princess said.

"In a cage, too," Nicky said.

"No! Not just Gabi. I have the robots. They're in the broom closet. I can signal them with my digital watch," his sister said.

While they ran, Andrea pushed 13x13=169 on the tiny buttons with her claws. She stopped to catch her breath.

A chipmunk fell through a hole into the log beside them. Chippy dropped his notepad and stared at Andrea. "Frost on the pumpkin! Can I take over for you, Princess?" he said.

"Oh dear me! I was trying to get Thith from the closet in the palace," Andrea said.

"Well, you got me. My number is 169. What a story I'll have when we get out of here! Try again. You might even get that old goose down here," Chippy said. The knocking on the log became louder than ever. The bubbles drifted lower and lower. Chippy climbed on the wheel and started running.

"But I used the right numbers for gold. The numerical value of the letters AU is 13," Andrea said.

"Try the atomic number for gold. That's 79," Nicky said and jumped off the wheel.

Andrea pushed the button on her watch for seconds and then punched in the number 79. "Bring my golden loving cup!" she said into her watch.

In just one Ziv second, Thith peered into the hollow log. A cloth duster hung over her right arm. "Your Highness! You're in a mess. I can't help. There is nothing but an old log here. I can't even dust it," she said.

Before Andrea could say one word, Thith rolled away across the grass. In her left hand was a golden cup the size of a teacup.

"Guess the old goose cast a spell on that, too. What are you going to do now, Sis?" Nicky said.

The knocking on the hollow log became violent. The log shook so much everyone fell off the wheel. Andrea caught up her tail in her paws and looked up.

Mrs. Pennyweight peered at them through the cloud of bubbles. "Come out quickly. The magic spell is broken. You will all get stuck inside," she said and rolled the log on its side with her big beak. Everyone scrambled out of a big hole on the side of the log.

When they looked for Mrs. Pennyweight, she was disappearing into the orchard with the loving cup held tightly under her wing. The golden globe floated out of the hollow log followed by the cloudy bubbles. They floated into the orchard and disappeared.

"Your beautiful surprise is gone," Chippy said. He sat on the log and wiped one eye with his tail.

Andrea started to do the same, but noticed that her paws had become hands, and she was getting bigger. Nicky and Gabi were changing form as well.

Gabi sat on the log beside Andrea. "There is no loving-cup to drink apricot nectar from either," she said. She scuffed her golden tap shoes in the sand.

Nicky sat on the ground near the hollow stump. "Some festival. All I can see being there is a bunch of mice," he said.

"The mice! That's it! The pumpkin is even bigger than my loving cup. We can make a drink in it!" Andrea said. She jumped up and down and clapped her hands.

"Mrs. Pennyweight won't let us have any apricot nectar now. I know her," Chippy said.

"But we can get lots of milk from Angie. We can make crème de pumpkin. That can be our surprise, too," Princess Andrea said.

At the bottom of the garden on the other side of the orchard, they found the biggest pumpkin they could ever imagine. Andrea ordered a shuttle conch to land close to the pumpkin. Everyone began pushing on the pumpkin, but it wouldn't move.

A huge black bull stood in the field pawing the ground. He bawled. "Moo-oove! Pardon me, Princess, I'm Angus McPail at your service. I can moo-oove anything," Angus said. He lowered his head and gently pushed the pumpkin to the shuttle conch. There he stopped. "I can push, Princess, but I cannot lift for I'm a polled Angus. You need someone with horns like Jerry Jersey from New Pasture," the bull said.

"How can I call Jerry? There is no phone and there's not much time. The festival is scheduled to start soon," Andrea said. She needed to think so she sat down on the mound of earth Angus had pawed up.

A furry face poked out of a hole beside the Princess. "If it pleases Your Highness, I can whistle," Chucky Woodchuck said. When Andrea nodded he whistled through his teeth.

In a Ziv minute a golden Jersey bull trotted up. He hooked his horns under the pumpkin. Gently lifting he set it in the rocket shuttle.

"Thank you Chucky. Your whistle was a wonderful gift. Thank you everyone," Andrea said as she, Gabi, and her brother climbed into the giant shuttle.

Many guests had already arrived when the shuttle flew over the palace garden. The princess waved and disappeared into the palace. A few minutes later, her golden gown shimmering in the sunlight, she stepped from the glass capsule on the side of the building.

A flock of songsters from the Lands of Vligan had arranged special music for the festival. At the sight of the princess Drake nodded to the choir. They began to sing.

"Golden is this day so fair.
Golden is the gown you wear.
Happiness we now will share,
As we taste a golden pear," they sang.

Softly Ming came up on slippered feet. "Welcome to your Golden Jubilee Festival," she said and bowed low. She held out a crown of marsh marigolds.

"This way, Princess," Donald said. He wore a golden sword in a sheath at his side.

Andrea followed him to a table covered with a golden cloth. The huge pumpkin shell filled with crème de pumpkin sat in the middle surrounded with nasturtium blossoms and golden leaves. There were nuts of all kinds along with raisins, pumpkin seeds, and currants. A golden pear hanging over the pumpkin swung lightly in a spice-laden breeze.

Donald slid the golden sheath from its belt and laid it on the table where the loving cup had been. "The sword will take a special part. You will know it in your heart," he said and bowed.

"A toast to our Princess!" Drake said. His voice was broadcast to the whole garden as well as the park beyond.

"Long live Princess Andrea!" the Zivites shouted as one.

The dancing dolls passed around trays of sweetmeats rolled in grape leaves. Everyone helped and everyone shared. Looking around Andrea noticed her friends from Golden Globe weren't there.

Disappointed she handed a tray filled with carrot sticks to Gabi. "I wish I could get my hands on that silly goose," she said.

Mrs. Pennyweight landed on the edge of the golden pumpkin. Ripe pumpkin seeds scattered everywhere. She stood up and flapping her wings fell into the crème de pumpkin. The drink splashed all over the golden leaves decorating the table. In her amazement the goose's beak stayed wide open.

The music stopped. The singing stopped. All the Zivites stopped dancing to stare at Princess Andrea.

She unsheathed the golden sword raised it high and chanted. "Happiness is best when we share. So have a taste of my golden pear," she said. Neatly she sliced the pear in half. A drop of nectar fell into Mrs. Pennyweight's open beak.

Quickly the adjutants filled tiny gourds with drops of sweet pear nectar. The chipmunks scampered everywhere to serve the guests with them.

"My goodness, Your Highness, I've been so selfish. Just think! I nearly missed this wonderful festival," the goose said.

"Knoh!" Mrs. Pennyweight said. Angie and Angus McPail, along with the Jerseys appeared in the park. Chucky and Chucka Woodchuck came behind with the mice. Princess Amber followed with a sparrow on her shoulder. In the Ziv light her light-brown hair shone like amber honey.

"Knoh!" Mrs. Pennyweight said and climbed out of the golden pumpkin. The golden loving cup full of apricot nectar appeared on the table.

"Knoh!" the goose said the third time. A pumpkin-shaped golden globe surrounded by a myriad of bubbles floated over Princess Andrea's head.

"The surprise is a piñata!" everyone said and clapped. As one every guest began moving toward the park.

With everyone gathered around the princess and her adjutants, Andrea lifted the golden sword. Deftly she struck the golden Piñata, and treats fell to the ground. Covered in candy foil they shone like gold. Golden grapes and little candy pumpkins lay beside clover blossoms. The myriad of rainbow bubbles turned into marbles that tasted like honey. Flocks of brightly colored Vligan swooped low to pick them up. The sparrows and finches preferred the seeds that scattered in the warm breeze.

The golden rays of the late afternoon sun began to play over the park. When the breeze became quite cool, Andrea decided it was time to go. Tired and happy she thanked Buttercup and Mrs. Butterball. Quietly she ordered her coach to take her home. *My next trip can't be any more fun,* she thought.

The silvery shell settled on the parking lot. Wrapped in her golden bath towel Andrea circled above the palace to wave goodbye. As she flew, she spelled out words in puffs of milky white vapor. Her message was: Happiness is best when we share.

Love, Grandma Schoe

43

Andrea Flies to Yellow Satellite

ANDREA, HER YELLOW JUMP SUIT shining in the morning sun, hopped first on her right foot then on her left. *Today is going to be a great afternoon to sit on the swing in Grandma's garden,* she thought.

"That is if those pesky gnats stop bugging me," she muttered to herself. She hated insects.

The lilies by the goldfish pond were heavy with yellow blooms. The vines that wound their way over the wooden trellises were filled with yellow buds and bright blossoms. Andrea sniffed their delicate fragrance. Several honey bees crept over the flowers, and a few dragon flies hovered over the small pond.

Andrea began to sing. "Tum, tum, tiddley tee. Tee, tee, tiddley tum," she sang.

She was thinking about her trips to Ziv where she was a princess. She hadn't been there since she had been awarded a golden globe by her happy subjects. Snowpink, Andrea's pink- and-white teddy bear, hadn't talked to her for a long time. No rainbow had brought her one of her pearly-pink conch coaches. Andrea sighed.

Just then she noticed that one of the dragonflies hovering over the pond was bigger than all the rest. It stopped circling and made a bee-line straight for the arbour where Andrea was sitting. She told herself that perhaps if she stayed very still and quiet it would go away.

Instead the ugly creature got bigger and bigger. The whirring of its double wings grew louder and louder. Princess Andrea clapped her hands over her ears.

Soon the young princess was getting smaller and smaller, and she fell off the bench onto the grass where the dragonfly had landed. She thought she saw a small boy astride the back of the bug. Rubbing her eyes in disbelief Andrea stared. Surely this was Drake, Adjutant of the Vligan in the Princessdom of Ziv.

The boy wore fringed yellow buckskin. His straight dark- brown hair was held by a pink headband. The pink flamingo feather stuck in his headband brushed his dusky face. It just had to be Drake, but Andrea wondered whatever he was doing in her grandmother's garden astride a huge very yellow dragonfly.

"All aboard, Princess," the boy said. The whirring of the twin pair of wings was so loud, he had to shout.

"No way! I hate bugs," Andrea said. She remembered climbing the elevators when she first went to Ziv. The window by the third elevator had been swathed in yellow chiffon. The room was full of yellow daffodils blooming by a tranquil pond.

Fine, but the bugs, she thought. Those horrible dragon flies had scared her then. She wasn't about to climb aboard one now.

"Hurry, Princess! We don't have much time," Drake said. The wings of the dragonfly hummed louder and louder.

"Why can't I order my coach?" Andrea said.

"We have immediate clearance to land on Yellow Satellite. Do hurry! The Princessdom of Vligan needs you. Just climb up behind me," her adjutant said.

If I'm needed I have to go, Andrea thought. Taking a deep breath, she reached for Drake's hand and swung up awkwardly onto the dragonfly's back. Almost immediately a yellow glow up ahead caught her eye. She watched as it grew bigger and bigger.

In moments they were circling a small pond, and the dragonfly settled in a patch of maidenhair fern. A clump of lily-of-the- valley nearby wafted sweet perfume into the air.

Drake punched some numbers into the computer on the bug's back. "I'm sending Yeager for your twin flame," he said.

"My twin flame! Whatever is that?" she said. She hopped off the bugs back and became her right size.

"Not whatever. You mean whoever. Your twin flame is a girl about your age who is coming to help you. In fact here on Yellow Satellite you will have two twin flames. Twin twins you know," Drake said.

"I don't need any help. Certainly not from some little twits my own age," Andrea said.

"They're coming anyway," Drake said. The dragonfly took to the air.

"I forbid it," Andrea said. No way did she want anyone to interfere in her Princessdom.

"Sorry, Princess, this is something you can't do by yourself. You need Karah for this job. Kadence will join you both later," Drake said.

"So! What is my job here? What do I have to do for the Vligan on Yellow Satellite that I can't do by myself?" Andrea said.

"Look around you! See what a beautiful world Yellow Satellite is," Drake said.

A huge yellow butterfly landed on the back of Andrea's hand. As it rested its wings opened and folded. *I've never seen anything so lovely,* she thought.

"Butterflies are insects, too. Each bug has its own job to do," Drake said, as the butterfly flew to a fern.

Andrea crossed her arms over her chest. "Does everyone here on Yellow Satellite have a twin?" she said.

"They certainly do. Everyone but Outlanders has a twin. Not everyone has a twin flame though. That's special. Most are twin souls," Drake said and scuffed his moccasins in the soft grass.

A sudden breeze wafted the scent of lavender over them. Andrea wished she could take some home for her bath. "What are twin souls?" she said to her adjutant.

Drake turned his soft brown eyes from the lavender to Andrea. "Perhaps you will find a twin soul someday. That's someone with whom you spend most of your time, someone with whom you feel you belong. Twin flames are different. A twin flame is someone who shares a duty. You are lucky. You have two. There's a poem about it," he said. He brushed the pink flamingo feather out of his face.

> "We have an unknown task, we two.
> Something special we must do.
> This duty cannot be done by one.
> It's unique and needs two for fun," he said.

Fun! How can it be fun to have two girls you don't know and don't like helping you? Andrea thought. She let the thought drift through her mind.

A whirring of wings in the hazelnut tree caught the princess' attention. Its branches were filled with yellow budgies. Dozens of bright hummingbirds hovered around her. Their tiny wings bathed her in the scent of the nearby lavender. Yellow butterflies, their soft wings at rest, covered the stand of fern between them and the pond. The air seemed alive with mystery.

Two tawny faces appeared among the budgies. Two tawny tails wrapped around a low branch, and two monkeys dropped to the ground chattering together. Andrea could hardly make out what they were saying.

"Welcome. Highness. Happy. Here. Now," they said. On cue the budgies voices blended into one chorus, and they began to sing, "Welcome dear Princess. We're glad--"

The song was interrupted by the whirring of wings. Yeager lit carefully just a few feet from where Andrea was standing. In a Ziv moment the girl who slid off the dragonfly's back was just the same size as Andrea.

"Hi! I'm Karah," the girl said and held out her hand.

"Go away!" Andrea said. Karah had spoiled her welcome song. No way did she want this intruder to stay.

Karah was wearing a yellow jump suit just like Andrea's. She had a yellow scarf tucked in at the throat and another hung from her pocket.

Yuck! She shaved her head, Andrea thought. Before Andrea could turn and walk away, she noticed Drake beside her.

"This is Karah. She shaved her head because one of her friends has cancer. Eden felt different than everyone at school because she lost all her hair," Drake said quietly.

Smiling Drake turned to the girl. Placing his right hand over his heart he bowed low. "Duchess Karah, I am Drake, Adjutant of the three Zivoids of Vligan in the land of Ziv. Welcome to Yellow Satellite," he said.

"Duchess!" Andrea said. She was about to order Drake to send Karah away, when a rather large myna bird settled in the hazelnut tree. The feathers on the bird's black wings were tinged with a yellow powder. It smelled awful just like rotten eggs. Andrea wished the bird would go away.

Straightening its feathers a bit the bird squawked. "Help! Help! Princess, we need your help! They've taken Mervin! They're already draining Marigold Swamp! Next thing they destroy will be the lemon grove on Myna Ridge," she said. She shook her tail feathers.

Drake picked a few leaves from the tree and began wiping the yellow powder off the bird's feathers. "Calm down, Ervina," he said and continued to stroke the exhausted bird.

"Who are they? Who is Mervin? And what have they taken him for?" Andrea said. She wondered what, if anything, she could do about it.

"They are the Rushers. Roland Rusher and Lola Rusher are twins from the monkey tribe that lives on the Plain of Cyn," Drake said.

The two monkeys came up. "Roland is my cousin," Fernando said. He twisted his tail around his legs.

Ernanda sat back on her haunches. "Lola is his twin. They run Cyn City. The wasps that are building Cyn City are on a building frenzy, and they never stop working," she said.

"They'll never stop. The Rushers are using my twin Mervin to find more sulphur," Ervina said and settled on a lower branch.

"What do they use sulphur for?" Princess Andrea said. She knew now why Ervina smelled like rotten eggs.

"Here on Yellow Satellite they have found that by mixing yellow sulphur into their concrete it will power their beetle- boards," Drake said.

At that moment Yeager dropped to a branch on a yellow-green fern. Another girl about the age of Andrea and Karah slid to the ground. "Hi! I am Kadence. What do we do here for fun?" she said and tied a yellow scarf more tightly around her very short very blonde hair. Her scarf matched her slacks and top.

"Donated your hair didn't you? My friend Eden cried when she saw I'd shaved my head like hers," Karah said to Kadence and smiled.

"That's what friends are for," Kadence said. A shy smile lit up her face.

Drake and the monkeys came up to where Andrea stood glaring at the two girls who had just been dropped off. The monkeys, each carrying two yellow velvet boxes, stopped in front of Andrea.

Your celliPhone, Princess," Drake said. He handed her one of the two yellow boxes he held.

Eagerly Andrea removed a pair of yellow quartz earrings. A small yellow ball dangled from a larger one. Inside each ball, colored bands seemed to dance in the light. Andrea looked for clips to attach them to her ears. There were none.

"Just put them on, Princess. They will stay as long as you think them there. On Yellow Satellite thoughts are things. The earrings are tourmaline, and these yellow balls are your celliPhone receivers," Drake said.

The other box contained what looked like railway tracks or braces. Set in the front was a row of tiny tourmaline marbles. Sure that she didn't need braces, Andrea handed the box back to her adjutant. "The earrings are peachy keen, but--" she said.

"But you do need these. They will send everything you say to the other receivers," Drake said. He handed two identical boxes to Karah and Kadence. In moments each girl's smile was studded with the tiny gems, and tourmaline earrings hung from their ears.

Both monkeys began dancing up and down. They chattered to each other, but Andrea couldn't understand a word they said.

Drake laughed. "Yes, you shall have earrings, too. Be sure you obey orders from both your princess and the duchesses," he said.

The monkeys disappeared into the trees. Soon their happy chattering could be heard, as they preened in front of their reflection in the pond.

Moments later Fernando swung down from a low branch in the tree. "Princess, Duchesses, the water in the pond is much lower today," he said.

Ervina squawked. "I told you so. It's just like Marigold Pond this side of the ridge. Something must be done to stop the Rushers. They will destroy everything beautiful on Yellow Satellite. If you make yourself small enough, Princess, I can carry you to Cyn City," she said. She pulled out a tattered feather and let it float to the ground.

The last thing Andrea wanted to do was go to Cyn City. The next to last thing she wanted to do was get on Ervina's back. The bird still smelled like rotten eggs. She was just about to give an excuse when Karah took a step toward the big myna bird. No way could Andrea let Karah get ahead of her rotten eggs or no rotten eggs.

I must make myself the size of a budgie, Andrea thought. As she began to shrink Ernanda handed her a handful of hazelnuts.

"Chew on them when you need to think deeply. The ancient Druids used them for that all the time," Drake said.

Andrea climbed onto Ervina's back. As the myna bird circled over the ferns, Andrea saw the two girls stomp away into the hazelnut grove.

The princess of Yellow Satellite felt herself sliding from the myna's back. She grabbed a wing feather and hung on.

"Be careful, Princess. We're coming in for a landing. This is Myna Ridge," the bird said. She ducked low under a lemon tree and landed by a vegetable patch.

Sliding to the ground Andrea caught her breath. The view back from Myna Ridge was of verdant valleys, ponds, and treed hillsides.

A breeze from the valley on the other side of the ridge brought the distinct smell of sulphur. From her vantage point, she could see yellow towers sticking up through a dirty yellow cloud. As she watched, the nearest tower grew higher and higher. Clouds of sulphur dust thickened around it.

"The wasps are really at it today. The Rushers won't let them have a bit of rest," the myna bird said.

Andrea's earrings began to ring. "Where are you, Princess?" Drake said.

Quickly Andrea tapped the number two marble on her braces. "I'm on Myna Ridge. I can see Cyn City from here," she said.

"The tallest tower you see is Roland's palace. Lola's is next highest," the voice in Andrea's ear said.

"I suppose I have to go down there. I need to find out why the Rushers can make everyone do what they want," Andrea said.

Ervina squawked. "There is a landing pad on both towers. I can't land there. It's for the dragon flies," she said.

I'll need Yeager then, Andrea thought. She was about to order him sent when a whirr of wings cut through the sounds in her ears. She grinned. "Thoughts really are things. That's really fast service," she said. Her grin changed to a scowl when Kadence and Karah slipped off the dragonfly's back.

"I thought you might need a good set of wings. Guess I was right. The poor old myna looks exhausted," Karah said.

"So take her back to the hazelnut grove. You should be able to make yourselves small as a gnat. You both bug me enough," Andrea said.

"Wow! Aren't we the grateful one?" Kadence said. She put her scarf over her nose as a sudden gust brought the stench of sulphur.

"If you're going down there you'll need this," Karah said. She pulled a bit of yellow cloth from the pocket of her jump suit and handed it to Andrea.

Snatching the scarf Andrea punched some coordinates into Yeager's computer. In moments she was circling over the pond on the roof of Lola's castle. "Wow!" she said. She couldn't believe her eyes or her ears.

Dragonflies of every size flit from roof pond to roof pond. Wings folded by their side, damselflies rested sedately on yellowed maidenhair fern. Clusters of wasps buzzed over building after building. The potter wasps, busy daubing mud onto rising towers, ignored the paper wasps. The paper wasps were frantically building layer after layer of condos. White-faced hornets flew in and out of apartments nearby. The two main towers were covered with a moving mass of black dots. Andrea wondered what they were and what they were doing.

Yeager paused just long enough for Andrea to slip to the yellow grass by the roof pond. She felt herself growing as the dragonfly disappeared over the bigger of the two tallest towers. Yellow jackets began buzzing around Andrea's head. She wanted to crawl into the fern and hide, but she was getting bigger and bigger.

On Yellow Satellite thoughts are things, Andrea thought. She sat cross-legged and thought herself small, but nothing happened. She dare not move lest the horrible creatures sting her.

"Stop it! Shoo! Who are you and what are you doing in Cyn City? This is my city and I don't like pests," someone said. The buzzing of the yellow jackets stopped.

On opening her eyes, Andrea saw a perfect copy of Ernanda. This skinny monkey was as yellow as the dust that blew around them. "I'm l-l-ost. Perhaps you could show me your wonderful home. I've never seen anything quite like this," she said.

Because her teeth were chattering, she could hardly find the number two tourmaline on her braces. She pushed a button anyway. Her earring began to vibrate, but the noise from the streets below drowned out every sound. *At least Drake will be able to hear me*, she thought. Still she wished she could hear him.

Andrea slowly got to her feet. "I'm Andrea," she said. Very politely she held out her hand.

"You're nothing. I'm head honcho here. Everyone does as I say," Lola said.

A slightly larger monkey landed on the roof of Lola's tower. His yellow face twisted with rage. "Just who do you think you are?" he said and beat on his chest with his fists.

51

"I'm your sister, darling. I run things for you. You're far too busy for trivial matters," Lola said.

"Just so you remember who the head honcho is. What do you have here? She's not yellow! She's not one of us! Get rid of her!" the larger monkey said. Still beating on his chest he danced in a circle around Andrea.

This must be Roland, Andrea thought. She already didn't like the pair very much.

"I'll do it in my own time. She could be useful," Lola said. Her nasty grin terrified Andrea.

Roland stopped stomping around. "Just don't let her upset our plans. I want Cyn City to be so big it takes over the whole dump the other side of Myna Ridge," he said.

Lola glared at her brother. "I fancy a grand palace in the middle of the lemon grove," she said.

"Not your palace. It will be my palace. You can have the marigold swamp," her brother said.

"No way! Now get out of my garden! I'll deal with this pest," Lola said.

The tourmaline earrings clinging to Andrea's ears buzzed loudly. Clearly Drake was trying to tell her to do something. She glanced at the dirty cloud that covered the city below.

She needed to see what was happening on the streets. A ladybug floated from one stand of fern to another beside the pond. *I need wings*, Andrea thought. She saw no other way to get off the roof. A damsel fly hovered beside her. "Ladybug size," Andrea said, and she began to shrink.

Before Lola could turn around, Andrea was on the back of the damsel fly. Moments later they were flying through the thick cloud that came from the burning yellow sulphur. Another wave of nausea swept over Andrea. She held the scarf Karah had given her close to her nose.

The damselfly flew over the street below. Nowhere could Andrea see a spot where she could safely land. The streets were crammed with black stag beetles. They were standing with back feet on round yellow boards. With horns tooting and blaring, they bumped into each other. As they sped through the streets, clouds of choking dust rose in the wake of their wheels.

"This is so wow. There are hundreds of yellow ladybugs hitchhiking on the backs of hundreds of stag beetles. It's so dark here that the myriads of fireflies darting about are the only light," the princess said into her mouthpiece.

Karah's voice came back to her left ear. "I'll bet they're Bunch-buggies," she said.

The damselfly flew to the entrance of the first in a line of cone-shaped paper huts. Before she could fold her wings, Andrea hopped off her back. The honey bees flying into the top of the cones bumped into other honey bees flying out. Wings beating frantically they took off in all directions.

Princess Andrea watched closely as the damselfly tore off a bit of the paper wall for a cone and stuck it into a slot in the wall. A paper cup partly filled with nectar popped out.

A long line of beetles, flies, and bugs began forming in front of the hut. Paper wasps replaced each leaf of paper as soon as it was torn off. Soon only empty cups came from the slot. A loud angry buzzing began among the insects.

Realizing she was still as small as a ladybug, Andrea hopped on the back of the nearest stag beetle. Zigging and zagging she sped through the crowd and down the street. Her ride took a sharp turn, and she was thrown off onto a passing Bunch-buggy beetle.

When it swerved at the end of the street, Andrea fell onto a pile of wet black feathers. "What have we here? A ladybug in the shape of a little girl?" the pile of black feathers said.

"Mervin!" Andrea said. She was so excited to find Ervina's twin she almost forgot to grow. "Myna size," she said.

One of Mervin's wings had been clipped. Getting him to fly her out of here was out of the question. Both of them were in fact trapped. She wondered when Lola or Roland might find them and set the stinging hornets on them. *At least Kadence and Karah don't know what a fix I've gotten myself into. I'd just die if they did,* she thought.

Andrea caught her breath and looked around. Mervin was sitting beside a leaking water tower near a refuse heap. Hoards of dung beetles were pushing small lumps of refuse up a long hill to a larger dump. Disturbed by the activity a cloud of flies rose into the air.

"What's going on?" Andrea said. She had to find out what, if anything, she could do to stop the destruction of Yellow Satellite.

"It's the Rushers. No one is allowed to rest even for a minute. They must build, build, and build some more," Mervin said and tucked his head under his good wing.

Andrea thought that the Rushers had taken over too much of the beautiful satellite already. "Looks like too much is never enough for them," she said.

"I'm supposed to be getting more yellow sulphur for their paving projects, but since they clipped my wing I can't fly into the desert to find the stuff," he said. When he pulled his head out from under his wing a drop of water fell from his eye.

Andrea stroked his wet feathers. "No need to worry. I'm Princess Andrea of Ziv. I'm here to help you," she said.

The air was filled with an angry buzzing. "Princess, she's coming! You'd better hide. Lola has all her yellow jackets with her," Mervin said.

Andrea thought herself into the size of a lady bug. She whispered into her celli-Phone, as she shrunk. "I'll need help with this," she said. The celiPhone had become so small, she wondered if it would transmit anything at all to Drake or the girls.

The buzzing grew louder and louder. Andrea shook as she clung to the underside of one of Mervin's wing feathers.

"Move over!" Karah said. Ladybug-sized she crept onto Mervin's wing.

"Where's Drake?" Andrea said. She was so annoyed with Karah, she lost her grip on Mervin's wing and slid to the ground.

Karah dropped beside her. "If you wanted Drake you tapped in the wrong code. Anyway you've got me," she said.

"Cyn city is in a real mess what with the Rushers and everything. What makes you think you can help?" Andrea said.

"We're twin flames remember! Of course I can help," Karah said.

Kadence dropped down beside them. She handed some hazelnuts to Andrea and Karah. "We just have to think," she said and popped a nut into her own mouth. No matter how small they were, the tangy taste of the hazelnuts made them worth chewing slowly.

Princess Andrea grabbed one of Mervin's wing feathers and pulled herself up. "What's all that noise?" she said.

"The Bunch buggies beetles are trying to get out of Lola's way. She insists that the streets be lined with her subjects when she rides her jeweled Bunch-buggy," Mervin said.

"Lola's subjects! No way! Princess Andrea is ruler of Cyn City and ruler of all of Yellow Satellite besides," Kadence said.

The princess noticed a column of winged ants marching past Mervin's hiding place. "Whatever are they doing?" she said.

"They're being sent to the desert to look for food. They bring lots back, but everyone in the city is hungry," the bird said.

A huge Bunch-buggy decorated in polished hazelnuts stopped in front of Mervin. A cloud of yellow jackets settled to the pavement beside it. Lola, wearing a purple-and-yellow cloak of bittersweet flowers, stepped off the Bunch-buggy.

Her crown of a solid mass of caraway seeds slipped over one eye. She stared at the wet bird with her other eye. "There you are you useless thing. You haven't found a bit of sulphur. Have you seen that pest that invaded my palace?" she said.

Mervin shook all over but said nothing. Andrea and her twin helpers clung tightly to his protective wing.

An even larger bunch buggy screeched to a halt. Roland flung his lemony yellow cloak over one shoulder and shouted at Lola. "What's going on here? I'll not have slackers in my kingdom. What has this mangy-looking creature done for us?" he said. He cracked a walnut with his teeth and popped the nutmeat into his mouth.

Lola poked the myna bird with the jeweled stick she used for walking. "Onto the refuse heap with you then. My soldiers will deal with you just as soon as I find that pest," she said.

Karah crept closer to Andrea and whispered in her ear. "Seems like the Rushers have plenty of food and flowers," she said.

That's it! The towers must be full of food that's being kept for the rulers and their minions, she thought. "If I become my own size I will be bigger than Roland and Lola, and they will be too surprised to set the yellow jackets after me," she said.

Looking down on the rushers, Andrea spoke in her loudest voice, "I am Andrea, Princess of Ziv. I am ruler of Yellow Satellite and of Cyn City. Open up your storehouses and feed the Vligan folk," she said. The princess grinned as Duchess Karah and Duchess Kadence appeared beside her.

In a panic the two Rushers jumped off their Bunch-buggies. They tripped over each other as they raced off after the column of ants toward the desert. The yellow jackets followed them stinging them in their most tender spots as they sped away.

Andrea put one hand or her hip. "Guess we'll just have to feed them ourselves," she said. Together the three girls opened the doors to the twin towers. They discovered stores of honey, and seeds from marjoram, lemon, verbena, and bittersweet, as well as wild carrot.

The Vligan folk lined up and tearing paper strips for paper cones wrapped the food. Calmly they passed it down the long lines.

"Thank you Princess Andrea," the lady bugs said. They hummed while the stag beetles honked their horns. The wasps buzzed. "Thank you," they said. The damsel flies dipped their wings in a curtsey.

Princess Andrea tapped the number two agate on her celi-Phone mouth brace. "Please send Yeager. We are finished here," she said.

Andrea, Kadence, and Karah shrunk to fit on the back of the dragonfly. They asked him to zoom over the vacated palaces as they left Cyn City. Everyone in the city was dancing in the streets below.

Yeager landed in the hazelnut grove close to golden Marigold Pond. Andrea and her twin flames jumped from his back and began to grow to their normal size.

Ervina flew down from her perch at the top of the hazelnut tree. "Where is Mervin? I want to go to him," she said. She paced up and down in front of the girls.

"Right here," Andrea said. With a tug, she pulled the still wet myna bird out of the pocket of her yellow jump suit.

"What a way to go! Wish I could do that more often," he said and became his own size.

Taking the pink feather from his headband, Drake bowed and swept it before the three girls. "I declare you henceforth to be twin flames in all the lands of the Vligan folk," he said.

Andrea, Karen, and Kadence hugged each other and said their goodbyes. When the tired princess found herself back on the swing in her grandmother's garden, she wondered if one of her twin flames would share her next adventure. Dozens of fireflies lit the twilight as they flit through the air around her.

Love, Grandma Schoe

Andrea Visits Violet Orb

ANDREA SAT BOLT UPRIGHT IN bed. Snowpink was sitting on the bed with her head down. She was sure her teddy bear wasn't talking in her sleep. She pulled the pink sheet over her dark hair and tried to go to sleep herself. She heard the sound again: Tum, tum, tiddley tee. Tee, tee, tiddley tum.

Andrea had only heard these words when she was in the Land of Be Alive. In Ziv she was a princess where she had a princessdom. She jumped out of bed to see if some of her subjects were calling her. The room was empty.

She opened the window. Rain pelted down, but there was no rainbow in the very dark sky. There was nothing to take her to Ziv. She sighed and turning around bumped into the largest conch shell she had ever seen. The pearly conch shimmered and glowed in rhythm with the words: Tum, tum, tiddley-tee. Tee, tee, tiddley-tum.

It had been the shell she'd heard all along. *Someone in Ziv does want me to come,* she thought. Andrea grabbed her pink dressing gown and pulled it on over her pink sleep set. She crawled inside the conch, and felt the wall of air close around her. As she grew smaller and smaller, she wondered who had sent for her. Without warning Andrea found herself in the middle of a mud puddle. Her pink sleep set and gown were sopping wet.

A voice said, "Serves you right. You weren't paying any attention to where you were going."

Surely that's Snowpink, thought Andrea. She looked around, but there was no pink and white teddy bear anywhere.

"Look up! There are more places to be than one you know. I thought you learned to think about things," the voice said.

Andrea pushed her dripping wet hair out of her eyes and looked up. Sitting snugly inside a pearly conch shell was her teddy bear. The princess stamped her bare foot and splashed mud all over. It's your entire fault. You should have told me I wasn't on automatic pilot," she said.

"I told you that learning to be a princess would be quite difficult, but you chose to be one anyway. Now go to your palace and get one of your adjutants to help you. You're a mess," Snowpink said.

Andrea stomped across the dark parking lot to the palace. She stomped up the stairs to the huge double doors. She hated being alone in the dark. "I am Princess Andrea. Let me in!" she said. No light came on. The doors stayed fast shut, and no smiling adjutant came out to meet her. She pounded on the door with her fist. "I am Princess Andrea. I order you to let me in!" she said.

"Even a princess has to be polite. You could try being more gentle," Snowpink said.

Andrea stamped on the paving. "Ouch!" she said and hopped on the other foot. A few tears fell on the polished marble.

The door opened to a kimono-clad girl with a smiling face. "Princess! I am Ming, Adjutant of the Three Orbs of the Land of Eau de Phyn in the Princessdom of Ziv. Do come in, Your Highness," she said."

Brushing the tears out of her eyes, Andrea stared in wonder at what looked like a vision in front of her. The girl's kimono of violet silk was tied with a sea-green sash. Her very dark hair was cut short, and bangs fell to her eyebrows.

"Please take me to my private rooms. I'm a mess," Andrea said. Head down she followed the shushing sound Ming's navy slippers made, as they walked across the pink marble floor.

On floor thirteen an elevator opened to a hall of mirrors. An open door revealed a sunken tub filled with lavender-scented colored water. Bubbles danced over the sunken tub. Tossing aside her dressing gown and sleep set, Andrea raced across the floor and slid into the warm water.

"Now I know where we get the lavender scent. Karah and I saw it growing on Yellow Satellite," the princess said.

"Yes, Your Highness. This fine herbal bath comes from one of your own satellites. Perhaps when Your Highness has relaxed, you would like a milk bath. Shall I fill the Birthday-bath tub?" Ming said. She bowed and slipped a tub pillow under Andrea's head.

Andrea slid further into the tub of bubbles. "Yes. Please do. And I bet the milk comes from Angie McPail on Golden Globe," she said.

Her adjutant didn't hear her. Ming was already filling the gleaming white tub with a warm milk bath. She set a small jar of cream beside the tub for Andrea's facial.

"Tum, tum, tiddley-tee. Tee, tee, tiddley-tum," Andrea said softly to herself. *This visit to Ziv is going to be great*, she thought. She had her palace all to herself, and wondered if she might visit one of her zivoids but decided not to. It was too much fun just being at home.

The young princess was startled when the door to her bath opened, and some girls started filing in. *Surely I should have some privacy in my own bathroom,* she thought. Then she realized that each doll looked exactly like her right down to the dark almond-shaped eyes.

Before she had a chance to say anything Ming came in. "Please choose your gown, Your Highness. The tea ceremony begins in exactly one hour. Your guest is already on her way," she said.

"Guest? What guest? I didn't invite anybody. I just want to be here in Ziv all by myself. Please send whoever it is away," the princess said.

"Excuse, please. You promised Duchess Karah that she would be named Sarah-Karah in a special ceremony. Today is the correct day for the tea ceremony. Violet Orb will be giving its best light at exactly midnight, and this won't happen again for many Ziv years," the adjutant of Violet Orb said.

The dolls began filing around the porcelain bathtub. Each stopped and twirled in front of Andrea. Every gown was of fine silk in gorgeous rainbow colors. *I'll never be able to choose. I like them all,* Andrea thought.

A pale ivory gown with an empire waistline caught her eye. A bright lavender sash tied high under the bodice flowed to the hem of the floor-length skirt at the back. "This one is perfect, and I'd like a bunch of purple violets pinned to the shoulder. Please hand me my towel," she said.

A crash in the courtyard sent Andrea to the window to see what was happening. The bright orb overhead, now lighting the parking lot, showed a yellow conch shell on its side in the mud puddle. A young girl was crawling out from under it.

The dancing dolls crowded in behind Andrea. "Just fancy! She's like, you know, rather clumsy," a doll in red said.

"Imagine! She thinks she can come to a tea ceremony in a yellow jump suit," a doll in a green dress said.

"How very drolly! Does she think she's coming to a puppet show?" another doll said, as she smoothed down her orange sheath.

Princess Andrea clapped her hands. "Stop it! I'll not have you making fun of Duchess Karah. I want you to go down there and greet her for me. Bring her here so she can get cleaned up," she said.

"Please run a fresh bath and bring more towels. I know just how she feels," the princess said to her adjutant.

Andrea had chosen ivory shoes to go with her gown. Karah was wearing white Mary Janes that matched her long lace dress. They held hands as they followed Ming down a long corridor.

Ming waved her hand at the wall and a door opened. They stepped into a glass enclosure which immediately whooshed to the top of the palace.

As another door opened into a room carpeted in white plush, Andrea gasped in amazement. Soon the girls were standing under the partial glass dome of an open retractable roof. Myriads of bright lights twinkled in the sky around a bright sphere.

Violet Orb shone her light deeply into the room turning the white carpet into varying shades of violet. A shaft of light from Violet Orb's own moon flowed across the floor and lit up a circle in the center of the tea room.

"I once read a poem about the moon. I wish I could remember it," Andrea said.

Ming slippered up to the where the girls were standing. She said, "Excuse, please. It's like this.

> "*MOON MAID*
> Silent, slipping softly through silver strands
> Unfetted by majorettes and marching bands,
> You seem to hold wisdom warmly in your hands
> Measuring the hour with sentinel, shifting sands.
> Are you the mourning Mother of our erring Earth,
> Or did she secretly spawn bringing you to birth?
> Where languish Laughter, Melody and Mirth

Waiting for the stage, the set, within your girth?
If I could spring like a wayward wallaby
And in your arid arms haven happily
Would you, will you a shining shelter be
A modern manger where I can lay my baby?" she said.

Karah twirled around gazing at the backdrop of stars. "Wow! It looks just like a violet-colored melon. This is really rad. I used to think that the stars were melons," she said and skipped across the carpet. When she tried to twirl again, she caught her toe in the deep plush. Tummy-first she fell onto the floor.

Andrea ran over to help her guest up. Karah's face was very, very red.

Motioning for the girls to follow, Ming stepped quietly toward the center of the floor and knelt in the circle of silvery light. Andrea knelt to her right and Karah to her left. Andrea was sure Karah's heart must be beating as fast as her own. After all they were like twins in Ziv.

Across the room a mirrored door opened, and a very large lobster emerged. He was as black and shiny as the stack of three small lacquered tables he was carrying in his claw. It was all Andrea could do to remain kneeling quietly. Karah clamped both hands over her mouth.

Bowing slightly Ming sat motionless as the lobster set a table in front of each of the girls. Each table was inlaid with a design in mother-of-pearl. When the lobster clicked his pincers the door opened again, and three fiddler crabs sidled into the room. Each had a white linen cloth draped over his left claw. His overly-large right claw held a small silver tray containing a delicate porcelain cup and a white linen napkin.

A fourth crab emerged with a silver teapot on a silver tray. When the cups were set before each girl, he poured tea for each celebrant. The aroma of peppermint wafted from the cups.

Lights came on in the wall opposite the girls, and a large video screen appeared. A huge central circle was surrounded by twelve smaller ones. Andrea was surprised to see an image of Snowpink in the central circle.

"Dear Karah, welcome to the Land of Ziv. You will now be known as Sarah-Karah for you are now Princess of Violet Moon in the land of Ziv," Snowpink said.

Ming picked up her cup of peppermint tea and bowed. She took a sip. Andrea and Karah did the same. Ming bowed toward Andrea and took another sip. She bowed to Karah. Their eyes met over their sips of tea.

The image of a boy wearing western shirt, Levis, and boots appeared in three of the smaller circles. His boots shone like copper foil, and he had a silver buckle at his belt. The blue lapis lazuli stones which studded his belt and buckle glowed. He bowed. "Welcome to the Land of Ziv, Princess Karah. I am Donald, Adjutant of the Three Moons of Fyrh, he said.

Each of the girls bowed and took another sip of the special tea. A shiver of excitement went down Andrea's back when three more circles lit up. Each contained an image of Gabi in a golden jumpsuit.

Her voice came from the surrounding walls. "Princess Sarah-Karah, welcome to the Land of Ziv. I am Gabi adjutant of the Three Globes of the Land of the Folke de Terre," she said. Her jump-suit glowed as she bowed to the new princess.

Karah smiled when she saw Drake appear in the next three circles that opened up. He pulled a pink flamingo feather from his headband, bowed and waved it toward Karah. "Sarah-Karah, you are indeed welcome. You have earned the right to be a princess. Now you must learn to be a princess," he said.

Music from the computer-organ filled the room. Hundreds of budgie voices joined in singing.

> "Tum, tum, tiddley-tee.
> Tee, tee, tiddley-tum.
> You are welcome Sarah-Karah
> To this wonderful princessdom," they sang.

Ming stood up and bowed to each of the girls who stood up also. "Excuse please. You go now," she said.

Andrea felt that her feet were on nothing. Her gown was floating inches above the carpet.

Karah grabbed her hand. Less than a Ziv minute later, they were looking out over the Land of Be Alive from above the ceremonial tea room. Before Andrea could point out how vast the countryside was, the palace became a mere speck below them.

Realizing that they were being beamed up to Violet Orb, Andrea wondered if they would land head first. The quick flip in mid-flight left her a bit dizzy.

She took a deep breath when her feet touched down near the edge of a huge ice floe. The sea beside them was green, but the ice reflected the violet of the clear sky. A salty tang filled the crisp air, and rhythmic waves sloshed gently against the ice.

Karah was shivering so much her teeth were chattering. "Think warm. This is Ziv. Just think warm," Andrea said. It wouldn't do to let Karah know they were both freezing.

"What are those creatures, Mummy?" a small creature said.

Andrea heard the splash of water at the side of the ice floe but saw no one. Both girls peered over the side of the ice. Round dark eyes gazed at them from a furry violet-tinted white face. The baby seal's black nose twitched as if the girls smelled nasty.

"Just practice your diving, dear. I'll check them out," a larger creature said. The pup immediately dove into the water and disappeared. A small gray face followed by a large floppy body hurled itself onto the ice. "I'm Phoca. You wouldn't hurt my baby would you?" she said.

Andrea noticed a harp shape amid the black markings on the seal's back. "Of course not, you're a harp seal aren't you?" she said.

"Certainly am. You're an Utlander aren't you? Surely you'll stay for lunch? We have fresh fish," the seal said.

"Um, no thanks," Andrea said. The thought of swallowing a whole raw fish appealed to her not at all.

"Surely you and your pup aren't out here all by yourselves!" Karah said. She looked at the water where the baby seal had disappeared a few minutes before. There weren't even any bubbles left on the surface.

"Oh! Look!" Andrea said. She stood with her mouth open in amazement.

Dozens of dark gray bodies were leaping into the air like dolphins, as they swam toward the ice foe. Dozens of pups with violet-white fur coats followed their mothers onto the ice. One of the pups tried to nurse at Phoca's milk bar. Sniffing his fur she pushed him away. Another pup flopped its way over to Phoca. One sniff and she let it cuddle up to her and nurse.

"I guess that's how they know their own baby. They certainly all look alike," Karah said. Together the princesses picked their way among the squirming bodies to the edge of the ice floe.

A squishy sound caught Andrea's attention. She knelt down and peered over the edge of the ice. A spray of water caught her squarely in the face.

The eyes in the large fat face with its big whiskers and long tusks seemed to be laughing. "Well, well what have we here? Utlanders I suspect," the creature said. He dug his tusks into the side of the ice and pulled his huge body up beside the girls.

"I'm Wally Colly. You Utlanders don't need to be so scared," he said, as he balanced himself on his flippers.

Andrea guessed that her face must be as white as Karah's. She knew that they were both shaking. After all this cinnamon-brown animal was over six feet long and must weigh nearly a ton. "Of course, we're startled," Andrea said. She had no intention of letting Wally know she was terrified of him.

"And we're scared. You're a bull walrus and a bully, too, or you wouldn't have sprayed us like that," Karah said.

"It was just a jolly-fun greeting. I guess I'm supposed to call you 'Startled' and 'Scared', or do you have other names?" Wally said.

Andrea stood up as tall as she could and straightened her silver tiara. "I'm Andrea, Princess of Ziv, and this is Princess Sarah-Karah. Violet Moon belongs to my, no our Princessdom," she said.

"Oh well, that's your problem. Can't say as I'd want a princessing job myself," the walrus said.

A slightly smaller body pulled itself up onto the cold ice. "Jolly good, jolly good. I'm Jolly Colly. You'll be staying for lunch, of course. We'll bring up a few shrimp or some snails if you'd like them better," she said.

"Oh no, thank you. I much prefer vegetables," Andrea said. She was sure even seaweed would be more to her taste than raw crustaceans.

"In that case we'll eat out. There's a lovely sand bar just across the way that features fresh coconut milk. Hop on. We'll be there in no time," Wally said.

Tossing aside her shoes Andrea slid onto Wally's back. When the walrus surfaced the young princess was sputtering and spitting, but she held on to the animal's neck. *After all Wally had said it wasn't far and the walruses knew the sea so what could go wrong*, Andrea thought.

Karah quickly tossed off her shoes and climbed onto Jolly's back. "This should be fun," she said, as Jolly slid into the deep water.

Andrea soon lost track of time. It might have been a few minutes later or forever later, when she saw that they were in the middle of a deep ocean. The ice flow and the seals were far behind. No sand bar was in sight. The only thing that was visible under the violet sky was Karah's white dress.

The waves sang to Andrea: Tum, tum, tiddley-tee. Tee, tee, tiddley-tum. That, and the motion of the walrus as his powerful flippers drove through the ocean, made Andrea sleepy. The young princess had never felt so filled with peace, then she noticed that Karah was far ahead of her. Between them a shark surfaced and dove again.

A Ziv minute later Wally climbed up on a sand dune. Andrea slipped off the walrus' back and caught her breath, as she lay shaking on the sand beside Karah.

"Did you see that shark out there? It nearly frightened the life out of me. I was just about asleep when I saw its dorsal fin," Karah said. Her voice shook.

"I told you it wouldn't be easy being a princess. We've got a lot to learn yet," Andrea said.

"Well I don't want to be a princess anymore. I want to go home," Karah said.

"I don't know how. You'll just have to wait until I figure it out," the princess of all of the Land of Be Alive said.

Above them coconuts swung in the top of a nearby palm, but there was no way they could ever climb the tree. *So much for snacking at the sand bar,* Andrea thought. In the distance leafy green trees bent over what she decided must be a shallow brook. "The first thing we need to do is find some fresh water," she said and pointed in the direction of the few trees.

"B-but we're surrounded by all this stupid sand. See how it shimmers! It must be awfully warm," the new princess of Violet Moon said.

Andrea remembered that she had taken off her shoes. "How are we going to walk across the hot sand?" she said.

"Oh, the sand is never too hot or too cold. Our moon Iloilo keeps it just right all the time," Jolly said.

A noise similar to the banging on a pipe with a hammer startled the girls. The tiny hairs on the back of Andrea's neck stood up. "Whatever is that?" she asked.

"Cousin Willy and his cows have a lounging spot on a small ice floe that is close to the beach. One of the calves must have got stuck again, and his mother is trying to chip him out. It seems she's refusing anyone's help," Wally said and chuckled.

Andrea noticed Karah shaking. "I'm sure there is nothing here that will hurt us," she said.

"You'll have to watch out for the crawdaddies. They've been in a mood ever since the fiddler crabs were chosen to serve in the palace of Ziv. They feel they could do a much better job than the crabs because they walk straight forward like a lobster. I can't see that it matters. Flippers are the way to go," Wally said and slid back into the ocean.

A pearly white conch shell caught Andrea's attention. *Surely it's a conch sent to take us home,* she thought. She raced across the sand to the shell.

Just as Andrea reached the shell, it began to move. Two hairy red legs were sticking out each side of the shell. Two larger ones with claws stuck out in front. Eyestalks, set in a yellow face, held striped black-and-gold eyes.

Andrea screamed and looked for the new princess of Violet Orb. She pointed her finger at the walking shell.

Karah ran up behind her. "Whatever is the matter?" she said. The creature moved again. Karah held both hands tightly over her mouth.

"I thought my conch had come to take us home, but it's the biggest hermit crab I've ever heard of. He's all of a foot wide and just as long," Andrea said. She was shaking so much she could hardly talk.

"G'day ladies. The name's Herman. You be Utlanders or you wouldn't think I should be screamed at, and this is my shell-house so bug out," the monster of a crab said.

Andrea shook a finger at him. "I'm Andrea, Princess of Ziv, and this is my orb so be polite," she said.

"That one eh? Thought a princess would have enough sense to be polite h'self," the crab said. He clacked his claws together.

Both princesses took a few cautious steps back. They knew Herman's claws could make short work of their toes.

"So you're the reason the crawdaddies are in a mood. Can't see their point m'self. I'm all of fifty years old, and I can get about just as fast as the crawdaddies do. You'll be havin' lunch, of course. I'll just scurry up that palm there and nip off a coconut or two," Herman said. He started his slow pace across the sand dragging his house with him.

"Coconut sounds wonderful. We'd love to stay for lunch, but how do you ever open their shells?" Andrea said.

For an answer Herman clicked his claws and started his slow crawl up the palm tree. It seemed like forever later when a big fiber-covered coconut fell from the fronds at the top of the tree.

After his slow crawl back down the tree, Herman cracked open the hard shell of his prize. The girls were brave enough to accept a large half which was still full of milk which was clear as water.

"Fer g'dness sake! Slow down! You'll choke eating that fast. We've got forever here on Violet Orb. There's nothing here worth hurrying a meal for," the crab said. To make his point Herman held up a tiny morsel and using his mandibles slowly put it in his mouth.

His black-and-gold striped eyes went from Karah to Andrea and back. "Guess you're the new un. New princess that is. Heard you're to be called Sarah-Karah," Herman said and put another morsel in his mouth.

Karah blushed. "How did you know?" she said.

Herman waved his antenna at her. "We don't have these for nuthin' here. We hermit crabs get all the news first. Told the cousins down the beach a ways that yo'all are here. They're anxious to meet you," he said.

The girls thanked Herman for their lunch and set off down the warm sandy beach toward the leafy green trees they saw in the distance. They hoped they would find a stream of drinkable water. Andrea stubbed her toe on something hard in the shallow water by the shore.

"Utlanders! You'd think that even an Utlander would watch where she's going," a husky voice said.

"Shush dear! These must be the princesses cousin Herman told us about. Welcome to our oyster bed. All the children will be happy to meet their princesses," a softer voice said.

"May I introduce our family. I'm Rosco and this is Oscara. We have 16 children so far, and another little one is joining us soon," the huskier voice said.

Andrea gazed in amazement. Rosco and Oscara were in the top center of the oyster bed. A series of smaller oysters were arranged in a semi-circle beside them. Each oyster sported an initial that had grown into its shell. The smallest smoky-gray oyster which was snuggling closely to Oscara wore the letter P. The largest oyster wore the letter A.

"This is Pearl. Show the princesses how wide you can open your shell!" Oscara said.

"Bravo! Bravo!" Rosco said, as each oyster from A to P opened its shell and gulped in a huge amount of water.

"This reminds me of a poem I read once, I think it goes like this.

> "THE OYSTER
> In the depths of the murky sea
> A capricious creature came to be.
> Nestled secure in a familiar bed
> Waves tossed restlessly o'er its head.
> Safe within a sturdy shell
> It feeds on gifts from ocean's swell.
> 'Family is first,' so 'tis said
> By each "creach" in the oyster bed.
> Despite the shell 'tis easily hurt
> By remarks sharp and curt.
> But when emotions are set a-whirl
> To protect self, it makes a pearl," Andrea said.

"That's me. I'm Pearl," the littlest oyster said. She opened her shell wide to show the tiny pearl she was making.

"She got a piece of sharp sea sand in her shell. The pearl protects her from the pain," Oscara said.

"Oh, I know just how she feels!" Karah said. She knelt in the sand by the littlest oyster. "Tum, tum, tiddley-tee. Tee, tee, tiddley-tum," she sang. The waves kept time to her sweet voice, and the oysters soon nodded their heads in sleep. The new princesses tiptoed away.

The two girls peered over the top of a sand dune and gasped in amazement. Hand in hand they raced down the hillside and through the tall amaranths that grew in the midst of a mosaic of wild flowers. Laughing they ran through the verbena. The crushed leaves wafted the aroma of lemon into the balmy air. The deep violet flowers of the verbena gave way to the purple of saxifrage.

Karah put her arms around a clump of white lilies. "They're so beautiful! I could stay here forever," she said and rushed from the lilies to a rosebush to sniff of the daintily scented white flowers.

Several branches of a tall green maple bent over a gently flowing stream. In an eddy by the far dark bank, white water lilies floated serenely among huge green lily pads. Andrea reached the stream first. She knelt down filled her cupped hands and drank deeply of the sweet clean water.

Kneeling beside her Karah dipped one hand into the cool stream. She screamed and jerked her hand out of the water. Hanging on to her fingers by one of its claws was a crawdad.

The new princess danced around trying to shake off the clinging crustacean. "I hate this place. I want to go home right now," she said. Immediately a huge yellow conch dropped down by the stream.

Andrea sent her thought to the shell as Karah climbed into it. The crawdad still clung to her fingers, as they were swept from Andrea's sight.

She peered into the clear water. Two reddish-brown crayfish were crawling out onto the shallow bank. They glared at her. "Utlanders! Crockford was only trying to get the princess' attention, and now see what you two have gone and done!" one of the crayfish said.

"Sarah-Karah has taken Crockford into the Utland. Now he'll never get to the palace in Ziv. We've lost him forever. And it's your entire fault. All he ever wanted was to serve in the palace," the other crayfish said.

At that moment Andrea's pearly conch settled beside her. Inside was a note from Ming. It read: Thanks for sending Crockford. He's very happy in the palace. Karah dropped him off just as you ordered.

Princess Andrea waved good bye to her new friends while they were thanking her for taking care of one of their own. She climbed into her conch shell and fell asleep wondering if her next visit to Ziv would be as much fun.

Love, Grandma Schoe

Andrea Has a Ball on Orange Moon

ANDREA PAUSED TO READ THE poem on her grandma's desk calendar before slipping out the back door:

> A ray of sunshine is coming your way,
> To warm the cockles of your heart I say.
> Let your mind wander and be at play.
> Your spirit will rejoice and be glad today.

Andrea repeated the words as she hop-skipped to the back garden. The orange lilies were in full bloom. Beside them spotted tiger lilies lifted their faces to the sun. The air smelled warm with a hint of sweet grass.

She was wearing her overall style shorts and orange T-top that matched her Kekk running shoes, and an orange barrette held her dark hair in place. Andrea decided to sit on the garden swing, where a ray of sunshine filtered through the trees. There she could read her wonderful new story about a cat.

Fuffle was a very special cat who knew all sorts of wonderful things. She could stalk through tall grasses playing hide-and- seek and even talk. *Wish I had a cat,* thought Andrea. She took a sip from her bottle of spring water and casually traced a kitty face in the spot of sunshine on the bib of her orange shorts-set.

"Meow," said the cat face. Fuffle jumped onto the swing beside her. The cat purred and rubbed its face against Andrea's arm.

"You're not real so please let me read," Andrea said and turned a page in her book.

"Of course I'm real, Princess," Fuffle said. She twisted her grayish body around to show off its black stripes and the letter M in her forehead.

"Princess!" Andrea said and sat up straight. She wondered how this strange creature knew anything about how she was a princess in the Land of Be Alive.

"Aren't you going to order your conch? There has to be a party going on somewhere in Ziv," the cat said. She sounded impatient.

"There's no rainbow and that means there will be no conch," Andrea said.

"Now what do you think makes a rainbow? It's sunlight shining through water," the cat said.

"So what! There's no water!" Andrea said.

"Why don't you try throwing a few drops from your bottle into the air. It should at least get a small conch," the cat said.

Andrea poured some water into her hand and threw it into the air. Something immediately began buzzing around her head.

"It is rather small! You'd best shrink and jump on my back. I can make it up there on my first try," the cat said.

Moments later Andrea was sitting beside the cat in the tiny conch shell. They were flying at a dizzying rate from flower to flower in the garden. "Slow it down for goodness sake. You're letting your thoughts spin through your head like some amateur," Fuffle said.

"Sorry. I was thinking about my cousins Karah and Lauren. We all had a really good time at the palace, but I'm afraid I'll never see either of them again. They went back to the Growns, and the Growns can't come to Ziv. They don't know how to live," Andrea said and tried to focus her thoughts.

"So! If you don't control this thing we'll crash land before we get anywhere near a party," Fuffle said, as the conch flew past a climbing rose and swooped over a pond full of cattails.

Andrea concentrated on her memory of the palace in Ziv. She soon saw the gold-and-white walls that towered over one of the parking lots. Almost immediately they were hovering over a flaming-red motorbike in one of the parking spaces. Andrea noted the silver letter D emblazoned on its side.

"Donald must be here! He's adjutant of the Three Moons of the Land of Fyrh," Andrea said.

"So! Watch out for the doors! We're going to crash!" the cat said.

Quickly, Andrea looked at the huge carved wooden doors. She remembered seeing them swing open and held that picture in her mind. The conch swept through the crack in the opening doors. They bounced like a ball at Donald's feet and up the steps of the escalators to the fifth floor.

A grinning orange-plush cat jerked the door open. The conch flew through and landed amid a pile of orange balloons. A black cat pounced on the small conch. "Stop that! Stop that!" Andrea said. She struggled to her feet and straightened her dark hair.

"Sorry Princess. I didn't mean to scare you. I was just welcoming you home," the black cat said. He rubbed his sleek body against her legs.

"When's the party, Phantom?" Fuffle said, as she and Andrea grew to normal size.

The black cat grew along with them until he became a big panther. As the panther raked them with his claws, balloon after balloon burst. "We haven't gotten all of the invitations out yet. They're supposed to be in these balloons, but someone forgot to fill them," Phantom said and glared at an orange plush cat.

The cat pulled a radio receiver from his ear and sniffed. "Not my fault. Donald said to wait for the princess to arrive," the cat said.

Phantom paced up and down. "What Donald said was to get the balloons ready and wait until the princess can help deliver them," the black cat said.

"Sorry Princess. Guess I got carried away. Bucci and the K-Katz are the best jazz combo going," the orange Plushie said.

"You're forgiven, but what do we do now?" Andrea said.

The Plushie answered, "I'll call in all of the Plushies and the Patchworks and get started right away. I might as well get the Calicos and the Tabbies, too."

"Leave me out of this. I've got a party in my future," Fuffle said.

The cat puffed out his chest with pride. "Not you. I mean real cats. Like me. Cats stuffed with pure polyester filling," the orange Plush cat said.

"You'll never get the invites done in time for the jungle cats to find them. Princess Andrea will have to deliver the message in person if everyone is going to get to the party. Best get on my back Princess. We've a long way to go," Phantom said.

Avoiding the twitch of Phantom's tail Andrea pulled herself onto the crouching animal's back. "Where are we going?" she said.

Fuffle sprang onto Andrea's shoulder. "We're going to have a ball. Just mind you keep your wits about you. It's a jungle out there," she said.

Phantom bounded across the orange carpet and took a flying leap toward what looked to Andrea like a ray of sunshine. Fuffle put one paw over her princesses' open mouth and waved her tail in the air. "Take it easy, Your Highness. No need to scream. Just hold your balance like I do and don't look down," she said.

Andrea took a peek at the vast nothingness surrounding them. "I wasn't screaming. At least I don't think I was," she said.

The cat dug her claws into the shoulder strap on Andrea's overalls. "Well, you were. Very un-princess-like," Fuffle said.

The shaking princess wrapped her legs firmly around Phantom's sides. Sure her heart was still in her mouth, she swallowed. "Just where are we going anyway?" she said.

"The Plushies didn't get their job done, so we have to visit the big cats in the jungle. On the way we'll visit the Domestics to be sure they got their invites," the cat said.

Phantom stopped short. Andrea tumbled over the big cat's head and landed against a solid wall of air. Looking up she saw a Tortoiseshell cat glaring at her. She was lying on a royal- purple velvet cushion, which was hovering over the wall Andrea had just bumped her head on.

"Princess, this is Stasia. She's matriarch of L'Arkville. This is the newest settlement here on Orange Moon," Fuffle said.

Stasia stretched out one paw. "Welcome. Do come in. The door is wherever Your Highness thinks it is," she said.

Taking a deep breath Andrea focused her thoughts. *This is Ziv,* she reminded herself and walked right through the solid wall of air into a beautiful garden.

A gentle breeze wafted the sweet scent of orange and lemon blossoms into the air. Ripe and ripening fruit hung on the green trees of a citrus grove. Small palm trees grew at the feet of a stand of very tall date palms. A clump of catnip nestled among some laurel bushes. By the wall orange sunflowers towered over several sprays of rosemary, and honey bees buzzed around a bed of yellow and orange marigolds.

The velvet cushion floated down to rest in front of Andrea's feet. Stasia stood up yawned and stretched. "Excuse me, Princess. This scrawny beast disturbed my nap," she said.

Phantom swished his tail back and forth. "Now just who are you calling scrawny? If I napped as much as you I'd look like a cushion, too," he said.

Andrea clapped her hands. "Stop it you two! This is no way to behave in Ziv," she said.

"Sorry Princess. We both used to live with The Growns. It takes some doing to get into the ways of Ziv," Phantom and Stasia said together.

"We're here about the party. Did you cats get the invites for the Domestics?" Fuffle said.

Stasia opened her mouth to reply. Instead she turned around and swatted at a small gray mouse that was pulling on her tail.

"Please Stasia, ask Her Highness why we weren't invited," the mouse said.

Andrea tugged the barrette out of her hair and replaced it. She had no idea just who had been invited to the party or why anyone had been left out.

Phantom was sitting behind a large potted plant twitching his ears. "The party is for us cats. Mice don't know how to enjoy a fun time," he said.

"You'd be a drag. What does anyone but a cat know about parades, dances, jazz, and stuff?" Fuffle said. She began to wash her right paw.

Stasia's green eyes opened wide. "We learn it all in dream- time. You mice don't even know how to dream. All you do is scurry around," she said.

Andrea fiddled with the clasp on the bib of her overall. "I don't think--" she said.

The mouse glared at her with his tiny brown eyes. "I think the princess should be a mouse for a day," he said.

Before Andrea could do anything, she felt herself shrink. Her body was covered with gray fur, and a tail stuck out of one leg of her shorts set. Her barrette fell to the floor. When she tried to pick it up, she discovered that she had paws instead of hands. "What have you done to me!" she said in a terrified squeak.

"It's only for a day. Come. Meet the family. I'm Chester. They call me that because I used to live in an old chesterfield couch," the mouse said and hurried away. Andrea had no choice but to follow him.

When she caught up to the mouse she tried to talk to him. "You used to live with The Growns. I was wondering--" she said.

The mouse wasn't listening. He was rustling through a wad of tissue paper.

"I was wondering about my cousins Karah and Lauren. They left Ziv to go to The Growns. Can they get back to Ziv?" the princess said.

"No way! Try this," the mouse said and passed a chunk of cheese over to Andrea.

The cheese tasted a bit old for her liking. What do you mean? 'No way'," Andrea said.

"The Growns can't come to Ziv. They don't know how to live," the mouse said.

The next thing Andrea knew it was dark, and she was standing in the middle of some tall green stalks. She sniffed. They smelled good. Good enough to eat in fact. She had an urge to climb a stalk and pull down one of the irresistible green- covered seed pods.

Something stirred in her memory. *Green corn! I just have to have some,* she thought. As she climbed she realized she was no longer in a mouse body.

In fact she was much larger and furrier, and her paws seemed more like her own hands. Andrea swiftly climbed the corn stalk and tore off a fresh cob. She threw it to the ground and pulled another. In a frenzy she backed down the stalk and began tearing the husks and silk off of the cobs. One taste and she just had to have another and another. Before long she had a pile of cobs strewn among a dozen broken stalks.

Soon she was thirsty and wondered if there might be some clean water close by. She ambled past a cucumber patch and a few hills of beans.

She could smell clean water and noticed a tub standing in the middle of a green lawn. Andrea looked into the tub, but she stopped short at the sight of her reflection. In the moonlight big brown eyes stared at her from behind a black mask.

Another brownish body with black-and-gray rings on its furry tail strolled up to her. "Sorry to snatch you away from the mice, but we raccoons want a chance to be invited to the party, too. We're already masked. We're just right for a masquerade ball," he said.

Suddenly a strong oily odour sent Andrea's head spinning. *What an awful stink,* she thought. Then she realize that it was herself she smelt.

A mother skunk was leading a family of four in single file across the dewy grass toward her. White stripes formed a cap on their heads and down their black backs.

"Please forgive me, Your Highness. I just thought you should know just how much we skunks love to dance," she said.

At a signal from their mother, the four baby skunks stood on their front feet. They waved their tails in the air and followed the steps of an intricate quadrille-like dance. In the moonlight the white stripes on their dear little faces stood out. Shadows gave an ethereal quality to the scene.

Andrea was enchanted by their movements. Her whole body ached to join them, but her bushy tail was trapped in the leg of her shorts. "Your children are beautiful and very talented, but I believe it's the cats who are having the party," Andrea said.

"But you're our princess. Surely you can invite whomever you wish," the skunk said.

The young princess thought for a moment. "You'd certainly add to the festivities, but I think we should have the cat's approval," she said.

Suddenly she was no longer in her black body with its white stripes and bushy tail. She was on all fours on the ground searching for her barrette.

Andrea closed her eyes for a moment. She took a deep breath to steady herself. Something cool and damp touched her nose. She opened her eyes and looked into two dark slits surrounded by golden pools.

"Princess. I'm Sundri. In my home in Bombay my name means 'a thing of beauty'," the cat said.

Stasia looked down at them from her purple velvet cushion. "You should have stayed there. Now everyone thinks every cat should be coal-black with huge golden eyes," she said.

Sundri rubbed her long sleek body against Andrea's arm. "I didn't hear that," she said.

"Well, your ears are big enough. You should even be able to hear a mouse breathe," Stasia said. She yawned and stretched.

Andrea sat back on her heels to put her orange barrette back into her hair. It was a relief to know that she was back in her own body. "Stop that!" she said.

Stasia and continued to glare at Sundri. She floated her velvet cushion to the top of a huge sunflower and let out a very loud "Meow".

Several cats began appearing from hiding places in the tall orchard grass of the citrus grove. A small grayish-brown cat stopped at a potted plant. She pierced its long leaf with her fang and ran the tooth down the length of the leaf. A cat, black as midnight with only three white hairs on her chest, sat in the shadows. She closed her eyes and nearly disappeared.

Sundri sat back on her haunches and perked up her ears. All the other cats turned in the direction of a sound which Andrea failed to detect.

Suddenly a red motorbike burst through the solid wall of air. The rider did a wheelie in front of Andrea and stopped. He dismounted and kicked the bike stand into position.

"Your Highness," Donald said and placed his right hand over his heart. He bowed low. He wore an orange shirt and Levis with boots that shone with fresh polish. A silver buckle held his belt, and blue lapis lazuli stones sparkled in the hilt of his sword and in his buckle.

Donald turned to the cats who had just left the coolness of the citrus grove. "May I present our staff, Your Highness. Tigger is in charge of the banquet," he said.

An amiable looking Tabby approached them. Tigger grinned and saluted Andrea with a twitch of her tail. She walked casually over to the shade of the sunflowers.

"Minx and Pixie will be our mounts when we visit the jungle. Fuffle will also accompany us," Donald said.

A small calico and a black cat strode over to Andrea. "Your pleasure, Princess," they said and bowed.

Our mounts!" Andrea said. It seemed impossible to her that they would be riding such small creatures into the vastness of the jungle. Immediately the Calico began to change. All the orange in her fur disappeared, and she became white with black stripes. In seconds Pixie became a white tiger, and Minx was a huge black leopard.

"Please choose your mount. I shall be pleased to ride the other cat," Donald said.

Andrea stroked Minx' sleek head and scratched behind her ears. "You're beautiful," she said.

"Always felt that I had a black leopard inside just aching to get out," Minx said. She licked Andrea's face and crouched so the princess could get on her back.

As Donald pet her head before mounting her back, Pixie began to purr. "Feels so good," she said and purred more loudly.

"Let's get the show on the road. We have a party to do some purring about," Fuffle said and sprang onto Andrea's shoulder.

The big cats leapt into the air and landed on a ray of sunshine. As their shadow appeared on the ground beneath them, Andrea caught her breath. In one twitch of a tiger's tail, they were bounding into a narrow path. On each side tall evergreen trees seemed to reach a sky ablaze with orange clouds.

Never had Andrea imagined the jungle on Orange Moon to be like this. Each tree hummed with a unique vibration. To Andrea it sounded as if they were singing the words from her grandmother's calendar: A ray of sunshine is coming your way to warm the cockles of your heart I say.

Suddenly Minx stood on her back legs. Andrea fell plop on the cone-covered ground. She sat up and pulled dry evergreen needles from her hair. Minx and Pixie began to dance to the rhythm of the trees.

Donald bowed low to Andrea. "Your Highness, may I have this dance," he said.

The evergreen trees stopped singing. "Your Highness!" they said. They bowed low. The forest became as dark as Minx' gleaming coat.

The next thing Andrea knew she was being picked up by the back strap on her orange overalls. The princess could feel an animal's hot breath on her neck. At the end of the tunnel it became much lighter, and Andrea saw the paws of a huge Siberian tiger under her dangling feet. She fainted.

When she came to the huge tiger was licking her face. "Sorry, Princess," the tiger said.

Andrea was about to order the huge cat away, when she heard a small voice. "Sorry to scare you, Princess, but we've a party to get to," the voice said. Fuffle was sitting beside her licking her paws.

The princess noticed that Fuffle had put her down on a moss-covered knoll. Trees with bright orange leaves dotted a vast valley in front of her. They bent over tall grasses in shades of burnt umber. Andrea watched the grasses move as though wild animals were prowling through them. She shuddered. *These must be the cats I'm to invite to the party, but how can I? I have no balloons to send them,* she thought.

A huge mountain, its top covered with orange-tinted snow, glowered over the valley. Half way up the mountain a dark cave was partially hidden by a cedar tree. A thunderous roar came from somewhere in its depths.

The hairs on Andrea's neck stood up. She felt cold and goose-flesh bumps covered her arms. She surely wouldn't have to invite these wild beasts to a party at the palace in Ziv. She turned to her adjutant. "Is that a lion?" she said.

"Yes. The cave belongs to Leon, King of the Cats," Donald said.

"Sounded like Noel to me. I guess the old man isn't home," Fuffle said.

Noel roared again, and Andrea noticed dozens of wild cats dropping from the trees where they had been napping. Their wild cries set up a roar of their own. Off to her right, a giraffe pulled his head from among the orange-colored fronds of a tall tree. He dropped the cluster of fruits he had picked and fled. On the other side of the valley, two elephants put their trunks in the air and trumpeted. Their baby crept closer to their side.

As Andrea watched great thorny trees sprang up from small bushes all around the grassy valley. Thorny vines were creeping up the side of the hill toward the mossy knoll where she sat. She wanted to turn and run. Dancing to the rhythm of the evergreens was more her idea of a fun time.

"What's happening?" she said.

"Nothing much. Noel has just sounded the alarm. There are strangers in Orange Valley," Fuffle said.

"You mean us? How can these wild creatures be afraid of their princess?" Andrea said.

"Your Highness, you have never visited Orange Moon before. Nor have the cats of Orange Valley ever smelled a human," Donald said.

The thorny vines were growing thicker and advancing faster toward the group on the mossy mound. The thorny trees were swaying as if in a strong wind. Andrea sniffed. The fear the trees wafted toward her smelled like burning cedar. Sharp, it stung her eyes, and they began to water. "Stop! Stop!" she said and rubbed her eyes.

When she opened them she saw that the thorny vines no longer advanced up the hill. The thorny trees still waved, and the acrid odour filled the air.

Andrea sat cross-legged on the ground. She rested her elbow on one knee and held her chin up with one hand. From the valley below the thorny vines, she could feel hundreds of pairs of eyes staring at her. The smell of fear still wafted up from the thorny trees. *How can we lose our fear of each other and become friends*, she wondered.

"What about the party? Time's a-wasting," Fuffle said and twisted around brushing her Princess' face with her tail.

Andrea sprang to her feet. "That's it! The party! But I'm sure none of the big cats would be happy in the gardens of Ziv," she said.

"You could have it here amongst us," a small evergreen at the edge of the forest said. She waved her branches.

Behind her the tall trees sighed in the light wind. They bowed. "Princess, we'd be most proud to have your party for the cats here," they all said.

Andrea spoke to her adjutant. "That settles it then. Donald, please find out if the orange Plushie has the balloons ready yet. We can attract their attention that way," she said.

"Minx, please take Donald back to L'Arkville. He'll want to take his bike back to the palace in Ziv. Be sure Stasia gets the word out to everyone. The party will start as soon as Plushie gets here with the balloons," she said.

Turning to Pixie who was still a white tiger she stroked the big cat's head. "It would be best if you stayed here and practiced your purring," she said.

Pixie settled down on the mound beside her princess. As she purred the thorny vines gradually retreated down the hill.

"Fuffle, you can take me back to L'Arkville, too. I want to be sure all the animals who want to come to the party know they're welcome," Andrea said.

Moments later the Siberian tiger and the black leopard were bounding into a sudden ray of sunshine. In a Ziv second they were speeding through the solid wall of air that surrounded L'Arkville.

Two Ziv minutes later Donald was back from the palace on his red motorbike. He was towing a cartful of colorful stuffed cats. Each Plush cat was holding a bunch of bright orange balloons. The message tied to each balloon sang a song when touched: Come and play. There's a party today.

Oh, I do wish Cousin Lauren and Cousin Karah and her sister Becca could come. We had such fun when they visited the palace, Andrea thought. But Lauren had gone back to the Growns like Karah and Becca had. She sighed. There was no way back to Ziv from the Growns. At least there was none that she knew of.

At that very second a large grayish forest-cat with a tiny girl on her back dropped in front of Andrea. "Hi Cousin! Fauna and I are going to Orange Grove. See ya," Lauren said, as she grew to her own size. With a hug, a smile, and a wave of her hand she and the cat danced away.

Andrea nearly fell over when a small animal pounced onto her back. The furry tawny-buff creature began chattering into the princess' ear. When it swung to the ground huge eyes peered at Andrea from two black circles in the gibbon's blonde face. A third black circle opened and closed as the animal chattered.

Another primate swung down from a tall date tree to the citrus orchard. She also had three black circles surrounded by a halo of blonde hair that framed her face. Both began to dance in circles around Andrea. Their chattering attracted the attention of everyone in the L'Arkville garden. "Why are you here? What do you want?" Andrea said.

The first gibbon sprang into Andrea's arms. "Oh, Andrea, don't you know me? I'm Karah's sister Becca. We've come for the party," she said.

"Oh Becca, I am so very glad to see you and Karah that I could just dance and dance," Andrea said. She swung around in a circle until she dropped to the ground panting.

"Princess! It's party time! Let's get everyone to Evergreen Forest," Fuffle said.

"Sure thing! Everyone grab a balloon!" the princess of all of Ziv said.

Donald unsheathed his sword. The rubies in the hilt shone, as he cut a ray of sunshine into ribbons. Fast as a ray of sunshine appeared, one or another of the gathered animals hopped on. They flew away with the bright orange invitations dancing in the light.

At last, Andrea landed beside Pixie who was still on the mound overlooking the valley. Evergreen Forest had arranged itself in a semi-circle behind the purring cat. The mossy mound was now in the middle of a large clear space covered with evergreen needles.

In the valley in front of Andrea, thorny vines were again creeping up toward the hillside. Behind her the trees stood silent and still.

In their midst everyone who had come from L'Arkville quietly looked from one to the other. The Plushies from the palace in Ziv clung to the low branches of the evergreens. Each sent an orange balloon into the breeze that blew over the valley.

In the distance a roar came from the cave belonging to Leon. A second roar louder than the first came from the grasslands of Orange Valley. Clearly Noel was still in the cave, and Daddy Leon was on the way home. A third large cat was pacing back and forth in the valley below the hillside.

From her vantage point on Andrea's shoulder, Fuffle looked over the valley. "Looks to me as if that's Lena down there. I suspect she's been out hunting geranos," she said.

"Whatever is a gerano?" Andrea said. She had never heard of such a thing before.

Donald took a step closer to his princess. "Their vines only grow here on the tall trees in Orange Valley. They look like orange grape-tomatoes," he said.

"They're really good. They taste just like whatever you like best," Fuffle said.

"We'll never have a party this way. Everything is too full of fear," the princess said to the little gibbon beside her.

Becca pointed to the tallest evergreen on the edge of the circle. "Sarah-Karah is in that tall tree," she said and sprang into a tree close by. Moments later the sweetest sound Andrea ever heard came from the tallest evergreen. Princess Karah's song was answered from the tree Becca had sprung into.

The evergreens joined in. Their song echoed from the snow-topped mountain. The trees from the forest floor below the hillside where Andrea sat with Pixie began to sing. The music filled the whole of Orange Valley.

The roaring in the lion's cave stopped. The thorny vines wilted. The thorny trees stood still. Hundreds of pairs of eyes turned toward the evergreen trees. No longer was there a smell of fear in the air.

Andrea stood up beside Pixie and took a step toward the valley. The princess of all the moons of Ziv stopped and held her breath.

Lena was pacing slowly up through the thorny vines towards them. Leon, his golden mane flowing in the sunlight, was bounding through the valley toward his mate. From the treetops Princess Karah continued to sing her sweet song to Becca. The only other sound was the trees singing to the wind.

The attention of every wild cat as well as the elephants and the giraffes was on their leaders. Every one of the domestics sat still and silent watching the drama before them.

Pixie stood up and walked forward as the lady lion came up the hill. Soon they were pacing around each other sniffing as they went.

"Wish I knew what they're saying to each other. Watch to see if they touch noses," Fuffle said.

The white tiger reached out to the golden lion with her nose. They touched just as Leon raced roaring up the hill. He stopped abruptly and watched his mate.

Pixie and Lena settled down on the mound together, and Pixie began to purr again. One by one the rest of the wild cats came out of hiding. They began slowly making their way up the hill.

Leon strode toward Andrea. "The white tiger tells us that you're our princess. Welcome to Orange Valley, Your Highness," he said and bowed.

"Welcome to our party," Andrea said. She bent down and touched Leon's wet nose with her dry one.

A song rose up from the roots of the evergreens. They rubbed their branches together. From all across the hillside the thorn trees joined in.

"Sounds even better than the K-Katz," the Plushies said. They began dancing in a Congo line through the trees.

Donald tapped Princess Andrea on the shoulder. "Your Highness, may I bring you a glass of citrus punch," he said.

The happy princess danced with Donald onto a broad ray of sunshine and onto the swing in grandma's garden again. *How can another adventure ever top Orange Moon,* she wondered.

Love, Grandma Schoe

Andrea in Midnight Globe

WHEN ANDREA FELL ASLEEP, SHE was in her room at her grandma's house. Her short dark hair framed her face which was pale in the moonlight streaming in through the soft white curtains at the window. A beam of light reflected from the dresser mirror onto her pink-and-white teddy bear. Snowpink was on the bed, where she always sat when they visited Grandma.

Andrea was clutching the new glass globe her grandma had given her. The outside of the globe was clear, but on the inside a snowy landscape was lit by silvery stars that clung to the dark blue top. It had been such fun for Andrea to shift the tiny flakes back and forth.

A soft purring in her ear made Andrea sit bolt upright in bed. Bright golden eyes were staring at her from a black cat- face. "Sundri! Whatever are you doing here at Grandma's house! You belong in Ziv," she said.

"We are in Ziv," Sundri said. She twisted around and swished her elegant tail.

"How did I get here? I don't remember any rain or a rainbow," Andrea said.

"You wanted to come, so I brought you. I brought company, too," Sundri said.

"Did I say I wanted company? I'd really rather explore Ziv by myself this time," Andrea said and rolled the glass globe around on the bed.

"But Princess, you have such a wonderful adventure waiting for you. Don't you want to share it?" Sundri said.

"I can have lots more fun alone," the princess said.

The sleek black cat said nothing. She merely stalked around on the bed twitching her long tail.

"Why don't you just go back to Orange Moon and annoy that bossy cat, Anastasia. And please send my company back where she came from," Andrea said.

Sundri gazed at the princess for a moment. Her golden eyes held a look of 'I know things you don't'. With a flip of her tail she stalked out of the open door.

Everything in the room looked different. The pink cover on her bed was now deep blue. No pink-and-white teddy bear sat beside her. No moonlight streamed in though the open window. A Tiffany-glass lamp by the bed lit the room. Andrea's navy-blue pajamas were dotted with bright silver stars, which crinkled when she touched them.

A smiling girl tiptoed into the cozy room. "Hi! I'm Cousin Diana," she said and closed the door softly. Her long brown hair brushed the back of her pink pajamas. The silvery stars on them sounded like crumpled tissue paper, as she climbed onto Andrea's bed.

Andrea rolled the glass ball in her hands. "You don't belong here. You can't come to Ziv unless I invite you, and I didn't. Ziv is my princessdom, and this is my palace," she said.

"I've been to Ziv before. I came from Casa Luna in a jet, and I always knew I'd come back someday. Where is the castle? I saw a castle when I was here before," Diana said.

"You must mean this palace. It's my palace and it's not a castle," Andrea said.

"No. It was dark but there was a high wall around it. There is no wall around your palace. You must have a castle, too," Diana said.

"You must have been dreaming. I've never seen a castle in Ziv," Andrea said.

"I would like to be a princess and have a castle. That would be better than just having a palace," Diana said and tossed her long dark hair over her shoulder.

"You look just like Sundri. She is always swishing her tail, and you don't look like a princess to me," Andrea said.

"I'm sure I am. I am a princess because my grandma is a Queen in Ziv. That's how it works," Diana said. She pulled a few stray strands of straight hair from over her dark eyes. Her hand touched a ring at her ear which fell onto the rumpled coverlet on Andrea's bed. Carefully Diana picked up the shiny earring. A tiny crystal hung inside a white-gold hoop.

Andrea stared at the crystal which sparkled and shone in the lamplight. Colors of a rainbow danced on the bed covers.

"Peachy-keen! Where did you get them?" Andrea said.

Diana rolled the earring from one palm to the other. Gently she put it into Andrea's hand. "My grandma sent them with a note saying they are very special. You may wear it if you like. It's really easy to put on. Just touch the hoop to your ear. It will stay," she said.

"Thanks. It's very beautiful, but what does it do?" Andrea said. She touched the ring to her ear. To her surprise it hung firmly in place.

Diana picked the glass globe up from where it had rolled on the bed cover. "What is this? It's humming," she said.

"My grandma gave it to me. Isn't it the peachy-keenest? Look at the snowflakes falling inside," Andrea said.

Diana stared at the glass ball in her hand. Tiny stars were falling gently from a midnight-blue sky to the snow-covered base below. A dark-robed figure strode up and down on the snow. A small spotted owl on her shoulder bounced up and down as she walked.

Cousin Diana held the globe out to Andrea. "There is someone inside. See! There by the trees," she said.

Andrea peered into the globe. A black girl, wearing a shiny gold jump suit and navy-blue robe, stared up at her. "Gabi, how did you get trapped in there? How can we get you out?" Andrea said.

"Meow. Not out. You have to go in," the cat said from outside the door.

"What! Go into that little thing! There is absolutely no room. No way will I go in there," The princess of all of Ziv said.

"Listen for a special tone. You each have a special tone that will take you inside Midnight Globe. A great adventure waits for you there," Sundri said.

The little ball in Andrea's hands hummed even louder. The chime of the earring became one long tone. Andrea grasped at the earring to shut off the sound. Suddenly she was following Diana through the glass to the inside of the globe. They drifted among the falling snowflakes and fell softly to the ground beside Gabi.

The black girl adjusted her green headband and placed her right hand over her heart. "Welcome Princess Andrea and Princess-in-training Diana. I am Gabriel, Adjutant of the Three Globes of the Folke de Terre," she said, and handed each girl a bundle. "You will need these. The hard dry snow called firn is extremely cold when it falls," she said.

Diana slipped on her pink mukluks and cloak. "Gabriel, is there a castle? I remember seeing one," she said.

Gabriel bowed low. "Please, your Highness, call me Gabi. Yes. You have--" she said.

"Well Snowpink didn't tell me anything about it," Andrea said. She wrapped herself in her navy-blue cloak pulled it tightly around her shoulders and stomped away.

I suppose she thinks it's hers, Andrea thought. She hadn't heard Gabi say that Diana had only seen the castle of Midnight Moon and had said nothing about it belonging to Diana.

A snowy owl, her wings whispering like a gentle breeze, swooped down from the trees. She settled quietly on the crisp snow in front of Andrea. "Go away! I want to be by myself," Andrea said. She shooed the owl away with her arms.

Instead of moving away the owl spread out her wings in front of the princess. No matter which way Andrea turned the owl was there stopping her.

Andrea flung herself on her back in the snow. The dark sky was studded with a myriad of stars. A granular snow began falling that was not a bit like the soft flakes the princess had expected. Soon she could barely see the oak trees a few yards away. Branches creaking they swayed like ominous shadows in the icy wind.

The owl was no longer visible through the drifting white. Loneliness crept over the princess who shivered in the bitter cold. She cried out but she knew the wind would whisk her words away. She had no idea of how to get back to Gabi and Diana.

This is Ziv. I am a princess in Ziv and I must think like one. Perhaps if I touch the earring Diana will hear the tone, she thought. She rubbed the gold rim between her thumb and fingers.

A dark shadow looming over her made her pull her cloak tightly around her. She covered her face. A monster with dozens of feet began walking all over her. Its claws were digging into her cloak. Go away!" Andrea said.

"Coo, coo, coo," the monster said.

Andrea sat up quickly. A flock of mourning doves flew up and settled on the snow.

"Don't they look just like a sewing circle of little old ladies all dressed in gray?" Gabi said beside her.

Andrea jumped up and was about to hug Gabi, when Diana rushed up and hugged her cousin. "I heard your tone. We followed it," she said.

The wind stopped, and the snow became stars in the sky again. The spotted owl settled on Gabi's shoulder. "The Children of the Tuatha de Danan need your help. You don't have much time," Adjutant Gabi said.

"Who are they? I've never heard of them," Andrea said.

"I think the Tuatha de Danan used to live in Ireland. I've read about the little people at school. When the Celts came to Ireland, they disappeared into a hill called a tor. I think some of them became elves," Diana said.

"Yes. Some of them came to Midnight Globe where they could do the work they love," Gabi said.

"Was it elves I heard tinkering at the palace? I was never able to open the sixth door," Andrea said.

Gabi spoke quietly. "You will have to open the right door here on Midnight Globe. The elves have been locked away by a leprechaun," she said.

"Nasty creature! He should be locked up," Andrea said.

"He's not really nasty you know. He just thought he would have a bit of fun," Gabi said and allowed a white-coated ermine to climb up her robe. When the ermine had settled down around her neck, she spoke again. "The trick didn't work the way he thought it would," she said.

"What happened?" What can we do?" Andrea and Diana said.

"Deep in a dungeon in the Castle of Tor is an oaken door set with six sardonyx stones. One will open the door. One will cause an earthquake which will seal the castle shut. Good luck Your Highnesses!" Gabi said.

Andrea looked toward the forest where Gabi had said they would find a path to the castle. When she turned back her adjutant was gone. In her place was a whirling vortex of firn. The granular snow fell to the ground and revealed a twirling form. The movement stopped suddenly, and a red-bearded man of about four feet tall stood beside them. He was leaning on a crooked black stick.

The stranger was dressed in a green hat, coat, and breeches. The black band on his hat was decorated with a shiny gold buckle. Another held his belt and two were on his black shoes.

"Mookie's the name. And wot d' ye be doin' 'ere? Ye best be goin' before I looses me temper," the little man said and shook his blackthorn stick at the girls.

"I'm Princess Andrea of Ziv, and this is my cousin Diana," Andrea said.

The man glared at the girls. "Faithe, but 'tisn't Ziv. 'Tis my land. 'Tis the home o' Mookie O'Tor," he said and shook his shillelagh at them again.

"We're glad to meet you Mr. O'Tor," the girls said. Andrea held out her hand.

Mookie glared at the girls. "Ye be here to steal my pot o' gold. No way will ye be gettin' it," he said.

"You're a leprechaun! So it was you who locked the elves away in a dungeon," Andrea said.

"Nasty creature! How would you like to be shut up in a dungeon?" Diana said.

"We demand that you let the elves out right now," Andrea said in her best princessing voice.

"And just who d' ye be to demand anything o' me? I d'na invite you here to The Tor," Mookie said.

"You could at least let us see the elves," Diana said in a sweet tone.

"And just what d'ye be wantin' of those worthless creatures? I shut them up because they refused to make me a new pair of shoes," Mookie said.

"Why would they refuse? I thought they liked making shoes," Andrea said. She brushed back the hair the wind blew in her face.

"I wanted a pair o' purple zogzs. They said such fancy shoes weren't right fer me," he said and began to twirl again.

"Wait! How do we get to the castle?" Andrea said to the dizzying figure.

"Ye'll never! I change ye into a pot o' gold!" the Leprechaun said and faded into the swirling storm.

Andrea wondered just how they would find a path through the oak forest. All she could see was clean snow with no trace of a trail.

A small bird with a gray body and a black cap flitted among the branches of a nearby tree. "Chick-a-dee, chick-a-dee," the bird said.

"Oh! It's calling to us to follow it. Let's go," Diana said and darted in among the big trees. The silver stars on her navy-blue pajamas crinkled under her cloak.

Andrea ran close behind. She certainly didn't want to be left alone even if this was Ziv. They soon entered a clearing where the narrow path became two. Each branch pointed in a different direction.

"Let's take this one. I think it's the shortest path to the castle," Diana said.

"No! I think we should go to the right. Follow me!" Andrea said and started up the trail. The swirling snow closed in around her. When she looked back there was no sign of Diana. She listened for Diana's tone, but no sound disturbed the falling snow. Even the chick-a-dee had disappeared.

A shadow loomed up in front of her. *I'll bet that horrid owl is back,* thought Andrea. She shivered and took refuge in a nearby grove of small trees. The path had been swept clean by the wind and was strewn with long sticks. When she bent to pick one up it wriggled.

Andrea screamed. She hated snakes. She touched her earring, but no answering tone came from Diana.

The huge owl was behind her. She was all alone with these horrid reptiles. Reminding herself again that she was Princess Andrea of Ziv, she held up her head took a deep breath and stepped forward.

"Watch it Princess!" You nearly trod on Kips," a voice from the ground said.

Andrea looked at her feet. Long brown sticks were wriggling all around her. Terrified that one might try to crawl up her pajama pants she screamed.

A snake, who was all of a yard long, held up his head. "I'm Mips. "We're on our way to the castle of Tor," the snake said.

Andrea found herself staring into the snake's unblinking dark eyes. She wanted to run, but her feet wouldn't move.

Mips turned her head away. "Sorry about that. Come along if you want to reach the Tor," the snake said.

Andrea began cautiously walking along the path with Mips and Kips slithering along beside her. "Who told you that I wanted to get to the Tor? And how did you know that I'm a princess?" she said.

"Here in Enchanted Hazelnut Grove we know things. Even in Otherworld we snakes are wise," Mips said.

Suddenly Andrea realized that she was walking up an incline. Right before them were the three turrets of the castle. No snow fell instead the air was cold and crisp. The young princess pulled her cloak more tightly around her, but she still shivered.

Seeing no gate Andrea wonder how she would ever get over the outside wall to the castle. *I have to find some way if I'm going to free the elves,* she thought.

"Shape shift. You can slither up the stone wall if you become a snake like us," Mips said.

Andrea shuddered. No way was she going to change into a snake, not even if she never got over the castle wall.

"No other way for it. Mookie has changed your friend into a yellow cat's ear. She is hidden in a pot of other golden flowers." Mips said.

"You can't let the old leprechaun see you, or you will be next to sit in a pot beside the castle door. No worse being a snake than being a tiny cat's ear. Coming?" Kips said and crawled up the side of the first gray stone.

If I'm going to release Diana from the leprechaun's spell I have to find her first, the princess of Ziv thought. She took a deep breath. "Okay! Okay! I'm coming," she said. Her legs and arms shrunk and finally disappeared. Her body became long and slim like Mip's. With her cloak and pajamas gone, slithering soon became as easy as climbing. In almost no time she reached the top of the cold wall.

Forgetting to cling to the rough stone, Andrea slipped on some ice and fell. In mid-air she felt the owl's talons close around her long slender body. Silently the owl set her down by a pot of golden mums beside the castle door. Unaware that she was back in her Andrea body and her clothes, she began searching for Diana among the mums.

A cat's ear is such a tiny flower I wonder how I will ever find her, she thought.

"I'm here," Diana said. While they hugged each other, Diana said she guessed that Andrea had broken the spell by agreeing to become a snake. "You were very brave," she said.

Andrea leaned against the stone wall of the castle. A very loud croaking by her ear made her jump. Tiny bright eyes stared at them from a small grayish lump clinging to the gray wall.

"Excuse me. I'm Princess Andrea. Just who are you?" she said.

Watching its tiny sides heave up and down as it croaked fascinated her. She didn't see the other frog on the wall beside her.

"Hi Princess! I'm Hyla. I'm a tree frog," the creature said and started creeping backward down the edge of the castle door.

The princesses followed as the tree frog took short leaps along the top walk by the castle wall. At the end of the walk, an open door squeaked as it swung on its hinges.

Diana clapped her hands over her mouth when she saw the spider web. Its delicate lace covered the doorway from side to side. "A web means a spider, and I'm really scared of them. I can't go in there. I just can't," she said.

"Why can't you? It's just a little old spider web," Andrea said and glared at Diana.

Diana was shaking so much her teeth chattered. "Spiders bite, and they're poisonous," she said.

"So! Do know of another way to get inside the castle? We have to get to the dungeon. Remember!" Andrea said.

The tree frog croaked as it climbed the wall by the old door. The air coming from inside smelled dank and dangerous. An answering croak from the tree frog's mate became louder and louder. "In here! In here! Mookie is coming! Mookie is coming!" Hyla said.

We'll have to get in there without touching the web or he'll follow us, but where else can we hide, Andrea thought. Then she noticed that some little animal had torn a hole in the bottom of the web. She pointed it out to Diana.

"We're too big to go through that," Diana said. Her teeth still chattered.

A white rabbit stuck his pink nose through the hole. His nose wriggled as he sniffed the air. "Get small! Get small! You'll be safe in here," he said and twitched his nose.

Diana started to cry. "I can't go in there. And I hate being small. It was horrible being such a tiny flower. I wasn't even as big as a penny," she said.

"We can't stay here. Mookie will turn us both into cat's ears. We'll be in a pot of golden mums forever. Think small! Be a rabbit! This is Ziv! You can do it!" Andrea said.

Grabbing Diana's arm she lunged toward the opening the rabbit had made in the web. Before Andrea could take a breath her body shrank and became covered with fur. Diana followed her through the rabbit hole into the semi-darkness. They heard Mookie's walking stick thumping along the stone steps.

"Whew! That was close! But we're okay," Andrea said in a whisper.

Diana twitched her rabbit nose. "I don't feel okay. Just how am I going to get out of this bunny suit?" she said.

"I'll figure it out later. Right now I sort of like being bunny," Andrea said.

The odor of carrot tops, lettuce, cabbage, and all that good stuff, was coming from somewhere deep in the castle. Another spider-web curtain hung at the end of a long passageway. When Andrea leaped through a hole she saw in the netting, she landed in the biggest greenhouse she had ever been in.

Glass walls soared to the dome of this turret of the castle. Crystals hung in the glass dome and studded the walls. Light rays bouncing from crystal to crystal gave the healthy environment the plants needed. Spider webs shone in the fine spray sent down by miniature jets. Nature spirits that Andrea knew were called naiads frolicked in the rainbow hues.

She was right beside a row of the most mouth-watering orange carrots she had ever smelled. By them rows and rows of crisp celery were almost buried in moist sand. By the tall stalks stood rows of ruby red beets, white potatoes, and creamy turnips.

About to pull a carrot out by its top, she was startled to hear a voice. She looked up into the hairy face of the largest spider she had ever imagined existed.

"Who invited you to lunch?" the spider said. She waved a long black foreleg in Andrea's face.

Another hairy spider with long legs was pulling itself out of a hole in the sand. "And who are you anyway?" she said.

Andrea was speechless. She couldn't believe she was actually hearing a couple of spiders talk. The tarantula-like creatures were so big she was afraid to move. She lopped her long ears down and twitched her rabbit nose.

A delicate shiny-black spider swung down on a thread which she pulled from her body. "Well!" she said.

Andrea crouched down on the sand between the rows of carrots. She hoped the spiders didn't think she was an enemy.

A sweet feminine voice spoke. "Leave her be! She's no rabbit. She is Princess Andrea of Ziv," the voice said.

Andrea looked up to see a most beautiful being. She looked like a tiny human with gossamer wings. Her purple gown hung to her knees, and bells on her tiny green slippers rang as she danced on the carrot tops.

Another winged being in a green gown drifted down from a blueberry bush nearby. "Hi Princess! I'm Perri and this is Winkle. Please feel at home, Your Highness. This is your castle after all," he said.

Andrea wished she had her human voice and could talk to the naiads.

"We know what you're thinking. Of course, it's your castle. You are Princess of Ziv and all the Zivoids of the Land of Be Alive. Diana will be Princess of Midnight Moon," Perri said.

"The dryads watched you come through the oak forest. They sent word that we should expect you. Please help yourself Princess," Winkle invited.

Andrea had just taken a big bite of carrot top when she heard Diana's tone in her ear. She turned around and leaped back through the hole in the web woven in the doorway.

When she reached Diana they both became themselves again. Andrea spit out the carrot top. Somehow it didn't taste as good as when she had been a rabbit.

When the two girls had hugged, they reminded each other that they had to find the dungeon as quickly as they could. They followed the passageway and came to an alcove where a huge door led into deeper into the castle.

With a little tugging and pulling on the bar holding the door shut, it opened to reveal two passageways. They led down into the depths of the stone castle.

"Which way?" asked Diana who was still shaking.

Andrea sniffed the stale air coming from the depths of the castle. "This way," she said. She raced down a passage to the top of a set of stone stairs. A faint light from somewhere above lit the rough steps.

Diana hesitated. "I can't see a thing, and there is icky moss growing all along these walls," she said.

Her words were lost on Andrea. She had already disappeared past the first curve in the winding stairs. Diana's mukluks shushed softly on the stone steps as she made her way into the gloom. On the sixth step she stumbled and fell.

"Remember six!" a voice said. When she caught up to Andrea she had counted another 156 steps.

Andrea was standing on tiptoe in front of a huge oaken door. "It's too dark to see much. I don't see even one sardonyx stone let alone six of them. How are we going to find out which one to touch?" she said.

The girls noticed a spot of light high on the wall opposite the oaken door. Slowly it arched downward.

"Maybe it's like the ancient ruins in Ireland. Maybe the sun will light the door in a few minutes," Diana said.

"I hope you're right but we'll have to think fast. If we touch the wrong stone the dungeon will be sealed forever," Andrea said.

She hopped from one foot to the other while she watched the ray of light creep down the door. She wondered what a sardonyx stone looked like. The light gradually showed a brownish stone set in the door. Finally a panel of six appeared in the shape of a rectangle.

"Look! These brownish stones have a lighter band going across them. I suppose the last one must the right one," Andrea said. She was about to touch the stone when Diana stopped her.

"I fell on the sixth step coming down, and a voice somewhere said sharply, 'Remember six!' so I'm sure we'll fail if we touch it. Let's see. I counted a total of 162 steps," she said.

Andrea thought for a minute. "If it's not the sixth one we must have to go back to number two," she said. The light was fast disappearing from the sixth stone as they talked. Heart in her mouth Andrea felt for the second stone.

The girls jumped back as the heavy oaken door parted in the middle and swung open. Bats, hundreds of them, streamed out.

Diana covered her hair with her hands. The girls watched as the bats circled higher and higher. "I think we must be under the central tower," Diana suggested.

Andrea held her breath for a second. "Listen! I think I hear tapping and hammering just like I heard behind the sixth door in the palace," she said and moved through the gloom along the wall to her right.

Her fingers touched a wooden door from which a ray of light was escaping. "Must be bolted," she said, as she tried the handle.

"Shush! Mookie's coming. I can hear his walking stick on the stone passage," Diana said.

Mookie came up behind them. "Ye be the peskiest girls ever. Here let me help you. Just promise ye'll tell the elves to make me a pair of zogzs," he said.

"Of course we'll ask them! Please just pull the bolt," the girls said together.

"Oh 'tis you! 'Bout time," the nearest elf said when he saw Mookie. He turned back to his work.

A willowy elf in a navy leotard and flowing top looked up from her sewing machine. "Princesses! Everyone look! Princess Andrea and Princess Diana are here!" she said.

Every machine stopped humming. Every hammer stopped tapping. Every shuttle stopped weaving threads into the fabric on the looms.

The elves crowded around their princesses. "We're so glad you've come!" they all said and led the way to the workroom.

Andrea and Diana gasped. Bolts of cloth of every fabric and color imaginable stood by cabinets full of patterns. Easels had been set up with drawing paper and markers. Twelve animated mannequins filed past. Each was wearing a pink body suit and pink toe shoes.

Diana ran over to a stand heaped with bolts of cloth. She put her arms around a pink one that smelled like cotton candy. "A tutu, first I want a tutu for myself. Then a clown suit for one of the dolls. And--" she said.

Head down, Andrea wandered around the room. She didn't want to design costumes, but this wasn't the way she had imagined it at all. *Diana is going to have all the fun,* she thought.

With nothing to do the princess walked out the first door she could find and into another long passage. She spied a jar of hazelnuts in an open cupboard. While she chewed she thought about all the things she could do to make her feel better.

What good is a parade without a crowd to watch it, she thought. She decided to bring her dancing dolls from the palace to watch the parade. In one Ziv moment the dolls were dancing around their princess. Andrea sent them to Diana to have dresses made for them in rainbow colours. She set some of the elves to work making a throne for herself where she could watch the parade as everyone danced by.

When the festivities began a flock of chick-a-dees lit on the wall. The gray doves settled down beside them. White rabbits seemed to be everywhere, and spiders hung from silken threads high on the castle wall. A cluster of snakes were clinging to the rough stones of the outer wall.

Diana in a fluffy pink tutu and diamond tiara led the grand parade. She twirled her baton to the croak of dozens of tree frogs. Elves in brown leotards and flowing tops tumbled and pranced along the route. Each bowed to Andrea as they danced past her throne of twinkling stars.

Mookie in his new pair of purple zogzs danced along twirling his walking stick. He winked at Andrea and bowed.

The mannequin dolls did pirouettes as they passed Andrea and her dolls which sat on two benches beside her.

Andrea stood up and clapped. "Peachy-keen," she said. As she moved she heard a crinkle like the sound of the wrapping paper on her bed. *Sundri was right an adventure shared is more fun for everyone,* she thought. Andrea went to sleep wondering who would share her next adventure.

Love, Grandma Schoe

Andrea and the Indigo Satellite

WHEN ANDREA WOKE UP IT was dark. She could see nothing not even a star. She listened for the crickets which had been chirping in the garden but heard nothing. Taking a deep breath she sniffed the air but smelled nothing. The heavy scent of the dew-kissed evening flowers was missing.

Very clearly Andrea remembered falling asleep on the couch her grandma kept on the summer porch. She was still in the pink shorts and T-top she had worn while dancing around in the garden. Warm and cozy when she went to sleep, she shivered now in the chilly air.

Andrea had borrowed a white crocheted spread from her grandma's closet. She felt carefully around herself for it. Her hand touched something that felt like dry grass. The young princess sat bolt upright. "Is anyone here?" she said, but no sound came back to her out of the stillness.

Something grabbed at her dark hair and pulled. She screamed or at least thought she did. There was still no sound. She grabbed at a handful of her hair and tugged.

The thing holding her felt like a low branch of a bush. When she pulled herself free it snapped in two. Several thorns stuck in her pink hair band, and the leaves crumpled in her hand. *It's only a shrub,* thought Andrea.

The princess took a deep breath. The air felt dry, too dry. Thoughts of exploring by herself with no one to bother her drifted through her mind. She did nothing to stop them.

"You've a lot to learn young lady," a voice said.

That sounds like Snowpink, but she is on the bed where she always sits when I visit Grandma," thought Andrea. She was glad her teddy bear was there because she was always telling her what to do.

The princess leaned back and put both hands on the dry grass where she was sitting. Something cold and damp touched her arm making the tiny hairs on her neck stand up.

Gingerly she felt for whatever was by her arm and touched warm soft fur. She sent her thought to whatever animal was there. "Who are you? I am Princess Andrea, and I demand to know who you are," she said.

"Easy does it, Princess. Remember the great time you had on Orange Moon," the animal said in Andrea's mind.

"Surely you are a cat," the princess said.

"Of course I'm a cat. I'm a calico cat. Just call me Pix," the cat said.

Andrea picked the small body up and cuddled her. "I'm really glad it's you Pix," she said to the cat while gently stroking the animal's silky fur. She felt the cat begin to purr.

"Ready whenever you are, Princess, but I could just sit here being petted," the cat's sent her thoughts to Andrea.

Andrea snapped at the cat. "I can't see a thing, and I can't even hear you purr," the princess said.

Pix stopped purring. "Easy does it, Princess. Your thoughts hurt. It's just as if you were yelling," she said.

"Sorry. No use trying to go anywhere if I can't see," Andrea said.

"That's okay. I can see just fine," the cat said.

"What do you see?" Andrea said. She wasn't sure she really wanted to know.

"Lots of dead stuff. Nothing's moving a whisker. Everything smells like a dead mouse that's been a long time dead," the cat said.

"I remember a story Grandpa told me. It was about a huge underground cavern in Arizona. It was very, very dry just like this. They put a dead animal in the cavern to see what would happen to it. In three days it was absolutely as dry as a long-time dead mouse. Which is what we will be if we don't get out *of* here. But I can't order a conch shell to take us home to the palace in Ziv. There is no water and there is no rainbow," Andrea said.

Putting her head in her hands and her elbows on her knees, Andrea tried to think. "Let's see, I have four adjutants. Each is in charge of a different zivoid. This one must be attended by Drake. Surely he will come if I call," she said to the cat.

The princess stood up and cupping her hand over her mouth shouted into the emptiness. Nothing happened. No sound broke the silence. No movement disturbed the stillness. Andrea stamped her bare foot and stepped hard on a thorn.

"Easy does it, Princess," the cat said to Andrea's mind. When Andrea pulled the thorn out, she began licking the wound left.

Anrea pouted to her pet. "Oh I wish Drake would come. He picked me up on a dragonfly and took me to Yellow Satellite once. It was such fun!" she said.

Suddenly a ray of light struck the ground in front of them. Andrea closed her eyes and covered her ears. The very bright light still shone in front of her, so she covered her eyes with her fingers.

"Greetings, Your Highness! I am Drake, Adjutant of the Three Satellites of the Land of Vligan in the Princessdom of Ziv," Drake said.

Andrea peeked through her fingers. A boy wearing fringed yellow buckskin stood in front of them. As he bowed he swept the flamingo feathers which brushed his dark face close to the sand.

"It's about time! Get us out of here!" Andrea said.

"Easy does it, Princess," the cat said in a very soft voice.

"What right do you have to always be telling me to take it easy? I'm the big enchilada here," Andrea said to the cat. She was surprised at how loud she sounded.

"Highness, I've only come to remind you about the computer- organ in the palace in Ziv. Remember how you refused to take Donald's instructions? The wild music you played came to this place. This is a zivoid of peace and harmony. You destroyed the balance here. Now you must find out how to restore Indigo Satellite to its natural state," Drake said. He stood for just a moment, folded his arms, nodded his head, and disappeared.

In the darkness that followed, something light as a cobweb drifted over Andrea's face and settled on her hand. "Can you see what this is?" she said to the cat. She daren't move in case it was an insect that might sting.

"It's a feather I think. It looks gray to me but could be any color," Pix said.

"Do you see anyone? Is Drake still here? Is this a feather from his headband?" Andrea said.

She picked up the feather and waved it in the air. A pink glow began to creep across the sky above them.

"Fantastic! Do it again! I can see even better now," the cat said.

Andrea's eyes opened wide as the dark sky became a soft purple. The growing light cast grotesque shadows from tall palms, whose fronds hung limply from their tops. The bushes seemed to be hanging their heads in leafless shame. Everything was a dull gray just like the ashes in Grandpa's fireplace. The air was still as dry as Grandma's wash on a bright and sunny Monday afternoon.

The princess ran her hand through her dry and lifeless hair. "I'm thirsty. How about you?" she said to her companion.

"Me, too. Can you make it rain?" the cat said.

Andrea shook her head. She had no idea how to find any water. *We've got to get out of here,* she thought. She wished there were some way she could order her conch. "Without rain there will be no rainbow. No rainbow, no conch, no way out," she said to Pix. A teardrop ran down her cheek and fell on her wrist. It glistened in the growing pinkish-purple light.

Immediately a pearly-pink conch shell swooped down and settled on the dry sand just down the slope from where they sat. Andrea picked her pet up in her arms and raced for her chariot.

"Easy does it, Princess. Are you going to jump ship? Any rat can do that," the cat said.

"You can stay here if you like. I'm out of here," Andrea said. She plopped the cat in the dust and walked toward the pearly shell.

"Toodles," the cat said. In a flash of light and a puff of dust Pix disappeared.

Small loss! She was always telling me to take it easy just as if I don't know what I'm doing. Besides she'd just be a nuisance at the palace, thought the princess.

"Take me to Ziv! I want to go to the palace," Andrea said to her shell, as she climbed in.

The shell didn't move. Andrea tried again. Nothing happened. The shell didn't budge even one inch. "I hate it here!" the princess said into the dry air. She beat her fists against the side of the shell. The conch still didn't move.

Andrea sat cross-legged on the floor of the conch and pulled her knees up to her chin with her arms. She looked around at the trees and shrubs. As she watched the light from the sky turned bright pink. The sand where the conch sat glowed with a pinkish-golden tint. Even in the shelter of the conch she could feel the chill air turning warm.

She looked at the dull gray thorn bush which had pulled on her hair. A shadowy form was slowly creeping away from it toward the shell.

The young princess screamed at the conch. "Get me out of here! You have to take me home," she said.

The shell tipped and dumped her out onto the ground. The heat of the sand under the flamingo sky felt as if it were burning her hands and knees.

Andrea found herself staring into the beady black eyes of a huge lizard. Small bead-like scales stretched from his blunt black face across his back. His back and blunt tail were black with orange blotches in a somewhat striped pattern. Almost half a yard long he swayed from side to side as he slowly advanced across the hot sand.

The monster stopped in mid-step and yawned. "Howdy, ma'am," My name is Gila and I live here. Who are you? And why are you in the desert of Indigo Satellite?" he said.

The young princess wanted to run, but she couldn't even stand up. The black, beady eyes held hers in a steady gaze.

"I am Andrea, Princess of Ziv and ruler of all the Zivoids. Go away," she said.

The monster's body swayed back and forth. He continued to stare at her. "Princess, eh? Not very polite I'm afraid," he said in a slow drawl.

"Whatcha got here? Anything good to eat? I'm starved," another voice said.

Andrea turned toward the sound. Another monster with beady eyes and a bead-covered body was slowly advancing down the slope.

"Nuttin', nuttin' but a princess, Liga. Not even a nice one at that," Gila said.

"Mebby she can help us with our rain dance. Another dancer sure can't hurt," Liga said.

"Sure can't. Follow me, princess!" Gila said and lifted his left front foot.

Andrea felt safer being behind the creatures than in front of them. She lifted her left arm. *I can't see that this will do any good,* she thought. Liga moved into step behind Gila and began chanting.

> "Humpa. Rain. Mumpa. Rain.
> Lac bush grow leaves again.
> "Humpa. Rain. Mumpa. Rain.
> Cactus grow big blooms again," she said.

Slowly as the lizards swayed from side to side Andrea crept behind them chanting.

> "Humpa. Rain. Mumpa. Rain.
> Lac bush grow leaves again.
> "Humpa. Rain. Mumpa. Rain.
> Cactus grow big blooms again," she said.

In the distance a flash of lightening split the air. The clap of thunder following it left Andrea shaking.

"Humpa, said Gila.

"Mumpa," said Liga.

Andrea watched as the monsters crept back up the slope to their burrow under the thorn bush. Glad to be rid of them she got up and searched for the feather she had dropped. An orange- pink pebble shone like copper in the sand beside the flamingo feather. She picked both up and turned toward her coach which had righted itself.

The moment Andrea stepped inside a solid wall of air closed behind her. She looked toward the top of the slope where the lizards' blunt tails were disappearing. At the bottom of the slope a solid wall of water was rushing toward her.

When the roaring water hit the conch, Andrea fell to the floor. The torrent poured over the shell and swept it down an ancient wash. Andrea thought someone had turned the sky dark again. The princess soon realized that her coach was falling. She wondered if they had been swept into a dark hole.

Frantic, she stuck the flamingo feather into her hair band and rubbed the small stone. It was flat smooth and just right for rubbing between the thumb and fingers. A soft glow came from the walls of the shell, and she could see the cascades of water as it swept over them.

Suddenly she noticed that they were no longer spinning downstream. The dim light from within the conch showed only that it was resting in a small pool of water. She rubbed the stone between her thumb and fingers again. Immediately a myriad of tiny lights lit up the outside of the shell.

Little calcium crystals were bouncing off of the walls of the huge cavern she was in. They flew through the air like a brightly colored snowstorm. The young princess stood up to watch as the crystals formed snowballs. One by one they hit the ceiling and clung there.

The snowballs became blood-red and began to melt and drip over the floor of the cavern. Dark shadows clinging to the walls flew to the floor and began lapping up the thick shiny liquid.

Glad for the safety of the shell, Andrea leaned against the solid wall of air that held her in. There was nothing there. She fell out into the pool of water. Immediately the conch and the light disappeared.

The princess was alone in the dark with these blood-thirsty creatures and had no idea how to get out of this mess. She wished there was someone, anyone there with her.

Andrea put the smooth stone in her pocket. On her hands and knees the princess crept out of the water. She felt her way to the wall nearest where the conch had left her. Over the years rushing torrents had swept the stone floor smooth, but left tiny pebbles which hurt her hands and knees.

When she reached the wall, she noticed a sliver of pinkish glow at the far end of the cavern. Quickly she walked toward the light. The sounds of the shadowy forms hovering over their feast faded behind her.

She began to wonder if she was trapped in this horrible place. If so she wondered why. She remembered that Drake had said she needed to find out how to turn Indigo Satellite to its natural state, but she hadn't a clue as to what he meant.

The first time she was in the palace of Ziv it had been such fun finding out that she was a real princess and had a princessdom. Everyone had come to see her, their princess. It had been wonderful!

But Drake had reminded her of the office in the palace and the huge computer-organ that stood there. She was still aware of the scent of the shelves full of books and the single rose on the desk. She had been so excited she just couldn't wait for her adjutant's instructions. She had simply gone ahead and done it her own way. Donald had patiently waited until she had made a real mess of the music before he stopped her. She shuddered at the memory of the horrible vampires she had made with the music.

She walked faster. The farther she got away from those blood-thirsty creatures the better she felt. A huge shadow loomed up in the pink glow at the mouth of the cavern. She could hear wings flutter.

"Help! Help! I'm so thirsty," a faint voice said.

Andrea peeked out of the dark cave into the pinkness. A butterfly with wings the shade of a black tulip lay on the ground. As big as Andrea, the butterfly's legs were curled up, and her antenna drooped. The princess remembered that the only water anywhere around was in the pool back in the cavern. *No way can I go back there,* she thought.

"I'm so thirsty," the butterfly said. She was clearly getting weaker.

Andrea felt she just had to do something. "There is a bit of water back in the cave. I'll bring some somehow," she said more bravely than she felt.

Rubbing the small stone gently, she stuck it into her head band and followed the beam of light it made. She found a path back to the pool. Using her hands as a saucer, she scooped up a bit of water. When she reached the mouth of the cave again, the butterfly took a few sips and sighed gratefully.

"You must be my princess. I've been waiting a long time for you to come. I'm Emma but please call me Indira. I like being a butterfly," she said weakly.

Now Andrea remembered what had happened at the computer-organ. She had fallen asleep before she got to the indigo note.

"Aren't you the butterfly I danced the Ziva with at my coronation party?" Andrea said.

"Yes. I was the only one who stayed after the party. When I got back here everything was dying," the butterfly said in a whisper.

"It's still very dry and we need rain. Do you think we could do a rain dance?" Andrea said.

The butterfly slowly lifted her left foot, fluttered her wings, and chanted.

> "Rain, rain, gentle rain,
> Fill the clouds and come again.
> Rain, rain, gentle rain,
> Make sweet flowers grow again," she said.

Princess Andrea followed the butterfly very slowly around an ancient maple tree. Stark against the pinkish sky the tree had long since shed most of its leaves. As they walked the leaves crackled and turned to powder under Andrea's bare feet.

A light breeze sprang up and blew the few remaining maple keys around. A pink cloud appeared above them, and gentle drops of silvery rain began to fall. Andrea stuck out her tongue for a few drops.

She caught some water in her hands and ran to the butterfly with it. *The air smells so good, and it's so fresh!* she thought. The princess became absorbed with watching the rain and listening to its gentle patter.

A sudden gust of wind startled Andrea. From somewhere a very tiny figure floated down on a maple key. "I'm getting wet," a little voice said.

Andrea picked up the golden key and looked at it closely. "Diana, is it you?" she said. Carefully she set the key down beside the butterfly and watched as her cousin grew to her right size.

"Of course it is. You'll never believe what trouble I had getting here. You left your earring at the castle in Midnight Globe, and I had no way to call you, so I decided to bring it myself," she said.

She stuck the tiny earring on the lobe of Andrea's ear and handed her a pair of Kekks. "The elves made these for you. I don't know how they knew that you're barefoot. They just did," Diana said and giggled.

Andrea opened her mouth to say something, but Diana continued. "Finally I asked the leprechaun what I could do. He told me that there is an ancient story about a princess and a key. So he took some of his gold and made this homing key. Who's your friend?" she said.

"I'm Indira and you are very welcome to Indigo Satellite, but I've nothing to offer you for refreshment," the butterfly said. She fluttered her dark-purple wings.

Andrea sighed. "It's my fault there are no flowers, Indira, and I'm so very, very sorry. I just didn't know how powerful the computer-organ was," she said.

Diana turned to Andrea. "What computer-organ? Is there one at the castle on Midnight Moon?" she said.

"No. The computer-organ is in the middle of a huge office in the palace in Ziv. I needed a stool to reach the keys it is so big, then I could hardly touch the pedals," Andrea said.

"Well? Go on!" Diana said. Impatient she picked up the small golden key and rubbed it.

"Don't do that!" Andrea said, but Diana had already disappeared. *It's a homing key so perhaps she landed among these maple keys again,* thought Andrea. As she began to search, the earring buzzed loudly.

"I've absolutely no idea as to where I am," Diana said.

"Are you back in Midnight Globe? You just got here you know," Andrea said. She was very annoyed with her cousin.

"I don't think so. The key is stuck to something gold, and I'm stuck up here with it. I can't get any bigger either. You've got to help me," Diana said.

"How can I help you if I don't know where you are," Andrea said and sat cross-legged on the sand at the mouth of the cave. The pitter—patter of the rain did nothing to make her calm. *Surely Diana is somewhere in Ziv but where,* thought Andrea.

Quietly Indira folded her satiny wings. "Princess, I think I can help. I remember what your friend said about the key," she said.

"Yes, go on," Andrea said. She wondered just what Diana had said. She'd been so excited she forgot to listen.

"She said it's a homing key so I guess that's why she landed among the maple keys, but it's also gold so perhaps it went to a golden key this time," the butterfly said.

"Sounds good but I don't know about any other golden key I have," Andrea said.

The butterfly opened and closed her wings. "You were talking to Diana about a computer-organ. Do computers or organs have keys?" she said.

"Of course! That's it! I didn't even think of that. I wonder why I was so slow to remember. The keys on the computer-organ in the palace were color coded, so it would be easy for me to learn to play," Andrea said. She touched her earring again as she spoke.

"Look around you, Diana. Do you see something green on one side of you and something yellow on the other?" she said.

"Guess so. The thing in front of me and below me is yellow and flat. There's a green flat thing right beside it. I'm on a long golden thing in between. Just where am I anyway?" Diana said and paused for breath. Clearly she was very tiny.

"You must be on the computer-organ in the office at the palace," Andrea said.

"This doesn't look like an organ. There are no black keys that I can see. It doesn't look like any computer either," Diana said.

"You're in Ziv. Everything is a bit different here. Just don't start playing until you know what you're doing!" Andrea said. She wondered just how Diana was going to play the organ if she was no bigger than the key that had clung to the maple leaf.

Indira proposed that perhaps Diana could jump up-and-down. "There is a rumour that musical tones from the palace created the flora and fauna on Indigo Satellite," she said.

"I suppose I could run the length of my key and jump up-and- down on the golden key. I'll try that," Diana said.

A golden tone echoed from the cavern behind her, and Andrea thought she had never heard anything so wonderful. The maple tree beside the cave began to shimmer. New golden leaves started to sprout on the bare limbs. Sure she could see better in the maple tree, Andrea climbed it.

Fascinated she watched as golden moths left their golden cocoons, and bright butterflies emerging from golden chrysalises flew from golden flower to golden flower.

The princess of all of Ziv touched the ring on her ear. "Whatever are you doing? You're just playing the same key aren't you? Everything is golden. There is no color," she said.

"I'm having fun jumping. This key is a perfect C#. I just love it," the organ player said.

Andrea snapped into the earring. "You can't just play one note all the time. Try flying over to the other keys!" she said.

"I don't know how. I need help," Diana said.

A golden hummingbird hovered by the princess' ear. "I think I can help. Just be. Just be like me and keep your cool," she said into Andrea's ear ring.

Thoughtfully Diana stroked her golden key on which she was standing. Just like the hummingbird it began to hover. "I'm aloft! Now where to?" she said to Andrea.

"Find the indigo key. Then I think you have to play the other notes," the princess of Ziv said.

"Oh! I see it now. I'll land there and see what happens," Diana said. When she touched down on the indigo key, she began to get larger.

She floated to the organ stool. When she was her own size, she carefully put the golden key into her pocket. First she played the scale up the organ. Next she played the scale down. Then she picked out a few cords.

Andrea was delighted. She rubbed the smooth stone she took from her pocket and shone its light on the maple tree. The golden leaves on the maple turned green.

"Send more green! I want more green," Andrea said into her earring. She shone her light on the sand, and watched amazed as green grass as smooth as her grandpa's lawn sprang up in the golden sand.

"Can you please send some red and some yellow. I want tulips," Andrea said. When the bed of tulips she wanted was full, she called to Diana.

"Pink, please send pink, I want some roses," she said.

"How do I make pink? There isn't any pink key," Diana said.

"I used the pedals to soften the tones, but they were awfully hard to reach," Andrea said.

"Well I can't reach them either. What can I do?" Diana said.

"Meow, I can help. Just tell me which pedal to press," a cat said.

"Pix, is that you? I'm glad you came back, and I'm sorry I dropped you in the dust," Andrea said to her pet.

"No problem, Princess. I love you. Now which pedal is the soft one?" the cat said.

Andrea waved the flamingo feather that had fallen from Drake's headband. The golden butterflies became all sorts of shades and delightful patterns.

Colorful hummingbirds flit from flower to flower. "These taste great. They have a perfect fragrance, and they're just exactly sweet enough," they said to the princess of Indigo Moon and all of Ziv.

"This is much better than Indigo Moon was before, but something is missing," Indira said.

Andrea sat down under the maple. She wondered what could possibly be missing from the wonderful garden she and Diana had just created. She waved her hand toward the distant trees.

A few poplars stood near a clear stream which wound its way through fields of grain. Gentle rains had recently watered the apple and pear orchards.

In the vegetable garden tender green asparagus plants raised their spears on high. Rows of beans were already fat with seeds. Sweet strawberries and bright red raspberries glowed under the warm sky. Blueberries ripened in their patch.

By the tulips big blue hydrangeas nodded to huge scented roses of every hue. Bluebells danced through the grass in the daisy field, and purple flowers on a clump of Jacob's ladder tempted all sorts of tiny insects.

Of every size colorful butterflies flit from flower to flower, while gentle moths rested on the trumpet vines. The hummingbirds' wings seemed to sing as they dashed in and out of the spray from the fountains.

While crickets chirped in the shade of the maples, small lizards raced through sandy paths. When Andrea walked by, they hid among the leaves in the herb garden. She loved to rub the rough leaves of fresh mint between her thumb and fingers even though the sharp scent made her sneeze.

"What could we possibly need? Haven't we thought of everything?" Andrea said to Indira.

"The Sidhe-folk left," Indira said. Her wings drooped.

"Whoever are the Sidhe-folk?" Andrea said.

Beside her Diana hopped off her key and became her right size. "There are some of them in the garden that's in the castle. They are devas or nature spirits. The Irish call them Sidhe-folk," she said.

Indira folded her wings and sat beside the two princesses. "They are the highest of the order of the faerie folk. They are the people of peace," she said.

"The garden is so beautiful! Won't that make the Sidhe-folk come back? Diana said.

"We brought rain with a rain dance. Perhaps they would come if we danced for them. We could dance the Ziva. It is both lively and graceful," Andrea said and clapped her hands.

Drake suddenly was standing beside her. He bowed low, and the remaining feathers in his headband brushed his face. "May I have this dance, Princess," he said.

Crickets chirped while moths, butterflies, and hummingbirds danced the Ziva with Andrea, Diana, and Drake. Gradually a few faeries slipped quietly into the garden and joined them.

The crickets were still chirping in the garden by her grandma's porch when Andrea woke up. She felt in her pocket. The copper-colored stone was still there. It was just like the pebble she found by the garden path that morning.

She heard Drake's voice in her mind. "It's called Vliganite. You must keep it safe. You will need it the next time you visit Ziv," he said.

Love, Grandma Schoe

Andrea on Scarlet Orb

THE NIGHT AFTER HER TRIP to the zoo Andrea was thinking deeply about the various birds she had seen there. Something stirred in her memory.

In her first trip to Ziv she had stood a few moments in front of the eighth floor exhibit watching the birds nesting there. The birds with their scarlet plumage and black wingtips had fascinated her. None of them had moved so much as a scarlet feather.

All at once she was there again, but this time it was different. She now knew they were scarlet ibises. One of them turned and looked at her. The young princess could not stop herself. She took a step toward the door.

Silently it swung open, and a smiling girl greeted her. "Welcome, Your Highness" she said. Ming's kimono was scarlet with heavy gold embroidery, and she wore matching scarlet slippers. With a very serious look on her face, Ming placed her right hand over her heart and bowed low.

"Your tea ceremony is ready, Highness. Come this way please," she said and led the way to a red carpet. It took off down a hallway and out of sliding doors, where it hovered over the courtyard for just a moment.

A Ziv minute later it lit on an ice floe. The tiny patch of ice was surrounded by water, and waves sloshed against the side of the ice. Andrea who was wearing only her red cotton pajamas and matching headband shivered.

She was glad her piece of Vliganite was safely tucked into an old watch she was wearing. She had a feeling it would be needed.

Ming led her to a nearby mound of ice-covered snow. She motioned for Andrea to creep inside. "Choose wisely!" her adjutant said.

Andrea wondered just what she could choose. The room into which she had crept was very dark. She rubbed the glass that covered her copper-colored stone. A warm glow immediately came from the walls of the igloo.

I will need something warm to wear, Andrea thought. One of her dancing dolls appeared wearing a one-piece bathing suit in scarlet latex. The princess of all the orbs of Ziv shouted at the doll. "That's not what I wanted. I'm not going in that freezing water. Never! Not ever!" she said.

Instead of leaving, the doll held out a swim suit exactly like the one she was modeling. Ming's words, 'Choose wisely', echoed in Andrea's mind.

Grumbling all the while Andrea slipped into the suit. It fit perfectly. "Now I need something warm," Andrea said to whoever might be listening. Another of her dolls appeared. She held out a faux fox robe with matching white slippers.

"Beautiful! It's absolutely gorgeous! Thank you," Andrea said. She slipped the warm kimono over her new swim suit and tied it with its long scarlet sash.

The princess heard Ming's voice in her mind. "Please, Your Highness, come out now. The tea ceremony is ready," she said.

Careful not to spoil her new robe, Andrea crept through the short tunnel. She could hardly wait for the tangy taste of mint tea. She expected to see her adjutant kneeling by a low ebony table laden with tea things.

The ebony table was there all right but it was empty. There was no steaming tea pot, and there was no sign of Ming. Instead a girl with medium brown hair and brown eyes, who was wearing blue shorty-pajamas, stood by the low table shivering.

Andrea's demands were loud and cross. "Who are you? Why are you here?" she said.

The girl was stamping her feet in an effort to keep warm. "My name - my name is – Leah, and - and I've no idea why I am here wherever – wherever this is," the stranger said.

"So go home! You don't belong here. I am Andrea, Princess of Ziv, and I don't allow intruders on my Zivites," the annoyed princess said.

"I would if I could. I don't want to be in this horrible place. I was just putting my baby dolls to bed and found myself here instead. It's cold. You're being nasty and I want to go home," she said.

Wrapped her arms around herself, she stomped over to the edge of the ice. She jumped toward Andrea screaming.

A long wriggly thing pulling itself up by suction cups was coming up over the side of the floe. A single eye in one side of a large body, which was pale as death, peered over the side of the ice.

Andrea grabbed Leah by the hand. "This way," she said, and motioned for the strange girl to creep into the igloo.

The young princess couldn't believe her eyes. The inside of the igloo was much larger than when she had just left it, but it still glowed with the soft light she had created with her stone.

Ming stood at one side her arms folded into her kimono sleeves. She bowed low. "Your Highness, your cousin Leah has come to accompany you, while you explore Scarlet Orb," she said.

Bowing to the brown-haired girl Ming smiled. "I am Ming, Adjutant of the Three Orbs of the Land of Eau de Phyn in the Princessdom of Ziv. You are here to prepare for your role as a princess in the Princessdom of Ziv, the Land of Be Alive. We adjutants are sure you will want to do your very best," she said, and bowing low she disappeared.

Because of the warmth that came from the lighted walls of the igloo, Leah soon stopped shivering. But she was still shaking and was mumbling something about not ever being a princess.

She looks just like a plucked chicken in those shorty pajamas, and I'll bet she's cold, thought Andrea. She clapped her hands, and one of her dolls came in holding a one-piece bathing suit exactly like Andrea's.

"Choose wisely! It looks as if we're in this together, Miss Princess-to-be. First you'll need a swimsuit," Andrea said.

Leah backed away. "I'm not going into that cold water. No way! Not even if I never become a princess," she said.

"It seems we must. Then you'll need something warm," Andrea said.

Another doll stepped forward holding a white, faux fox kimono with a scarlet sash and white slippers. A third doll held out a dark-red track suit and matching jogging shoes.

"When you're changed we'll have tea," Andrea said and started down through the tunnel, which soon curved upward again. She hoped the creature from the sea had vanished.

Andrea looked around for the ebony tea table. Two pair of eyes stared at her from two white furry bodies that nearly covered the table.

"Love your gown, Princess. It looks almost like our fur," one of the creatures said.

The other twisted around to show off his white, bushy tail and barked. "We're Artic foxes. I'm Icy and my mate is Floie," he said.

"The ice-worm cometh. He's really boring into the ice flow this time. It will soon be gone. The snowy owls have already left," Floie said sadly.

The ice Andrea was standing on was quickly melting, and the little island of ice was also drifting in a fast current. The princess looked over the side of the ice to see if the nasty creature had gone to his lair in the depth of the sea.

"If you're thinking of Topus, he's gone for now at least. He's been taking all the scarlet ibises to his lair. Everyone is hoping you can free them from the bubbles he has created for cages. We just came to wish you luck before we left," Icy said. He hopped down from the little table.

"Bye, bye," Floie said. She raced behind her mate to the side of the ice. With a flying leap and some frantic clawing at the snowy bank they were ashore.

The floe began drifting further from shore. The edge of the ice was getting softer and thinner. Leah crept from the igloo. She was wearing the dark-red jogging suit and matching shoes.

Andrea grabbed the tiny table and overturned it. Climb aboard!" she said.

Leah stared at Andrea. "Don't be silly. We're much too big to get into that thing," she said.

Andrea yelled over the sloshing of the water. "Try to think small! Just think small! Things are different in Ziv you know," she said.

When she grabbed her new friend's hand, they both started to shrink. Just as they stepped into the overturned table, the ice disappeared. The last thing they saw behind them was the tip of the igloo as it melted into the sea. Their little boat began to rock on the waves.

"Where to now?" Leah said and shivered. She told her cousin she was sure she wouldn't like this adventure a bit.

Andrea jumped at the sound of a hoarse squawk beside her. A scarlet-breasted macaw was perched on one leg of the overturned table. The huge bird's weight was tipping the small table dangerously low in the water. The young princess waved her hand at him. "Go away! Shoo! Scram! Beat it!" she said.

"Nuttin' doin'. I'm McGee Macaw an' I'm stayin'," the macaw said and balanced by shifting his green wing feathers.

"You'll get us all drowned," Andrea said, as she moved to the center of their small make-shift craft.

The macaw flapped his wings. "I got blown out here by a sou'easter, and there's nothing else for miles around. Word on the tzivine is that you're a princess, Princess of Ziv even. If you're so smart make the table bigger. I can hardly stay upright," he said.

"I can't do that. I don't know how," Andrea said.

"Sure you can. Just think big," Leah said. She stood up on one side of the overturned table, began to grow, lost her balance, and fell overboard.

Andrea stared over the edge of the tiny table at the sputtering Leah. "Now what? You're too big. I'm too small, and I can't swim!" she said.

Leah splashed around. "The water isn't awfully cold. If I can get my shoes off, I can tow you toward that little island over there. It's not far," she said.

Clicking his beak the macaw jumped into the air and snatched up Leah's shoes in his huge claws. "Didn't see that. Tide must be going out. Follow me!" he said and flew ahead of the girls.

Andrea untied her scarlet sash and threw it to her cousin. "Use this for a tow-rope," she said and held her end tightly in both hands. She moved to one corner of the table and stood up behind the leg. The wind and waves drove the make-shift boat toward what looked like a red-rock island. The waves were very choppy.

The young princess hoped she wouldn't take flight like the bird she saw overhead. The albatross floated effortlessly against a bright blue sky before disappearing beyond Andrea's sight.

When they reached the atoll, they discovered it was bright red coral surrounding a bit of land. Leah swam through an opening in the coral and dragged the little table ashore.

Andrea climbed out of her makeshift boat, and as soon as she became her own size she up-righted the table. "Leah, you were wonderful! But you're shivering. You can wear my kimono while you dry out," Andrea said and hugged her.

"We need some hot peppermint tea," the princess said to whoever might be listening. Just as she expected a beautiful china tea service appeared on the table. Golden dragons wound around the bright red pot and around four tiny tea cups.

Andrea knelt at the ebony table and motioned for Leah to do the same. The tantalizing aroma of peppermint tea filled the air.

"Could do with a spot meself. Mind if I join you, my dear Princess?" McGee said. He sidestepped over to the table opposite Leah.

Andrea was about to shoo him away when Leah put her hand on her cousin's arm. "Let him stay. He was a great help in getting us here," she said.

Even while wondering why there was a fourth cup on the table, Andrea poured tea into it. She wrapped her hands around her bowl-shaped cup, and closing her eyes she inhaled the fragrance of the peppermint leaves.

"Well! What have we got here? And who is the green guy in the scarlet vest?" someone from across the table said.

The princess of all the Zivoids of Ziv looked up from the warm cup she held in her hands. "Diana! However did you get here?" she said and watched as her other cousin put a golden key into her pocket.

Diana smoothed down the navy blue jump suit she was wearing. "I had a bit of trouble peeling this key off the golden dragon on the teapot. It was getting awfully warm there," she said.

She turned to the open-mouthed girl sitting beside her. "You're cousin Leah aren't you? I was wondering when you'd become a princess in Ziv," she said.

Leah closed her mouth and opened it again. "Do you really think I'm a princess?" she said. She bent her head over her tea and took a tiny sip.

Diana curled both hands around her steamy cup of tea. "I know that you're a princess. Your grandma is a queen in Ziv, and that makes you a princess. That's how it works," she said.

"Never been a queen in these parts, nor a princess neither. I'm McGee Macaw, and I'd have known. I get around you know," the bird said. He shook a drop of tea off his beak.

"I'm the only princess of Scarlet Orb at the moment. Diana is princess on one of my other zivoids, and Leah has never even been to Ziv before," Andrea said.

The macaw cocked his head on one side and remarked, "Blimey, it'll take more than you three princesses to outwit Old Topus," he said.

Diana brushed her long dark hair out of her face. "Whoever on a zivoid is Old Topus?" she said.

The macaw burst into a torrent of speech. "He's an old slippin' slider. He went and got h'self caught. Was a-slippin' between the cracks in these here atolls and lost all o' his red color. He thinks he can get it back.

The volcano in the center of these atolls makes bubbles that harden. Old Topus stole a bunch. He's caught almost all of the scarlet ibises and put them into bubbles," he said.

Andrea buried her face in her hands at the thought. "Won't they smother?" she said.

"Naw. They got lots of air to do for at least another few days. When he gets them all, he's a-gonna suck all o' their color out before he releases them," the old bird said.

"Then they'll be white just like when they were babies. It's no fun being different than you really are. I know," Diana said.

The macaw twisted his neck around and preened his feathers before he answered. "Worsn' that. They will be gray as the ash from a volcano. Best you figure out how to get off this here bit of an island. Tide's a-comin' in. And it's a-comin' real fast," he said to the princess of all of Ziv.

As she finished her tea, Andrea looked at the ocean that surrounded them. A surge in the tide sent water lapping at the macaw's feet. He flew up and perched on the lid of the teapot.

Andrea noticed that Leah had changed into her track suit. Quickly she slipped back into her white robe and tied her sash. The three girls grabbed each other's hands. "Be small," they said, and each girl jumped into an empty teacup.

The macaw lifted first one foot and then the other. "Blimey, you three aren't about to leave me here are you? This pot's too hot. It won't float neither, and I'm not a-goin' to ever fit into one of those teeny cups," the bird said and flapped his wings.

A second wave moved the table closer to the ocean. The macaw shrieked, as the teapot tipped over. A third wave swept them all into the sea.

"I'm too little to even swim now. We're all going to drown!" Leah said.

Andrea barely heard her. She knew she had to do something, but she had no idea what. *If only we had some horses to ride,* she thought.

She rubbed the glass in the watch covering her piece of Vliganite. The golden dragon that wound around the teapot slipped into the water and diving deep into the ocean came up under the squawking macaw. As it surfaced its dragon head became similar to a horse's head, but its body still appeared to be armoured right down to the tip of its curved tail. The creature had a short golden mane that floated on the water.

Andrea rubbed her watch face three more times. Soon three more golden sea horses were swimming beside the tiny teacups.

"Think big!" Andrea said. She leapt out of the teacup into the water beside one of seahorses and immediately grew to her own size. When the seahorse was big enough, she found a spot on the creature's back where she could hold on.

Another sea horse surfaced beside Diana. She quickly became her own size and got on its back. *She must have heard my instructions in spite of the wind*, Andrea thought.

Before the princess-to-be could take a breath, Leah's teacup began to fill with water. "I'm still too tiny. I have to get big," she said.

"Get big! Get big!" her tea cup echoed and sank.

Leah took a deep breath. One of the seahorses swam beside her with his golden mane floating around her. She grabbed it and tried to pull herself onto the horse's head.

Andrea leaned her mount to the right and turned toward the golden seahorse. "Leah, remember things are different in Ziv! You can do it!" she said to the struggling princess-in- training of Scarlet Orb.

"I am a princess in Ziv. I am as big as I need to be," Leah said. Immediately she began to get to her own size.

Andrea, whose mount had just swum up to Leah, called to her. "Wonderful! I couldn't have done better myself. It just takes time to learn how to live in Ziv," she said.

The macaw flapped his wet wings harder. "Look out for Old Topus! He's slipping through the water just like an eel," he said.

Andrea shouted into the wind. "Let our seahorses have wings!" she said. Tiny wings sprouted from the sides of the water creatures. They flapped them uselessly at their sides.

Andrea noticed a pale shape moving through the water toward her. It looked like a pale blob of jelly being pushed through the water by eight long arms. Its sharp beak grabbed at her white robe.

She pulled her legs onto the back of the seahorse and leaned over its mane. "Be a winged dragon! Please, be a winged dragon," she said and patted his neck. As her mount rose it changed into a winged creature with a dragon's head and short legs.

Old Topus had changed direction in the water. His pulsing arms were pushing him furiously toward the struggling wet bird.

Andrea pointed her piece of Vliganite at the macaw's seahorse. "Be a winged dragon! Be a winged dragon!" she said.

"Now we have to get to the golden palm on the island where the ibises are," McGee said. He flew beside Andrea and Diana, whose mount had also become a winged dragon.

"Did you say golden? I can get to golden things, but I don't know how to get all of us there," Diana said.

Andrea thought for a second. "Did you bring the earrings?" she said to Diana.

"Sure thing! Here! Catch!" Diana said and took the tiny crystal that hung in its white-gold hoop from her left ear. Deftly she tossed it in Andrea's direction. The earring flew straight to the lobe of Andrea's left ear and attached itself there.

"Thanks. When I touch it I can even hear you breathe," Andrea said.

"I get it now. I go to the golden islands, and you follow my sound waves," Diana said.

It was a Ziv minute before the princess of Midnight Globe called Andrea. "I guess I'm on an island. There looks to be sand everywhere, but my key stuck to a golden palm frond. I'm stuck to the key, and I can't get down. If I get big I'll fall," she said.

Andrea's attention was taken by a low rumbling in the distance. The sound was coming from the direction of the coral atoll.

"Old Topus has just stolen another bubble from the volcano. He must know where the last family of ibises are," the macaw said. The rumbling gradually grew louder and louder.

The trio was flying very low over a body of water. It was connected to the ocean by a small stream. The warm air was less salt and carried the scent of fresh water.

When Andrea looked down she saw a vast number of bubbles, each containing a bright red bird bobbing on the surface. She wondered where the rest of the ibises were, and was puzzled as to how they would be able to save them.

The distant rumbling of the volcano became a roar. A billowing column of smoke rose up from the volcano followed by an explosion from the depths of Scarlet Orb. The lava that spewed into the air looked like firecrackers lit for a special holiday. As it fell it became gray ash which drifted over the coral of the atoll.

"The legend must be true! 'Tis said that Madre Mountain will rise from the ancient sea bed. I never thought I'd live to see it," the macaw said.

Andrea's faux-fox robe billowed out around her. She stared at the bird. "You mean that pile of ash will become a mountain?" she said.

"It be a mountain. Madre sank beneath the waves many, many lifetimes ago. She's been waiting for someone special to appear. Or so the story goes," McGee said.

Andrea stared first at the macaw then at the bursts of fire and the plume of steam in the distance. "It looks to be in the direction of the little island where we had our tea," she said.

"So it is! So it is! The volcano is surrounded by a coral reef," the bird said and began to preen his feathers.

"What does all this have to do with Old Topus?" Andrea asked. She was still shielding her eyes from the fireworks exploding from the growing mountain.

"That's where he lost his color, when he was trying to slip through the cracks to get brighter color from the haws of a hawthorn bush," the macaw said.

Leah swung her winged dragon closer to the bird. "Why would he do that?" she said.

"Because he wanted to be more brilliantly scarlet," McGee said.

"Then it's the mountain that has his color. And he should get it back from her instead of stealing it from the ibises," Andrea said.

The mountain rumbled. "Princess Andrea. I am Sierra Madre. I am Mother of this realm," she said. The landscape around the mountain began to glow in shades of red, maroon and scarlet.

"I am Andrea, Princess of Ziv and of the Orbs of Eau de Phyn. Scarlet Orb is one of my zivoids," the frightened princess said. Her voice was so weak she was sure the mountain would never hear her.

"This is my home. If you want it you will have to take it away from me. You will have to get Old Topus color from me and give it back to him, or we'll all know you're not a real princess," the mountain said and spewed forth a burst of lava.

At that moment Andrea heard Diana's excited voice in her ear. "Do come quickly! I've found the ibises hiding in a clump of red cannas by this huge waterfall. They are so scared they are crowding close together now," she said.

Andrea touched her earring. "I've no idea how to do this. I don't even know where Old Topus' color is. Or how to get it back to him," she said to Diana.

McGee pulled his dragon up beside Andrea's again. "There is a hawthorn that grew in one of the cracks in Mother Mountain. Topus got stuck on its thorns, and his color bled into a bubble under the bush," he said.

Andrea turned from the fuming mountain to the macaw. "Where is this hawthorn bush anyway? And how can I get to it?" she said.

"It grew on the edge of the mountain. Now it's underwater and covered with coral," McGee said.

Andrea wondered just how she would ever get there. She wasn't even sure just which coral island it was.

"I'll take you there, Princess, but if you don't stop shaking you'll fall off," the dragon which was her mount said.

Just before they crashed into the coral of the atoll, Andrea's mount dove toward the water. Quickly she loosened her robe and let it fall into the wind, but before she could hold onto her dragon again she slipped and fell into the waves.

Gasping for breath the princess came up just in time to feel someone's arm slip around her. "Take a deep breath! I'll hold you up. Stop struggling. Just relax," Leah said. She was wearing only her scarlet swim suit.

"I can't swim! I've never tried," Andrea said between breaths.

"Then you don't know do you? Kick your feet," the princess- in-training said, as she swam beside Andrea.

"This way girls. The hawthorn is right under this bit of coral," McGee said. He settled down on the reef where the wind had blown Andrea's white robe. He was just a few yards from where Andrea and Leah were struggling in the water.

The princess soon caught on to the dog paddle, and with Leah alongside of her she made her way to the big bird. Andrea pulled herself up beside the macaw. "Do you know how far it is down to the bubble that holds Old Topus' color?" she said.

"You'll have to dive. It's only a couple of fathoms or so," McGee said.

"I can dive. Two yards is too much though," Leah said and pulled herself out of the water to sit beside the bird.

McGee stared at Andrea with one eye. "Princess, ye best be thinkin' o' somethin'. There isn't much time. I saw the old octopus going toward golden isle with another bubble."

Squid, Andrea thought. "We can be squid," she said.

"Squid? Did you say you're going to become squid?" the Princess of Midnight Globe said into Andrea's ear.

"Sure thing! We can get the bubble of color and get to the golden palm before Old Topus does. We'll be a lot faster than he is," Andrea said and rubbed the glass face on her watch.

When the Vliganite glowed she pointed it at her friend. Leah began to grow eight sucker bearing arms from around her mouth. Two became long and were like arms with spoon like tips and horny hooks. From her body where her feet had been a pair of small wings grew.

Scarcely feeling the same changes in her own self, Andrea dove into the waves after the princess-in-training. *This is not the time to be scared of the water I must try to think like a squid*, Andrea thought. She followed Leah deeper and deeper and swam around until they found the calcified thorn bush.

Andrea sent her thought to the princess-in-training. "Do you have any idea where it is? I can't see a thing," she said. She swam around deeper into the water and searched among the roots of the ancient tree.

Using the suckers of her mouth Andrea felt for anything that seemed like a bubble. Finally she found one of its haws which was a rose that had been calcified into a lump. Beside the haw was a bubble, but it was almost covered with lime.

"I think this is the bubble. Can you get ahold of it," the princess of Ziv said to her diving partner.

Leah grasped the bubble with her tentacles. Tugging with the horny tips on her long squid arms she pulled it free.

Andrea sped through the water toward the vibrations she felt coming from the waterfall. Leah clutching the precious bubble swam close behind.

When they caught up to the pale old octopus, they were within sound of the waterfall and the ibises' hiding place. He was clutching the clear bubble he'd just brought from Mother Mountain.

When he saw the scarlet filled bubble, he grasped it in two of his long tentacles and swallowed it whole. He immediately began to turn color and became gradually darker until he was a gorgeous scarlet octopus.

Old Topus sped away to his lair followed by Andrea and Leah. He tapped each ibis-filled bubble with his sharp beak. The bubbles burst and fell away like bubble bath floating on the sea.

Squawking loudly the birds flapped their wings and crowded around Andrea and Leah. They were now standing among them in their scarlet swim suits along with Diana in her track suit.

"Oh thank you, thank you, thank you," the ibises said. They stretched their long necks and their long legs.

"We don't know what we ever would have done without our color. Every other ibis would have shunned us if we were gray like the ash from Mother Mountain," one ibis said.

"Come join us for a lunch of krill," another said. The rest clapped their wings in agreement.

In the distance, a deep rumble came from Sierra Madre. Like gorgeous firecrackers lava shot from her core and filled the sky with scarlet and white sparkles. Above them small bursts of steam became little clouds. They spelled the words ANDREA, PRINCESS OF ZIV. A second burst of steam spelled LEAH, PRINCESS OF SCARLET ORB.

"Blimey, never thought I'd live to see the day," the macaw said. He flew in, dropped Leah's shoes on the sand, and clicked his beak.

Old Topus pulled in his long tentacles. "Welcome to Scarlet Orb. It's an honour to have been visited by even one Princess, and here we have three. I'll never again wish to be something I'm not," he said.

He turned to the scarlet birds. "I'm sorry for the scare I gave you. Please feel free to lunch in my lair. There are lots of shrimp here," he said.

He held out one of his bright red tentacles to each of the girls. Andrea hesitated for just a Ziv moment then took the octopus' flexible arm-tip in one hand. His skin felt soft and slippery to her touch.

At that moment the red carpet that brought Andrea from the palace in Ziv floated down to her feet. Diana took her golden key from her pocket and disappeared along with both earrings.

As the red carpet rose over the waves, the other two princesses were surprised to find themselves back in their shorty pajamas. Leah began to disappear exactly as she had appeared on the ice floe.

"When you want to come back to Scarlet Orb next time just say, "Ziva, Quiva, Liva," Princess Andrea said to her vanishing figure and waved.

Love, Grandma Schoe

Andrea Hunts on Blue Moon

ANDREA SUDDENLY FOUND HERSELF IN a deep darkness. Her body felt heavy and strange, and she was holding a stick in each hand. The one in her right hand was narrow and smooth, while the one in her left hand was much heavier.

When she touched the heavy stick with her right hand, she thought it felt like a bow. She decided she must be holding a bow and arrow. While keeping both in her left hand Andrea felt her arms and chest. They were bare. She distinctly remembered falling asleep in her old blue sweat suit.

The air smelled like the barn she and her grandpa had visited that morning. A stable-hand had been mucking out the horse stall. It smelled so bad Andrea had held her nose and hurried out into the fresh air.

She tried to take a few steps. Her feet clip-clopped like horse's hooves!

Andrea's heart began to pound in her chest. She felt for her legs and discovered that they were covered with horses' hair. *I'm a centaur,* she thought.

At first the thought scared her, but then she remembered. Before she went to sleep, she had been wondering what it would be like to be a centaur.

"Be careful what you wish for! You might get it," her pink- and-white teddy bear had said from her place in Andrea's room.

She had no idea of how to go about being a centaur. She tried to move around, but she had too many feet. She tried to go forward and bumped into a huge tree.

"Just where do you think you're going? You had better watch out. There is a whole forest of us oak folks here. Stop stomping on our acorns. If you crush them they won't grow into new trees," the huge tree said. She shook her large leaves in Andrea's face.

"You nearly stepped on my whole family. We mice snack on these acorns," a whiny voice at her feet said.

"S-s-sorry. I've never been here before, and it's so dark I can't see," Andrea said.

A bird flying over her head cried to the wind. "Go toward the light! Go toward the light!" the bird said.

In the distance Andrea saw a rim of blue light which was almost like a horizon with a blue sun coming up. She felt for reins to turn her mount's head toward the light, then she realized she was her mount herself. Slowly lest she trip over her too many feet the young princess made her way toward the blue horizon.

The light from the distant horizon began to penetrate dimly into the oak trees that grew everywhere. Various animals moved through the trees as dark shadows.

When she paused under an oak to rest for a moment, something dropped onto her back. "Well what have we here?" her passenger said. The creature ran a paw over Andrea's bare back. "You're a centaur for sure. A few stomp around in Brown Oak Forest, but they never venture this far toward the light," the creature said.

"Just who are you? And where do you think I'm going to take you?" Andrea said to the creature.

"I'm a Pine Martin, and you may call me Marty. Down this deer trail are some tasty acorns. If you don't mind, I'll hang on a bit. You sound like a girl. Are you a girl centaur?" he said.

Andrea ignored Marty's question, and turning her torso around felt for the creature. He allowed her to stroke his fur. In the dim light she saw an animal with dark brown fur which was about the size of her grandma's cat. He had a white-and-yellow bib of fur under his chin.

"Aren't you cold? Why don't centaurs have any fur up top?" Marty said.

"That's because centaurs are part human. I'm a human who got trapped in a centaur body because I wanted to find out what it felt like, and I am cold," Andrea said.

"Toodles! Got to go. I hear one clomping down the path. Guess he must have smelled you," Marty said and jumped down into a clump of fern.

Andrea made her way out of Brown Oak Forest into Dark Forest. She realized that she was hungry, but she had no appetite for the grass that grew around her feet.

She sniffed. There were ripe grapes somewhere close by. Quickly she made her way to the tangle of vines she could see in the dim light.

Just as she reached out for a big bunch of ripe grapes, something dropped over her head. It felt like a spider web. Right in front of her, hanging from another web, was the biggest black spider Andrea had ever imagined. She sat back on her haunches.

"No need to take on so. Marty said you were coming by and that you were cold. We creatures do talk to one another we do. Now hold still while I fix this. It's the finest gossamer you'll ever find," the big black spider said.

She began at Andrea's head and cut the fine threads of the web. When the spider was finished Andrea felt warmer. The spider web that hung from her arms and around her torso in billowing waves had become like the most delicate of gossamer fabrics.

"Fit for a princess it is. I hope you like it," the spider said and pulled herself back into her own web. The idea of being a princess stayed in Andrea's mind.

A dark shape loomed up in front of her. The animal that stood in her path was as big as Andrea. In the dim light his rack of horns looked huge.

"Please don't shoot me, my Princess. I've ventured into Dark Forest to lead you to the blue light," the big buck said.

"You are very kind, but I'm no princess. I'm just a girl who got stuck in a body I don't want," Andrea said. A tear ran down her cheek.

The big buck nodded his head. "I understand. I will walk with you when I can, but when the trail is narrow you will have to follow me," he said softly.

In the darkness Andrea could barely make out the antlers on other dark bodies that passed them. They were heading into the dark forest. She wondered if she could trust this one to lead her toward the blue horizon in the distance.

"They are going to find fresh acorns. The mice aren't the only animals that like the nutty taste. There are finer oaks with tastier acorns that grow under the bright blue sky. These deer, however, were born here and prefer to live in the dark," the buck said. It was just as if he knew her fears.

Andrea dropped her bow and arrow. "I'm so glad you came by. Please let's hurry," she said. In her haste Andrea forgot she had four feet. She got them so tangled with each other she fell to her knees.

A fox trotting by stopped and stared. "You're going the wrong way you know. I'll wait 'till you get up and you can follow me. I'm Reddy Fox, and I know where all the action is," he said.

Andrea got her front feet under her and stood up. "Thank you Reddy. You're very kind," she said. She hesitated just for a moment.

The big buck was just going around a bend in the narrow trail ahead. The steady rhythm of his hoof beats gave Andrea courage. Her own feet began to feel less clumsy, as she clip-clopped after her new friend.

At the very edge of the darkness Andrea stopped. She wanted to go for shelter to the blue-domed yurt she saw close by. She tried to take a step, but her feet got tangled. "I need help," she said.

A boy stood beside her. "I am Donald, Adjutant of the Lands of Fyrh in the Princessdom of Ziv. I am here to help you, Your Highness," he said. He placed his right hand over his heart. Drawing his sword he touched Andrea at the withers just below the torso.

Andrea was in her own body immediately. Her gossamer gown hugged her close and hung to her knees. It glowed with the blue light of sky.

Before Andrea could say a word, Donald handed her a smooth piece of lapis lazuli. "Welcome to Blue Moon, Princess. You will need this as a guide," he said.

The young princess took the stone. "Thank you Donald," she said. When she looked up he was gone.

Happy to have two feet instead of four Andrea ran to the yurt. The bottom half of a narrow door opened, so she crept inside and sat on the floor. The scent of blue violets made her feel safe, but she couldn't see a thing.

Without thinking she rubbed the smooth stone Donald had given her. A beam of blue light began to play over the walls of the yurt.

A mosaic of pictures in various shapes and colors covered the walls. Each showed someone she had visited on her various zivoids. Finally the beam stopped on a large circle.

A black cat leapt down from the circle and strode over to her. Purring the cat sat down beside her. "Welcome Princess. I'm Sundri. I know you didn't see me in Dark Forest, but I was watching you," the cat said.

A hundred bright budgies appeared and sang to her.

> "Princess, dear Princess
> We hope you will stay.
> We are happy to sing
> For you each day.
> Tum, tum, tiddley-tee.
> Tee, tee, tiddley-tum," they sang.

Andrea clapped her hands as she began remembering everything. The budgies had sung this very song for her in the roof-garden at the palace in Ziv. It was on the very first time she had ever come to The Land of Be Alive. When the portals closed she shivered.

Her dancing dolls appeared and circled around her. "The princess is cold poor thing. She is going to need a warm pair of blue jeans and a jean jacket," one of the dolls said. She took her princesses' hand and helping her to her feet led her to a small booth.

"Everything you need is in here Princess. Please pick up the blue tote beside your new running Kekks. You are to carry it with you," another doll said.

The young princess felt very fine in her new clothes. She slipped her lapis lazuli stone into the back pocket of her blue jeans and perched her smoke shaded goggles on top of her head.

She tried out her new Kekks by running around the inside walls of the Yurt. By her third round, a faint scratching on the walls outside had become louder and more frantic. The fear the young princess had felt in Dark Oak forest came back to haunt her. Wondering what was out there, she shivered in spite of her new warm clothing.

Her only answer was a distressed whine from near a low door on the far side of the yurt from where she had come in. "*I am Andrea, Princess of Ziv. I am in Ziv and this moon is mine. I am in charge. It is my duty to help whoever is out there,* she thought. She picked up her blue satchel and cautiously opened the small door.

The princess had taken no more than one step, when a large furry body hurled itself on her. It knocked her to the ground and began licking her face with its wet tongue.

The dog sniffed her ear then dropped belly to the ground whimpering. "I'm so sorry, Princess. Everyone I asked told me the girl in this yurt was the princess of Blue Moon, and I thought you must be my girl-person, but you don't smell right. You smell like lavender and violets. My girl-person smells like me. I am Ari the Artic Husky," he said. His white fur looked blue in the light of the domed sky.

Andrea got to her feet and looked into his sad green eyes. "I am Princess Andrea of the Land of Ziv. You are welcome to visit Blue Moon, Ari. But why would you think your girl-person was a princess here?" she said.

Ari stood up and sat back on his haunches. "Alexis is my girl-person and her grandmother is a queen in Ziv and that makes Alexis a princess. Everyone said that's how it works," the Husky said.

"So it is. But why are you looking for Alexis? Don't you know where she is?" Andrea said.

A few notes of a song hung in the chill air. The sweetest voice she could imagine was singing. "Blue," the girl sang.

Ari put his head up and howled. His mournful cry echoed from a mountain that loomed in the distance.

Chills went down Andrea's back. Ari's howl reminded her of the coyotes which howl near her grandma's cottage. Together the songs touched her heart more deeply than she had ever felt before.

"Isn't that your girl-person singing? And if you are an Artic Husky why are you blue?" the princess of all of Ziv said.

"I'm actually a white Siberian Husky now. I'm blue because the dome of the sky is so very blue. Even the snow looks blue," he said.

Andrea laughed. "That is because this is Blue Moon. But your eyes are green. I thought Siberian Huskies had blue eyes to help protect them from the dazzling white snow," she said and pulled her goggles down over her eyes.

"I guess my eyes are green because I'm still me. I'm used to the light dancing off the snow anyway. Will you help me look for my girl-person please. There are no trails in this new snow, and now I'm lost, too," Ari said.

There was nothing but fresh snow and big mountains looming up everywhere. "Where did you see her last?" Andrea asked.

"We were in the garden playing a game with Grandma. I think it was called, 'What would you be if you could be anything you wanted to be?' And I've always wanted to be a White Siberian Husky because they are so handsome," the Husky told her.

Andrea thought for a minute. "Did you see a rainbow? There is always a rainbow the first time," she said.

"It started to rain, and we all went inside so I guess there was a rainbow. Now I'm stuck here, and I don't know how to get home. I only know Alexis is here because I can hear her singing," he said.

"Of course I'll help," Andrea said quickly. After all it was only what seemed like moments ago, that she thought she was stuck here as a centaur forever.

Andrea picked up her bag and tried to think. Just beyond the yurt was Dark Oak Forest. They had to make sure they went the other way. She listened again but couldn't be certain just where the song was coming from. The notes rose and fell as they echoed off the mountains. She had no idea which way they should go to find Alexis.

A pair of small bodies covered with white fur emerged from the snow. Yapping and yipping they circled Ari sniffing. "It is you. Glad you found your princess," the larger of the two artic foxes said.

"But I didn't. It's great that I found Princess Andrea, but my girl-person is a princess in Ziv, and I still haven't found her. I can hear her singing, but I don't know where she is," Ari said sadly and hung his head.

The white fox picked up his ears. "We've never heard anyone singing like that here before. If she's your girl-person aren't you both Outlanders?" he said and sat down on the snow in front of Ari.

The other fox jumped up on Andrea. "Welcome to Blue Moon, Princess! "We saw you on Scarlet Orb. The ice worm caused so much melting we had to come here, but we like living on Blue Moon," she said.

"Thank you Floie. This is my friend Ari. His girl-person is a princess in Ziv," Andrea said and hugged the fox.

Floie started sniffing at the bag Andrea was carrying. "Where is the faux-fox robe you wore on Scarlet Orb? You'll need it here in this cold," she said.

Andrea pulled up the flap on the blue denim bag. Inside she felt a small furry object. When she pulled it out, it became a full sized faux fox robe with a hood and attached mittens. She put it on over her jacket.

Now that she felt warm she was aware that she was hungry. Reaching into her bag she pulled out a small thermos. As she watched, it became full sized with a wide-mouth top. "Will you join us for lunch?" she said.

"Oh no, thank you, Princess. We have just eaten. We feasted on acorns in Blue-green Forest. You can see the trees from here," Floie said.

Andrea noticed that Icy had his ears picked up. He was turning his head this way and that listening. "That's where your girl-person is! Her song is coming from the top of the granite cliffs, where the Northern Gannets have their nests," he said.

Ari jumped up and down in the snow and began running around in circles. "How do we get there? Which way is it?" he said.

"You can't get there from here without going through Blue Spruce Forest on that big mountain you see over there. That is unless you can swim across Blue Whale Bay," Icy said.

Andrea and Ari thanked the artic foxes said goodbye and started walking toward the mountain. Huge snowflakes began to fall thick and fast in the cold air. The rising wind drove the snow into a whiteout.

Ari soon turned his back to the wind and curled up in the snow, with his black-and-pink nose covered by his tail. "Best do the same Princess. We'll be here awhile," he said.

Awkwardly Andrea copied Ari and curled up close to him with her robe tucked around her. She pulled her hood around her face and used one of her mitts to warm her breath.

While the wind howled over her, Andrea forced herself to think of all the friends who had visited her in the yurt. Their love for her made her feel warm and safe.

When the wind stopped shrieking, Ari stood up and shook off the mound of snow that had covered him. "Let's go, Princess. I could hear Alexis calling me just as the wind started," he said.

Andrea got up, shook the snow off her robe, and looked to see where they were. It seemed as if they were in a snow bowl. High mountains nearly reached the blue dome of a sky on two sides. Oak forests were on the other two. Now Andrea couldn't tell which was which, nor did she know which mountain was the one they had to cross.

"I guess we will go this way," the young princess said. She sighed and picked up her bag.

They trudged through the deep snow until Andrea's feet and legs felt heavy. The numbness in her cold feet caused her to stumble. She fell into a drift and lay still to catch her breath.

Ari paused at her feet. Suddenly the dog climbed onto her back and began growling at something. Another deeper growl came from close in front of her.

Andrea lifted her head and looked into the enormous blue eyes of the biggest white tiger she had ever seen. Too scared to scream she put her head down and waited for the attack.

The growl changed to words. "Princess Andrea, I am Whitfield Tiger. Donald sent me to guide you over White Mountain. Jump on my back Princess and put your pet in front of you. I can easily carry both of you," he said.

He lay crouched in the snow until Andrea and Ari were in place. The young princess was soon busy dodging low branches of the spruce trees as Whitfield bounded up the mountain. He stopped suddenly at the top, and Andrea slid off his back and over his long tail into the snow again.

"Thank you Whitfield. This is Ari the Artic dog. He is looking for his girl-person who is a princess in Ziv," Andrea said when she got to her feet.

Whitfield turned to Ari and purred. "You were very brave for an Outlander. It isn't every dog who would face down a white tiger," he said.

"Forgive me. You are very kind. I was only trying to protect my princess," the Husky said.

"Princess Andrea needs no protection in Ziv unless she forgets. Like she forgot the blue stone Donald gave her for a guide," Whitfield said.

When Whitfield waved his tail goodbye Andrea felt in her hip pocket. Hidden among a wad of tissues was the lapis lazuli Donald had given her just before she crept into the yurt. When she touched it, her cold fingers felt warm from the touch of the letters Z, Q and L on the stone.

Ziva! Quiva! Liva! These three words came to her mind. She remembered that Ziva meant The Land of Be Alive. Quiva meant quit kvetching or complaining. And Liva meant live!

"Whatcha doing? Whatcha doing?" Ari said and danced around her. Clearly, he was impatient to be going.

"The stone was to remind me of who I am, and I am in Ziv. If I had remembered I would have known that Whitfield wouldn't hurt me. By the way thanks for trying to protect me. You were very brave," the princess of all of Ziv said.

Ari put his head down. "You are welcome, Princess. It was nothing but please where to now?" he said.

Andrea pulled her smoke colored goggles back down over her eyes. She noticed that the Whitfield had left them in a clear spot at the crest of White Mountain. Thick pine trees covered the far side and went from high above on the mountain to a snowy valley far below.

Snatches of a sweet song drifted on the wind. "I am lonely. I am blue," Alexis sang.

Ari circled Andrea frantically. "There are too many trees. I don't see a bit of a trail going down anywhere," he said.

A white leopard whizzed by them on something that looked like a snowboard or a mat. A few minutes later four snow chickens flew up from the valley. Each had a corner of a mat clutched in its claws. The quail flew to the top of the mountain and settled down with their burden.

The white leopard bounding up from the valley stopped by Andrea. "Did you see that? Wasn't that something? Faster than a leopard can blink," he said and cocked one ear to the wind.

A flock of snowbirds were twittering and twattering in the pine trees. "Your Highness, the news on the tzivine is that you are Princess Andrea. I am Leon Leopard at your service," he said. He crossed his right paw over his left and bowed his head.

"Please tell us how to get down this mountain as quickly as possible. Ari wants to find his girl-person. She is singing somewhere beyond White Mountain," Andrea said.

"You need a snow-skivia. You can borrow mine. The mice make the mats for us out of pieces of pinecones and needles. They simply fly over the snow in the zigzag path that goes down the mountain," Leon said.

Andrea hesitated for a moment. Even when she was at her grandma's cottage, she had never been on a snowboard.

"May we have one for Ari as well?" she said and picked up her blue bag. As soon as the ptarmigan dropped two snow-skivias in the clearing, Andrea and Ari stepped on them. They positioned themselves and pushed off.

When her snow-skivia stopped at the bottom of the mountain, Andrea fell into the snow laughing. The wild ride on the way down was more fun than she had expected it would be.

A big sloppy tongue licked her face. She sat up to stare at the black nose of the biggest hound she had ever thought existed. Black floppy ears framed his black-and-white mottled face. A few large black patches were among the same mottling on his body.

"Sorry, Your Highness, Ah'm just glad to see you. Royalty doesn't visit Blue Moon very often. Ah'm Big Blue. The word on the tzivine is that you and Ari are looking for a lost person. Ah'm the best tracker ever," the dog said in his deep bass voice.

He snuffed around Ari. "Ah ha! You smell like the Outlander that was here. Ah assume we're looking for your girl-person," the dog said.

Ari ran in circles around Big Blue and yapped. "Was she here? Did you see her? Where is she?" he said.

"Yep. Nope. And I dunno. But Ah can find her if she's still here," the big dog said.

Andrea was puzzled at Big Blue's self-confidence. "How did you know we were looking for a girl who is an Outlander?" she said.

The big dog puffed out his chest. "Ah'm a Bluetick Coonhound. The girl left a couple of small footprints. We don't have many visitors here on Blue Moon you know. She smelled of daisies and even dropped a petal on the ground. Ah found a couple of cookie crumbs by the petal, and she had been stepping in a bit of flour," the hound said. He sat down and scratched behind his left ear.

Ari sat down by the big dog. Clearly he was impressed by the coonhound's ability to interpret scents. "That's right. Alexis had been helping her grandma make cookies. Then we went into the garden," he said.

Big Blue got up and trotted toward a grassy field below the snow line. He stopped, sniffed the ground, and commented on the scent he picked up.

"Rained didn't it? Her shoes were damp. We never have rain here on Blue Moon except once in a Blue Moon. And that hasn't happened for dozens of dog-years," he said.

"Yes. We went inside to stay dry, and Alexis sat on the mat by the door with me. She was eating a cookie," Ari said.

"Looks like you touched down in different areas. Always in your own right place on Blue Moon Ah always say, but your girl-person smelled of fear. We dogs can always smell fear can't we Ari?" the big dog said.

The white Husky sniffed the ground where Big Blue said he had smelled Alexis' tracks. "Because I love her I can feel her fear, too," he said.

Big Blue looked straight into Andrea's face. "Pardon me Princess, but Ah smell a hint of 'old fear' on you. You've been to Dark Oak Forest haven't you? Everyone there fears one thing or another," he said.

Andrea was soon out of breath from running after the two dogs. She could hear Big Blue baying, and Ari yipping as they got further down into the valley and were soon out of sight. The princess flopped down on a grassy knoll to rest for a bit.

Far across the valley were the granite cliffs the foxes had talked about. She adjusted her goggles to shield her eyes from the bright light.

A huge flock of white birds with black wingtips were perched all over the face of the nearest cliff. Far above the gannets Andrea spied a bit of red that moved as if it was someone dancing. When the dancing stopped the flock of birds rose in the air as one. The dancing began again, and the gannets settled down.

"Pardon me Princess," said a voice behind Andrea. The princess of all of Ziv turned and stared into the soft brown eyes of another coonhound.

"Ah'm Lady Blue. Big Blue sent me to help find Ari's girl-person," the dog said.

Andrea jumped up. "I know just where she is, but I have no idea of how to get there. See that cliff with all those white birds flying around? She's in a red track suit at the top," she said.

Lady Blue put her nose into the wind. Finally she stared straight in front of her. "I can't see her, but she's there all right. Let's take this shortcut to Blue Whale Bay," she said. She trotted into a field of desert sage.

Tired when they reached the shore of the bay Andrea sat down on the sand. A huge sea turtle poked his head out of the water. "Want a ride, Princess? I took a little girl over there a short while ago," the sea turtle said. Andrea jumped on his back.

"Can you take me, too?" Ari said. He had skidded to a stop at the edge of the water. The sand shifted and the dog landed beside Andrea on the turtle's back.

Once they were on the other shore Ari picked up Alexis' scent. They followed her trail upward by a corkscrew path to the top. Ari raced to the little girl in the red outfit.

"Alexis! Alexis!" he said. All Andrea, who was far behind, could hear was his short sharp yips.

"Ari! My Ari! I knew you would come!" Alexis said and held out her arms. She sat down with the dog and cried. Ari dried her tears with his wet tongue.

The huge flock of gannets rose into the air. They clapped their wings and squawked.

"I was so scared. I thought they would hurt me. I just had to keep dancing and singing," she said.

A boy in western shirt and Levis appeared by Alexis. He bowed low. "Princess Alexis, the gannets were merely applauding. I am Donald, Adjutant of Blue Moon, and I am here to show you what you have created with your songs and dancing," he said.

Donald unsheathed his shining sword and pointed it toward the blue dome. A magnificent castle of glowing ice descended and hovered over the granite cliff. "This is your castle, Princess. And this is your key to everything," the adjutant said and handed her a blue stone.

A couple of breaths later Alexis was opening the towering door of her own castle. She and Ari raced from empty room to empty room. Ari skidded to a stop in the middle of a grand room. "Can we have rugs? I want a white one that looks like me," he said.

When Alexis returned from her private suite to the hall leading to the great room, she was wearing a flounced satin gown and matching blue satin slippers. The soon-to-be crowned princess was met by Donald who bowed and offered her his right arm. At the end of the hall they were greeted by Princess Andrea who was gowned in glowing white satin.

A huge section of the ice-crystal wall suddenly opened up into a room brightly lit by hanging icicles. In the center of the wall an open window revealed a circular balcony hung over the granite cliff of Gannet Cove. The blue-white cliffs were covered with white gannets that were tinted blue from the intense color of the sky.

"Presenting Andrea of the Land of Be Alive," Donald said into a microphone that was strapped to his chest. The gannets on the cliff rose into the air and applauded.

Andrea stepped forward to the thick white mat in the center of the room. She knelt and Donald drew the silver sword from his sheath. He tapped the princess of Ziv on the shoulder with the sword.

"I declare you, Andrea, to be Princess Royal of Blue Moon now and forever," he said. He bowed low.

A gannet flew in from the balcony and carefully set a tiara of frosted crystal on Andrea's head. The jewels inlaid in it sparkled like a rays of light.

"Presenting Ari of Blue Moon," the adjutant of Blue Moon said. The white Siberian Husky, who was holding his tail over his back, walked proudly to the white mat.

Andrea, Princess Royal of Blue Moon, took the silver sword from her adjutant and tapped Ari on the shoulder. "I declare you to be Sir Ari, Knight of Blue Moon, now and forever," she said.

The to-be-crowned-princess hesitated so long Andrea was sure Alexis had barely heard Donald announce her name. Her blue satin slippers nearly floated as she walked to her place on the white mat. She trembled as she heard Princess Andrea speak.

"Alexis, I declare you to be Princess of Blue Moon. May you rule your subjects well," the Princess Royal said.

A gannet flew in through the open window. He placed a crystal tiara set with blue Lapis Lazuli stones on Alexis' pigtails. She ran to the balcony. "Oh, thank you! Thank you!" she said.

Dozens and dozens and dozens of gannets flew about. Squawking loudly they clapped their wings and cheered.

Everyone hushed the moment Alexis began to sing. "I can never be lonely. I can never be blue. I have Ari and I have you," she sang in her sweet voice.

Andrea was still listening to Alexis sing when she found herself back her old blue sweat suit. A moment later she was in her room at her grandma's house.

That was a wonderful adventure. I wonder who will share the next one with me," she said to her teddy bear just before she went to sleep. Snowpink merely nodded and smiled.

Love, Grandma Schoe

Andrea Climbs on Green Globe

ANDREA CARRIED A COOL GLASS of lemonade into her grandma's back yard. Casually she walked over to the rock garden her grandpa was building. She sat down and leaned back against the mound of field stones.

It's very warm for so early in the season, she thought. A light breeze whispered through the green leaves of the weeping willow by the duck pond. It ruffled her straight dark hair and pulled on the neat green scarf at her throat.

High in the willow tree black squirrels were chasing each other through the waving branches. Andrea took a sip of her lemonade. Tangy yet sweet it was refreshing after eating so many cheesy sticks.

She thought of her cousin Lauren, and the time they had shared cheesy stick and lemonade in the palace of Ziv. Lauren had made it a lot of fun with her tales of pirates, Russian princesses, and magic lamps.

Her cousin Nicole startled her when she sat down on the rocks beside her. "Just look at that! I wish we could climb trees like they do," Nicole said.

Taller than Andrea her cousin's dark eyes shone with excitement. They were set in a perfectly oval tan face under a crown of kinky curls, which she wore in beaded plaits.

"Look! We match. You're in a green jacket and navy joggers, and so am I. And we're both wearing our green Kekks with their shiny toe-tags," Andrea said.

Nicole giggled. "Big deal! The toe-tags on my Kekks are shinier than yours are. Grandma bought us some bubble stuff. Here's your wand," she said. She handed Andrea a large wand and began to blow bubbles herself.

Andrea was happily blowing rainbow bubbles into the breeze, when she noticed one bubble was sort of green. Bands of various shades of green wound through it. Defying the wind the strange bubble hovered in front of her.

When it cleared away, the tiny figure of a woman stood where the bubble had been. Much darker than Nicole the woman had her black hair in plaits beaded with green gemstones. Two gold hoops hung from her ears to the shoulders of her dark-green jump suit.

The small figure bowed. "Princess Andrea, I am Gabrielle, Adjutant of the Three Globes of Ziv. I have come for Nicole who is Koa of Green Globe," she said. She smiled and disappeared along with Nicole.

Everything felt wrong to Andrea. The willow wasn't green anymore. Quite brown its leaves were scattered on the ground and were blowing with the dust across a dull landscape. The leafless branches seemed to be dripping as if the tree were crying.

Not even a stick remained of the squirrel's nest. The bare branches of the tree shook with the will of the wind. Scrawny squirrels were scurrying among the dry leaves looking for nuts they had hidden long ago.

A very bold one ran over to Andrea and climbed up on one of her Kekks. Reaching back among the heap of rocks, her fingers searched for a small stone to throw at him.

The squirrel sat on his back feet and crossed his front paws in front of him. His dark eyes looked up into hers. "Whatcha got? Got anything good to eat?" he said.

Andrea put the stone she picked up into her jacket pocket. "Sorry chum. I didn't bring lunch. Just this bit of lemonade," she said and set her wide-mouth glass on the ground by the heap of stones.

The squirrel put his little paws on either side of the glass and drank. "Nasty stuff but at least it's wet. Got anything else? Nothing grows here anymore," he said.

"Just this cheesy stick I found in my pocket," Andrea said. She set the morsel on one of the flat stones on the ground. Grasping the treat in both paws he sat up on his haunches and ate greedily.

"Whatever is the matter? Why is everything so dry and brown?" Andrea said to the squirrel.

The wind moaned in the weeping willow. "I'm so thirsty! There isn't even a drop of dew. All the water is gone," he said and blew a pile dust through the dry air.

As children, we are captivated by stories of huge, fantastical creatures, such as the wooly mammoth and the pterodactyl. The prevailing wisdom is these species are long extinct, but new evidence uncovered by author Gerald McIsaac casts doubt on these widely held assumptions.

McIsaac gathered stories from the elders of the First Nation—those who were formerly referred to as Indians, Native Americans, or Aboriginals. First Nation elders provided McIsaac with detailed descriptions of six species long thought to be extinct. These species include the "Devil Bird," the "Hairy Elephant," the "Wilderness Wolf," the "Rubber-Faced Bear," the "Lake Monster," and "Sasquatch."

In *Bird from Hell*, McIsaac separates fact from fiction by comparing eyewitness accounts of these species with scientific opinion concerning their identity. His conclusion is that these huge species are not extinct, but he needs assistance in gathering evidence to substantiate this claim. By following the simple directions provided in *Bird from Hell*, you can help prove these various species still exist.

****

Gerald McIsaac has lived and worked with First Nation people for over thirty years and has their trust and respect. His home is in the village of Tsay Keh Dene in the mountains of northern British Columbia.

Trafford
PUBLISHING®

ISBN 978-1-4269-6642-2
90000

9 781426 966422

When the dry dust swirled into her face, Andrea cried to the wind. "Stop! My hair is full of sand already! Whatever is the matter here?" she said.

"If you really want to know you have to climb higher," the squirrel said.

Andrea noticed a dry stream bed by the weeping willow. It twisted and turned past dull brown trees and disappeared high in a mountain that rose in the distance.

Not far from the willow stood a tall poplar with heavy branches. When the wind whistled through them they creaked and groaned. "Why do you creak and groan? You sound like an old man with arthritis," the princess of all of Ziv said.

The tree hung his branches lower. "We are old. All of us are dying. The soil still holds lots of food, but there is no water for us to make a drink out of it," the poplar said.

A few dry leaves clung to the branches of a nearby aspen, as it shivered in the wind. "It was really awful. All of us aspens were shaking in fear. We thought they would never go away," the tree said. Its voice quavered.

"Who wouldn't go away? Andrea said. The tree said nothing but continued to shake it's few dry leaves.

The squirrel didn't tell me his name. I'll call him Earl, Andrea thought.

The young princess of the Land of Be Alive climbed until she reached a yew tree that still had some of its evergreen leaves. As she sat on the bare rock at its roots, she could feel the mountain vibrating. The air began to fill with soft music which sounded like: Tum, tum, tiddley tee. Tee, tee, tiddley tum.

A black bird flew in from a tall elm and sat on a high branch of the yew tree. He flew to a lower branch and stared Andrea in the face. "Caw, caw, I know who you are. You can't fool me. You're supposed to be the Princess of Ziv as sure as my name is Crawlie. But if you are Princess of Green Globe why are you wandering around asking questions?" he said.

"How can this be Green Globe when everything is so brown!" the princess said.

When Andrea climbed as far as a tall elm, she walked through the deep dust to the base of the tree. "Can you tell me what has made this place so dry and dusty?" she said in a very polite tone.

The elm dropped a small branch and snapped. "What are you asking me for? I'm so dry I'm falling apart," the tree said.

From high in the tree a large black bird called from his nest. "Why? Why? Why? We rooks know why. But if you really want to find out the old redwood knows all. The old redwood tells all. See that tallest dark tree halfway up the mountain? That's the last one of The Ancients. He knows everything that has ever happened on Green Globe," the rook said.

Andrea struggled on up the mountainside toward the ancient redwood. A hemlock tree stood by what seemed to be an old racing track. Every bit of soil had been torn from all around the tree.

I wonder whoever did this, Andrea thought. She decided it must have been aliens. With a deep sigh she sat down on the bare rock.

Suddenly Andrea thought of her cousin Nicole. Gabi had said she had come to take her to Green Globe. When the princess wiggled her toes, the toe-tags on her shoes caught her eye. She wiped the dust off one until it shone. A girl with beads woven into her dark hair appeared in the shiny tag.

"Nicole is that you?" Andrea said, but she had no idea how Nicole could talk to her through a shoe.

Words began forming in her mind, "Me is it. That see you can't?" Nicole said.

The black crow hopped down through the tree and stopped just above Andrea's head. "'Cawn't you see that it's me? This is Ziv. Things are quite different here. You are inner-viewing a reflection." Crawlie said and hopped to another branch.

"You are where?" Andrea said as she spoke into her left Kekk in reverse order. The young princess held her breath for a long minute. Finally she heard a faltering voice.

"Mountain Majestic on am I. Agate serpentine green a for looking am I. Dusty. Thirsty," Nicole said and coughed.

The wind blew dust over the toe-tag that Andrea had been talking to. The image of Nicole disappeared.

I'm thirsty, too, but how will I ever find us a drink, Andrea thought.

"If I were you, but I am not, of course, I would order a drink from one of your other zivoids," Crawlie said. She hopped down pulled at the toe-tag in Andrea's right shoe and polished it with her wing-feathers.

The image of a young girl appeared. Andrea stared at the petite face framed in red hair and the brown eyes that shone from under her bangs. *Surely this is Cousin Lauren,* she thought.

A furry face rubbed her cheek. "Meow," the animal said.

"We're right here beside you. You called us didn't you? Fauna and I were dancing the Ziva in Orange Grove. We love it there," Lauren said and tossing her long auburn hair over her shoulder sat down and crossed her legs under her. In brown tights and matching long shirt, she looked like a pixie.

"Have a gerano. I love the fresh cream mine taste like," Fauna said. With her six-toed paw, she held out a small bunch of orange colored fruit that looked like grape tomatoes.

Eagerly Andrea took the geranos from the brownish-gray cat. While eating slowly she wondered just how to get one of the geranos to Nicole. *"Earl needs one of these, too,"* she thought.

The small animal began wriggling out of her pocket. Andrea held out one of the orange colored fruits out to the squirrel who took it greedily. "When you're finished I want you to take one to my cousin Nicole," she said.

While the squirrel ate Andrea polished the toe-tag on her shoe. "Drink a you bring will Earl," Andrea said to Nicole's image. In her cousin's place Andrea saw the black squirrel. He was holding the ripe fruit in his paws.

Lauren called over her shoulder. "What was all that about? Where is Nicole? Why are you here?" she said.

"Nicole is on the other side of this mountain looking for a green serpentine agate. As to why we're here the old redwood knows all. The old redwood tells all, but to find out we have to climb higher," Andrea said.

Lauren picked up a pointed stick from among the roots of the hemlock. Twirling it in her hands she followed Andrea up the dusty trail. Fauna walked sedately beside her.

The trio sought out the tallest tree and sat down gratefully by its gigantic trunk. Lauren scratched in the dry dust with her stick. Every once in a while she gazed into the distance.

The large very black rook flew down beside them. He paced up and down cocking his head to one side then the other. He peered at Andrea. "You are the princess of Ziv. I'd know you anywhere. I'm Rodney Rook. Welcome to Green Globe," he said.

He strode over to where Lauren and Fauna were sitting. "You two are from Orange Moon. Mind that the big furry creature doesn't take a fancy to bird-breakfast. The Elder, may His roots grow ever deeper into Green Globe, is willing to tell you his story, but you must learn to listen to his thoughts," he said.

Andrea and Lauren quickly moved to a spot where they could put their backs to the tree. When vibrations from the redwood's huge trunk went through Andrea, she felt that the tree was humming: Tum, tum, tiddley tee. Tee, tee, tiddley tum.

The princess of all of Ziv began to hum along with the vibrations of the tree. Then she sat very still so she could hear every thought the tree sent. She watched Lauren trace letters in the soil around her feet and wondered what her cousin Lauren was thinking. She wondered, too, about her cousin Nicole, and if she had found the serpentine stone.

The huge tree began. "My great-grandfather told me the story just as his great-grandfather told him. 'When Green Globe was first populated with plants, the song came from the grand palace in Ziv. Everything was beautiful then. We were all green with strong stems that would become strong trunks.

"Our roots went into the soil and drank from the water that sprang up from within Majestic Mountain. The wind picked up moisture from the pools which formed and sprayed it over everything.

"All the plants grew where they liked it best and thrived, but the elders knew what was to come. They prepared for the day that would follow the invasion," the tree said.

Andrea wondered what invasion, but she said nothing. She watched Lauren drawing furiously as the old redwood talked. The young princess remembered stories she had heard about the Anasazi women of the Arizona desert and their sand paintings. They drew pictures of things they wanted to create in their own life, and when the pictures were done let them drift away in the wind.

The ancient tree continued his story. "The Rushers came first. They brought their Bunch buggies from Yellow Satellite and rode them everywhere. They tore out all the small plants first then the small trees.

They were still here when the whole family of lizards came from Red Moon with their terriers. Belial and Belila turned everything into a race track.

"The vibrations were so bad the aquifer in Majestic Mountain stopped flowing. Everything that wasn't killed outright started dying," the redwood elder said.

So it wasn't aliens after all, Andrea thought. She had always wondered where the copper-plated lizards and the yellow monkeys from her other Zivoids had gone. Now she hoped they had left Ziv forever.

"The elders made a plan that would make everything right again. But we were told we had to wait until three princesses came. They would have to agree on how to carry out the restoration. You will have to get the rest of the story from the goats. They live higher up the mountain," the tree said.

Andrea sighed as she looked up the mountain. Above the redwoods bare rock dominated the landscape. "We apparently have to interview the mountain goats. They are much closer to that bare summit than the sheep," the young princess said to her cousin Lauren.

Lauren picked up the stick with which she had been scratching pictures. "I think Fauna and I ought to interview the big horns. The rocks look less jagged there. It will be easier on her paws," she said and walked off in another direction.

Andrea climbed toward the two goats who were high up on the stark rock face. The goat's sharp black horns curved over their heads, and they stared at her with their rectangular shaped pupils.

The nearest goat swallowed his cud. "What do you want of us, Princess?" he said. His beard quivered in the wind.

"You may call me Andrea. "May I call you Billy?" the young princess said.

The animal tossed his horns. "I'd prefer Bill if you don't mind. We're not true goats. We're actually of the family Bovidae. We're sort of an antelope, but you know that."

Andrea wasn't sure she did know what the goat had told her. She sat down on the nearest flat rock. "But the redwoods said you would tell us the story about what happened to Green Globe," she said.

The goat coughed up a new cud and started chewing while he talked. "We have to go back a long way to do that. All life began in the sea. The true goats were the first to climb out and live on land. We were next," he said.

The goat looked straight into Andrea's face. "We climbed out of the water because we wanted to climb higher, and that's why the Rushers came here from Yellow Satellite. They wanted to see just how fast they really could go. They made the soil into a dust that made them really fast.

"That's what attracted Belial and his bunch from Red Moon. Their terriers really tore up the countryside with the new fuel. The Rushers were afraid of the terriers, and Belial's lizards were afraid of the Rushers. And everyone on Green Globe was afraid for their lives," Bill said.

Andrea stood up. "I'm glad they're gone, but what can we do now?" she said and shivered in the wind.

Bill looked up the mountain at the faraway summit and nodded his horned head. "The rocks tell us that there are to be three princesses, three stones, and three tones. Once there the rocks will tell you what to do. But if you're going up there you had best be a mountain goat. Those silly shoes would never make it," he said.

"Be a mountain goat! No way," the princess of Green Globe said.

She realized too late what had happened. Her green Kekks were turning into yellowish cloven hooves. Her fingers joined in pairs with a split in the middle, as they became hard hooves. Strong shoulders which were covered with thick hair strained against her jacket. The joggers she had on flapped in the wind blowing around her short back legs.

I'm just a little kid. I'll never make it up that mountain, Andrea thought.

A small goat bounded down the mountain and came to a halt on the very edge of a ledge. He was just above the distressed princess when he stopped. "You may call me Bo. I'll show you how to get up the path to the top," he said.

Andrea looked up. The whitish kid was framed against a background of bluish-green rock that seemed to go up forever without a trace of a path.

"Follow me!" Bo said. He stood on his back legs, turned around and dropped onto all fours. He looked back to see if Andrea was coming. "You do it this way," he said.

He put his front hooves on a ledge just above where he stood. By hooking the dew claws on the back of his front legs on the rock, he pulled himself up. One ledge of rock at a time the young princess followed him.

In the meantime Bo was chattering. "The story is that three princesses are to meet at the very top of Majestic Mountain. Each one will bring a special polished agate. They are to go in the three streams that will flow again from Majestic Mountain. I can hardly wait. I haven't even had a bite of dry grass today," he said.

Nicole's cry penetrated Andrea's jumbled thoughts. "Please don't let him eat me. I'm a pansy," she said.

Andrea looked ahead to the ledge Bo had stopped on. A bit of a hollow just in front of him was filled with pretty gold pansies with orange faces. In the middle of the bed one pansy stood taller than the rest. Dark purple with very dark eyes it was waving frantically to and fro.

Andrea shouted at the kid. "Bo! Please don't eat them. One is a cousin of mine," she said.

She pulled herself up onto the large ledge and looked at the pansy bed. *There is still some moisture here. It must be coming from inside the crown of the mountain,* she thought.

Lauren came around the edge of the rock face that towered over the ledge where Bo and Andrea were. She strolled over beside the bed of pansies sat down and brushed a few strands of her auburn hair off her forehead. "Learn anything from the goats?" she said.

"Maa, maa, maa," Andrea said. As a goat she could say nothing else.

She was sure the nubs she had for horns were growing. They were very heavy and felt to be full-sized. *If I could just get rid of these horns I could be me,* the princess thought. She backed a few steps away from the sheer face of the rock's crown.

Head down she charged forward. Her head hit the rock hard and she fell backward onto her own princess butt.

"Ouch! That hurt," Andrea said. The horns she had just shed were rolling around on the ledge. Fauna swatted them into the hollow where the pansies were.

When Andrea got up she saw Nicole standing in the flower bed. Her cousin was bent over apparently searching around her Kekks for something.

By now, Lauren was sitting cross-legged with her back against the barefaced mountain. Silently she twirled the stick from the hemlock's roots in her hands and stared out into the vastness before her. Andrea and Nicole walked over and sat beside her. Gradually in the silence they shared, they felt the rock of the crown of Majestic Mountain talking to them.

Nicole whispered to Andrea. "The rock is telling us that we must bring three special green stones to the top of the crown. I've found the green serpentine agate. It was in the pansy bed. I felt it with my Kekks," she said.

Pulling the white-and-green tree agate from her pocket, Lauren whispered, "See! It's been polished into the shape of a cat. You must have the other stone. You do have it don't you?" she said.

Andrea moved around carefully on the ledge. "The only stone I have is this moss covered one picked up to throw at Earl," she said and got up to walk around the rock face.

As she walked Andrea got the feeling that it was circular and sort of a crown on the top of Majestic Mountain. At the edge of the ledge they were on the rock split into a deep crevasse. She assumed that was where the water would flow to the valley below. The princess of Green Glove walked back to the other side the rock and found another channel exactly like the first. The crown was too high for any of the group to reach the top.

When Andrea got back to the others she examined the moss covered stone that was still in her pocket. "This must be the moss agate the mountain is whispering about, but who is going to take the stones to the top of that sheer rock face?"

Claws from some kind of bird dug into Andrea's hair. "Shoo! Go away!" she said and reached up to pull the creature off herself.

The bird cawed. "I'm Crawlie. I came as soon as the wind brought the message from Majestic Mountain," he said.

"What message?" Princess Andrea said.

"Remember what the mountain told us. Crow is to place our stones in the pockets deep in the rock where the water flows," Nicole said, as she leaned back against the sheer rock face.

Andrea tried to remember what she heard from the mountain. "Lauren is to be first then Nicole. At least that's what the mountain told us wasn't it? I'm last, Andrea said.

Lauren stood up and held the cat-shaped agate in the open palm of her hand. "Tree agate will send water through the branches to water the land. New green life will begin," she said. She put one of the horns to her lips and blew a single tone.

Crawlie snatched up the stone and flew to the crown of the rock. He went to one side and placed the cat-shaped agate in a deep hollow.

Nicole held out her serpentine agate. Crawlie picked it up and flew to the other side of the ledge. He placed the smooth stone in the other crevasse. "The agate through which a serpent creeps will cause the water to rise in the mountain," Nicole said. She took the horn from Lauren, and putting the hollow horn to her lips blew a single tone.

Andrea took the horn from Nicole. She noticed that the horn was missing its tip. *No wonder we can blow into it*, she thought. The princess of all the Orbs of Ziv held out the moss covered agate. Crawlie caught it and flew away up to the very top of the crown of the mountain.

"Moss agate will relieve the stress known on Green Globe. The dust will become good earth again," the princess said. She blew a single tone on the hollow horn. A deep rumbling began in the depths of the mountain.

Water flowed through the mountain and down the stream beds to the valleys below. From the crown it rose in a mist. The wind swirled in and picked up the moisture which misted the trees and the fields, until they glowed with new green. The brown moss around the edge of the pansy bed became green and spread like a carpet over the ledge of rock.

"Party time," Andrea said and sent Fauna back to Orange Moon for more of the geranos which grew only in the deep valley there.

When she was passing them out Earl squirmed out of her pocket and took one offered to him. "I love tomatoes!" he said.

"They're whatever you like best," Andrea said.

"Peanuts then," the squirrel said. He raced over to the place where Nicole had been among the pansies and planted one. Everyone watched amazed as a gerano vine sprang up. Before their eyes it blossomed and green fruit grew on its branches.

Andrea was surprised to see her adjutant in a dark green jump suit standing by the crown of the rock. Gabi touched the rock dust clinging there. It became three silver crowns set with polished agates. They floated over and hung above the pansy bed.

The Adjutant of Green Globe bowed to Nicole. "Nicole, I declare you to be Princess Nicole of Green Globe for now and forever. Your gemstone will be green serpentine agate," she said.

Donald wearing blue Levis and an orange shirt appeared beside Gabi. He bowed to Lauren. "Lauren, I am Donald, Adjutant of all the Moons of Ziv. I declare you to be Princess Lauren of Orange Moon for now and forever. Your gemstone will be orange plume agate," he said.

Both adjutants bowed to Andrea. "Princess of the orange plume agate, and of the green serpentine agate, and the moss agate we declare you Princess Royal of Green Globe and all the worlds of Ziv now and forever," they said.

The three crowns settled on the heads of the three princesses who were now wearing flowing robes of silk that were green as springtime. They billowed out in the gentle breeze that played around the crown of Majestic Mountain. The breeze picked up the vibrations from the mountain, and Andrea heard it humming: Tum, tum, tiddley tee. Tee, tee, tiddley tum.

Gabi picked up the horn that lay by the crown of the rock. She held it high. "Lauren, Princess of Orange Moon, your deep thoughts have filled this horn with plenty. Nicole, Princess of Green Globe, your thoughts of beauty have filled this horn with plenty. Andrea, Princess Royal of all the lands of Ziv, your kindness has filled this horn with plenty," she said.

After dipping it into the flowing stream she passed the horn to each girl to take a sip. "You will now have plenty in your life. Plenty of whatever you allow your thoughts to create will always be with you," Adjutant Gabi said.

"Be careful what you think about my beautiful princesses," Adjutant Donald said and bowed to each of them.

After much hugging between the princesses Lauren and the cat returned to Orange Moon, and to the party they had left in Orange Grove. Nicole went back to her grandparent's home to catch a ride with her mom back to the city.

The princess royal sat with her back against the crown of Majestic Mountain and watched as the dry brown hills and trees below her turned a vibrant green.

Instead of smelling like choking dust the air became fresh and moist. *I wonder what the leaves are like now,* she thought. She called for Earl to bring her a leaf from one of the trees near the willow, where she first became aware of Green Globe.

In a Ziv second he squirmed out of her pocket with the twin keys of a maple tree in his mouth. "Is this what you want, Princess," he said and began to chew on the nut-like end of one the maple tree's keys.

Andrea laughed. "Not quite but this will do thank you. Now I know that my subjects on Green Globe have enough to eat. Even the goats have fresh grass springing up in the crevasses of the mountains," she said.

Happy, but tired the newly crowned princess closed her eyes for just a minute. When she woke up by the rock garden the willow tree was waving its long branches of green leaves in a gentle breeze.

I must ask Snowpink where the Rushers and the Lizards went, she thought. The answer surprised her. "There are ninety-nine worlds beside this in your universe. They went to one where they belong," Snowpink said.

Love, Grandma Schoe

Andrea and Crimson Satellite

"ANDREA, ANDREA LYN WHERE ARE you?" a cheerful voice called.

Surely that's Snowpink talking to me, Andrea thought and brushed a rose petal off *her* deep-pink mini-dress which she was wearing with matching tights. "I'm at home in my mother's flower garden," Andrea said even though she couldn't see her teddy bear anywhere.

"Your Highness, please excuse me. You must go to the eleventh body that shines over Ziv soon. Crimson Satellite needs you for a special task," a boy said and appeared beside her. He was wearing fringed yellow buckskin. He bowed low, and the flamingo feathers hanging from his yellow headband brushed his dark face.

For a minute Andrea thought about the first time she had visited Ziv. Then she had gone up an elevator from floor to floor in her palace. On each floor had been a different colored door. Echoing in her memory was the horrible buzzing she had heard behind the crimson curtain on the window by the eleventh door.

The princess of all the lands of Ziv smiled at her adjutant of all the satellites of Ziv. "I'm so very glad to see you, Drake! But whatever are you doing here?" she said.

He handed her a decorated egg-shaped box. When Andrea touched it the lid popped open, and a pair of earrings floated to her ears.

"They're crystal set in Vliganite. You will always have a rainbow when you are wearing them," Drake told her.

Andrea said, "Peachy-keen!" When she touched her copper- colored earring her conch shell flew into the garden, and it settled between the red rose bushes and the pink peony.

A Ziv millisecond after she and her adjutant got in, the conch was flying through the enormous front doors of the palace of Ziv. It zoomed through long hallways to the throne room. There the pearly conch paused and settled down on the plush raspberry-red carpet.

"The plan this time is for you to build a city on Crimson Satellite. It's to be for all the princesses of all the moons, globes, satellites, and orbs of Ziv. Call them zivoids if you like," her adjutant said.

Surely the princess royal of all the lands and worlds of Ziv has a choice, Andrea thought. "I would really like to assign the actual building to one of the cousins. Bryanna is rather young but she would make a great princess-to-be. If she messes things up I can send her home," the princess of all of the Land of Be Alive said.

"As you wish, Your Highness. Your Vliganite watch is now programmed for you to see Bryanna at all times. Her thoughts will come to you through one of the Vliganite arcs holding your crystal earrings," Drake said.

"I can see her now! Bryanna is sitting in the shade of a silk oak in the backyard of her Grandma's winter home. I hear her mumbling about the trip they took to see the Anasazi ruins, and she wants to meet a real Indian," the princess said.

"She is about to meet a real native of the Americas," Drake said. He clicked his buckskin-clad heels together and disappeared.

Andrea watched Bryanna who was leaning back against the trunk of the silk oak. Her dark hair shone in the sun that filtered through its leaves. Her hot pink top and shorts matched her Kekks sports shoes. A pair of "crazy socks" whose stripes didn't match finished her outfit. A shadow went over Bryanna's face which Andrea assumed was Drake. She watched him hold out his hand to her young cousin.

In a Ziv mini second the scene changed from the southwest desert to a windblown crimson desert. The future princess was now sitting cross-legged on a pile of crimson sand. Drake's flamingo feather brushed his face as he bowed low to her.

"Bryanna, I am Drake, Adjutant of the three Satellites of the Land Ziv. Your cousin Andrea has chosen you to be princess-in-training of Crimson Satellite," he said. He held out an earring much like the ones Andrea wore herself. It attached itself to Bryanna's ear.

"I don't want to be a princess. Especially not in this awful desert," Bryanna said.

Drake handed her two small smooth copper-colored stones. "These are called worry stones, but when you rub a piece of Vliganite wonderful things can happen. Be careful how you use them," he said.

Bryanna slipped a stone into a pocket of her shorts. She put the second piece of Vliganite into her other pocket. "I hear a bee. Make it go away!" she said.

"Hi Bryanna! It's only Bixbee Bumblebee. He has come to welcome you to Crimson Satellite. Bixbee and Honeybee will be your chief helpers in building Casa City," Princess Andrea said into her cousin's ear.

"I don't want any silly old bees helping me do anything. Just make him take me back to my grandma's house. Now!" Bryanna said.

Andrea decided to go from the palace to Crimson Satellite herself to calm Bryanna down. She landed her conch in the sand close to the princess-in-training. "It shall be as you wish, Bryanna. Cousin Amber will take your place then," Princess Andrea said.

Just then a golden goose lit on the sand and raced toward them. The princess-to-be jumped to Drake for protection and hid her head on his buckskin sleeve.

"Mrs. Pennyweight, welcome to the future city of casas on Crimson Satellite. You are to show Princess-to-be Bryanna the fantastic gardens on this Zivoid," Andrea said.

"I'm not a princess and I don't want to see any old gardens. Just take me home!" Bryanna said to Adjutant Drake and kicked at the sand under her feet.

"Very well, I'll go myself. I haven't seen the gardens yet. You can stay here and pout," Andrea said to her cousin.

She took a step toward the goose. Before she could get astride Mrs. Pennyweight's back, Bryanna got on from the other side. Bixbee lit on her right shoulder. Soon Honeybee was flying ahead of the goose and the two princesses who were on her back.

Bixbee buzzed from one to the other. "You'll have lots of tasty native plants for your casa gardens," he said.

"Peachy-keen! We have everything here. I just love those orchids down there. They will look great in my own casa's conservatory," Andrea said.

"Zowie! I want some of the pink ones in my casa, too," Bryanna said.

"Those green trees down there are an orchard of different kinds of apples. They and the pear trees ripen every time the zivoid over the castle in Ziv changes," Bixbee said.

"I'll want bright red apples and yellow pears in my garden. Please make a note of that," Bryanna said.

Andrea was amazed to see Bixbee stand on his back feet. In his front feet he held a small tablet in which he was making notes with a tiny pen.

The goose swooped low over a patch of tall elderberry bushes. Honeybee told them when they bloom the white flowers could be stirred into muffins. She also told them when the ripe berries were black and juicy they could be made into delicious jam.

I'll want some of them in the garden at the palace, Andrea thought.

Mrs. Pennyweight flew to a grove of ripening cherry trees. In their shade Bixbee found a clump of Solomon's seal. He searched under the leaves on their graceful stems for their fruit. When he hopped back on Bryanna's shoulder, he was covered with yellow pollen.

"They're yummy stuff. You wouldn't like it, but the little bells have seeds that the little chickens come here for," he said, as the goose lit on the ground beside a peach tree.

"It's time for Mrs. Pennyweight to go to Golden Globe to get Princess Amber. Princess Amber will build the twelve small casas while you are making my grand casa," Andrea said.

When Bryanna slid to the ground Mrs. Pennyweight raced across the sand with Andrea still on her back. Through her earring Andrea heard the princess-in-training grumble, "There is nothing for it but to walk back I suppose. Bixbee, please show me the way to the center of Casa City," Bryanna said.

"Can you make yourself small and as light as one of the bells on the Solomon's seal? If you can I think I can carry you," Bixbee said. Andrea's earring picked up the sound perfectly.

"I'd rather walk. I'm not going to be just a dumb bell off of an old plant," Bryanna said.

When Andrea heard that she checked the video function on her watch. Bixbee had his tablet in one foot and a creamy-colored bell in another. *Bryanna must have quickly learned shape shifting and size reduction. The kid is doing better than I did my first time in Ziv,* she thought.

She tapped the old goose on the head and told her to make a stop at the palace to let her off. The goose flew through the palace doors and down a long hall to the video room. The princess turned on one of her computers. The clicking of the unit indicated that her thoughts had been added to her diary.

"That was fun," she said as a tape recorded her words.

Andrea summoned Donald who was her adjutant of all the moons of Ziv. Immediately a boy in blue Levis and a bright red shirt appeared in the video room. He bowed low.

"Please get a seamstress from Blue Moon to make a flying suit for Bryanna. She needs to be able to take the suit off when she wants to. And she has to be able to blow-up the wings with the Vliganite stone she has in her pocket," Princess Andrea said.

When Andrea saw him next, he was standing by Bryanna with a small box in one hand. "I am Donald, Adjutant of the three moons of Ziv. The Princess Royal has decreed that you are to have a flying suit," he said.

"Zowie! I'd love to be able to fly like Bixbee does," the princess-in-training said.

"You will need to be able to get around Casa City as fast as Bixbee and Honeybee do, so I've brought you a seamstress from Blue Moon to make your suit," Donald said and set the small box on the sand. When he opened the lid, a large black spider crawled out.

Bryanna screamed. "No! No! Take it away! I don't want a flying suit. I'd rather walk. I hate spiders," she said and pounded the sand with her fist.

Donald let the spider walk over his hand and up his arm. "You have no need to be afraid of the creatures of Ziv. There is nothing here that will really hurt you," he said.

The black spider crawled back down to the box. "Rather a testy little thing isn't she? How can I make a flying suit for her, if she won't hold still?" she said.

"You can talk! I thought that spiders just stung people," Bryanna said.

"Not in Ziv. Things are different here I have to tell you. Now stand up and stay still while I measure you. I'll try not to tickle," the huge black spider said. She crawled across the crimson sand to where Bryanna sat with her arms around her knees. Lifting each of her eight legs high, she crawled onto the back of Bryanna's T-shirt.

She should have some entertainment to help her relax, Andrea thought. She decided to send Indira to keep her company.

While obeying the spider's command to stick her arms out, Bryanna opened her eyes. In front of her a butterfly of the deepest purple was finishing her dance with a pirouette.

"Hello. I'm Cousin Emma from Indigo Satellite, but you can call me Indira. It's really me. So you're getting a flying suit. Why don't you just turn into a butterfly like I do?" she said.

"Because I wouldn't be me, and I don't want to be any old bumblebee," Bryanna said.

The spider tugged on the web she had woven for princess-in-training Bryanna. "Please do stay still, Your Highness. I'm nearly finished," she said.

As Andrea watched her young cousin, Bryanna began jumping up and down. She flapped her arms. She stomped her feet. "This is a crazy idea," she said to Honeybee who was flying nearby. She flapped her arms again.

"I taught Bixbee how to fly and I can teach you. Weren't you listening to Drake? You have to use the Vliganite. Black Spider made a pouch for it," Honeybee said.

Bryanna stopped jumping around. She searched in her pocket for the worry stone Drake had given her. When she slipped it into the pocket of the spider web, she heard a hum. A buzz started in the webbing, and her wings filled with Ziv air. Soon she was floating in place.

Honeybee hovered beside her. "Now you have to think. Just think of where you want to go," she said.

"What good will that do me?" Bryanna said. She was slowly turning in a circle.

"This is Ziv you know. Things are different here. Now think," Honeybee said.

Bryanna tried to think. "I want to go to the orchard," she said. She spun around until she was dizzy.

"You want to go to which one, which orchard?" Honeybee said. She was flying around in circles, too.

"I want to go to the apple trees," the princess-in-training said. The words barely out of her mouth, when she was flying in a bee-line for the orchard.

"Mind you don't crash! Tell yourself to slow down or I can't keep up to you," Bryanna's flying coach said.

From the roof garden in the palace Andrea heard Bryanna's voice through her earring. "Slow down! Slow down!" Bryanna was saying.

The Princess Royal was happy to see the newest princess of Ziv drop safely onto the grass under the apple tree. "A little practice and she'll have flying down pat," she said to whoever might be listening.

The hummingbird who was hovering over a trumpet vine didn't answer. Neither did the cricket who was chirping on the palace wall.

Andrea zoomed up in the glass capsule to the palace's roof and the garden there. Colourful birds were drinking at the fountain, as it sprayed fresh water over the flowers and bushes. The princess picked a few ripe red raspberries. *These would be good in my garden on Crimson Satellite, but really I would rather have a huge lawn with a few shade trees,"* she thought.

Because she hadn't checked on Bryanna since she had come to the garden, Andrea wiped the drops of water off glass face of her wrist watch. The Vliganite stone in the watch showed Casa City clearly in the glass. The air seemed to be filled with black wasp-waisted insects. They were flying around a tiny figure in hot-pink shorts and top.

Bryanna was sitting on the crimson sand with her Kekks crossed in front of her. Beside her Bixbee was hastily making notes on his tablet.

"Be sure the wasps get the measurements right. Everything will be in kangaroo hops and elephant jumps," the newest princess-to-be in Ziv said.

"Queen Bee will have the wasps memorize the size," the bumblebee said. He made more notes with his tiny pen.

Whatever is that child doing, Andrea thought. She wished she had something to help her fly around Crimson Satellite to see what was happening.

At that moment an adjutant came in with a parcel. "Your cousin Lauren sent this. It came from her great- grandfather in Wales," Drake said to his princess.

The Queen Scallop mollusk was a peach-colored calcified shell about three inches in size. It had grown in a scalloped pattern of about twenty radiating umbones. *This is perfect,* Andrea thought. She slipped it into the pocket of her mini dress and ordered her conch. When she landed behind Bryanna on the crimson sand, she heard the princess-in-training's instructions to the bumble bee.

"I want all the pods to be a honeycomb unit. Each unit is to be two elephant jumps in length. That is three kangaroo hops to one elephant jump. Please give Queen Bee the instructions," she said.

Andrea touched her Vliganite earring and her Queen Scallop at the same time until the three inch shell was large enough for her to sit on. Grasping the sides of the shell she floated in front of Bryanna and asked what her instructions to Bixbee meant.

"Well, I don't know what this is in feet and inches because the instructions Drake gave me are in metric so I just call it kangaroo hops and elephant jumps then touch my Vliganite earring and watch the lines become the right size," the casa builder said.

I wonder when Mrs. Pennyweight will get back here from Golden Globe, Andrea thought. She was sure the old goose had left the palace in plenty of time to already be back on Crimson Satellite with Princess Amber. With much flapping of her wings Mrs. Pennyweight flew in at that moment with Amber on her back.

The young princess from Golden Globe was having trouble holding on so Ms. Pennyweight told her to pull a couple of her down feathers and put them on her wrists so she could fly. "Just think them there and they will stay," the old goose said.

With the feathers on her wrists, Amber flew from the goose's back to the ground on her own. She was wearing a golden jumpsuit with a matching belt. The light shining on her hair turned it to the brightest shade of amber.

The princess of all of Ziv greeted the princess of Golden Globe. "Welcome to Crimson Satellite, Amber. You are here to help me create the casa's for each princess of all the Moons, Globes, Satellites, and Orbs of Ziv. Cousin Bryanna will be building my casa with the help of the bees and wasps that live here," she said.

Adjutant Drake appeared from a swirl of sand and held out an earring much like the ones Andrea wore. It attached itself to Amber's ear. He handed the young princess one of the copper-colored stones and told her it was Vliganite. "If used with your thoughts properly this stone will do wonderful things on Crimson Satellite," he said.

"Honeybee will show you what to do with these," he said and handed the new worker a sand-pail and shovel. With a swirl of sand Drake disappeared.

Princess Andrea motioned for Bixbee to stop flying around them. "Amber has never been here before, and she might be afraid of you, Bixbee," she said.

"Of course I'm not afraid of the bees. I know nothing will really hurt me in Ziv. I actually thought Chucka Woodchuck was a teddy bear," the Princess of Golden Globe said. Her laugh set the bees to humming as they worked.

Honeybee flew through the swarm of wasps and settled on Amber's golden jump suit. "Welcome Your Highness. Your eyes look just like the sage that grows in the gardens on Crimson Satellite. You must be very wise," Honeybee said.

"Thank you Honeybee. I'm too little to be wise, but I do like to think about things before I do them," Amber said.

"The honeybees have finished drawing the straight lines to the pods," Honeybee said.

Princess Amber flew over to the end of one of the lines. She filled her pail with sand tapped it down firmly and turned it over. She made sure it was in the exact spot a new casa was to be built, then flew over to where Bryanna was constructing Andrea's palatial casa.

As Andrea had directed, the wasps formed honeycomb walls around the pile of sand Bryanna was sitting on. They worked in pairs. One wasp flew to the fields. She searched for woody plants to make the paper. When she flew back to the casa, the other wasp left for the orchard. When the wasps had finished one layer, Bryanna sprang up and flew around the circular walls. Andrea shone her piece of Vliganite on them, and they grew into a beehive-shaped casa.

The Princess Royal then touched her Vliganite earring and watched as the sand and paper on the walls melded into the finest crystal. She made the entrance to her private apartments through the top of the casa and made sure she could fly in on her Queen Scallop shell. She kept the lower floor an open plan for her guest's entertainment.

The princess of all the worlds of Ziv was pleased to see all the building activity she had set in motion. She envisioned a marvelous recreation site where all the princesses could come for a holiday from their duties on their own zivoids.

Princess Andrea paused in her work to talk to Drake. "Yes, of course, you may use the palace. It's a fine idea to have a party for your princesses of the satellites," she said.

The Princess Royal floated her Queen scallop shell to where Amber was working. She already had twelve piles of sand in the exact spots Honeybee had pointed out to her. The worker bees were mixing wasp-made paper with the crimson sand.

Andrea then shone her Vliganite on the casas until they became bubbled glass in a beehive shape. They glowed in twelve different shades of light.

To Andrea's surprise, a sparrow flew in and dropped a pumpkin seed on a spot in the sand Amber had marked near her casa. Another sparrow came from Yellow Satellite and brought a beak full of marigold seeds. Soon a flock of sparrows was bringing seeds from all twelve zivoids for the twelve casas on Crimson Satellite.

Amber then flew to each of the gardens and touched the seeds with the Vliganite stone Drake had given her. The new gardens began to grow and were soon blooming in brilliant colors.

While Andrea floated around on her shell overseeing all the activities, she heard the princess of Golden Globe talking to a sparrow who lit on her shoulder.

"Thank you for telling me about the party Drake is planning for the Satellites, but that means I can't come because I'm from Golden Globe. Don't you think I should be invited? We're working very hard here," she said.

Immediately the princess royal of all the lands of Ziv buzzed Gabi's stone, which was on the band of her celliPhone watch. "There is a change of plans. Everyone is to be invited to a really grand ball for all the princesses of all the Land of Ziv. Make sure the elves have enough white organza for each of the princesses. Also have food brought in from Golden Globe for our party," she said.

"Please bring in more crawfish from Violet Orb to help serve the many guests who will be invited," Princess Andrea said to Ming when she answered her tone.

"We will need your Vligan fliers as singers for the extravaganza. Be sure they have enough places to perch," she said to Drake.

Andrea asked her adjutant of all the moons of Ziv to bring Bucci and the K-Katz from Orange Moon as the band to play for the dance to the Ziva. "Yes, Your Highness," Donald said and jumped on his red bike.

The Koa of all of Ziv decided not to tell the princesses of her plans until her own dancing dolls arrived at their casa with their coronation dresses. *It will be a wonderful surprise,* she thought. She was so busy she forgot to check on Bryanna and Amber.

Andrea floated over to see how Bryanna was doing. The newest princess had employed a host of carpenter ants. They were cutting a doorway into of the front entrance of her casa. The ants were making the double doors from the old wall. They coated them with resin from the fir trees and polished them to a shine.

Satisfied as to the work being done, Andrea called for her conch and flew back to the palace garden where she found Ming. "The princesses from all of the Zivoids will each need an escort to the gala from her own Zivoid. And I want Crockford to manage the other crayfish with the serving," she said to her adjutant.

Andrea pressed the stone on her watch band to call Donald. "May I suggest that Melody from Red Moon be the first princess to enter the grand ball room," she said.

"We want to invite special guests to applaud each princess," Andrea said to Gabi. She had found her in the stitching room at the castle in Midnight Orb.

"The snakes want to come, but are afraid the guests may step on them. We must have some of the elves. They've worked very hard on these dresses for the princesses," Gabi said.

A loud buzzing in her ear caught Andrea's undivided attention. *Whatever is Bryanna doing now,* she wondered. The princess called for her conch shell. Without taking time to check her video screens she ordered it to take her to Crimson Satellite. She stepped out of her conch beside the door of Casa Bryanna.

The princess-in-training flew by followed by a very large wasp. She was buzzing into Bryanna's earring.

"Stop it this instant," Andrea said.

The startled wasp flew on by then circled Bryanna again. She lit on the shoulder of Bryanna's flying suit.

Immediately Bryanna folded her gossamer wings and dropped to the sand beside the Princess. "Don't blame me. Queen Bee is upset because she is not invited to the party. But what party is she talking about?" Bryanna said.

"It was going to be a surprise. I guess Queen Bee heard it on the tzivine," the Princess of Ziv said.

Queen Bee flew away. She came back with dozens of her workers. They buzzed around both Andrea and Bryanna. Queen Bee curtsied in mid-air. "We demand equal rights, Your Highness. We have worked hard and want to see our own princess receive her tiara," she said.

"Tiara! Is it going to be a really big party?" Bryanna said.

"Yes. It will be a really big party. And Queen Bee will present your tiara. That is if she and her workers can keep quiet in the flower arrangements in the ballroom. All the princesses of all my zivoids will be there. Each will have an escort from her own Moon, Globe, Satellite or Orb," the Princess Royal answered.

Bryanna flew in circles around Andrea. "I want Bixbee for my escort. Will he have to wear a tie?" she said.

"It will match the crimson ribbons on your skirt," Andrea said. She was glad Queen Bee and the worker wasps were buzzing happily around Bryanna's casa.

When Bryanna was dressed for the party, she looked into a triple mirror in her bedroom. Her ankle length dress was of white organza. A crimson bow with two streamers held her waist. On the bow was a crimson rose of silk.

When Bryanna stepped outside the casa, Drake motioned her to a shimmering pearly conch, which was resting on a landing pad by the casa. When she sat down inside, it rose like a feather and bee-lined for the palace in Ziv.

Just then Princess Amber stepped from her changing rooms that were in the outer wall of her casa. She was wearing a full-skirted organza dress, with a golden bow tied with two streamers at her waist. On her wrist was a golden rose she had picked from her own garden.

Adjutant Donald was there to escort her to her coach. Bowing to her he held his hand to help her into her golden conch. Her smile told Princess Andrea, who was watching from the palace, she had chosen well when she picked a helper for Bryanna.

Andrea, Princess Royal, was in the long hall of the palace when the twelve princesses were ushered in. Nearly floating in her white organza dress, she fiddled with the white silk rose at her waist. Just as she had ordered, the organ in the computer room of the palace was sending music into the grand ball room. "Tum, tum, tiddley tea. Tea, tea, tiddley tum," was what Andrea heard.

Chippy Chipmunk from Golden Moon tested his mike. "Honored Guests. May I present Andrea, Koa of all the Lands of Ziv, and Nicky, General of Red Moon," he said.

A white dove flew down with Andrea's silver tiara. The various colored stones gleamed as the princess and the general walked arm in arm to the center of the ball room.

"Donald, Adjutant of the three Moons of Ziv with his princesses," Chippy said.

His silver sword at his side, Donald walked proudly into the ball room. He was followed by Princesses Melody, Lauren and Alexis. Each princess wore a gown of white organza trimmed with sash and flowers in the color of her own moon.

Melody with her red roses was escorted by Zander Salamander. Behind her came Lauren with orange blossoms on her ribbons. Fauna strode beside her. Ari, the Arctic dog, accompanied princess Alexis from Blue Moon.

"Gabi from the Globes of Ziv with her three princesses," Chippy said.

Gabi, her shoes already tapping to the music, walked to the center of the floor. Head held high Princess Amber walked in with Chucky Groundhog. Chucky's bow tie matched the princess's golden bow and streamers.

Trying to keep a straight face, Diana of Midnight Globe came in with Mookie the Leprechaun. Mookie had refused to wear anything so somber as the deep blue of Diana's sash. Instead he was in Irish green with black brogues. Accompanied by Bo who walked on his back legs was Nicole. Her sash matched the green bow worn by the mountain goat.

"Drake, adjutant of all the satellites of Ziv," Chippy said.

The buzz of insects flying around Princess Kadence almost drowned out the chattering of the monkey, Ernando, who accompanied her. He proudly showed everyone his yellow bow tie. Behind them fluttered Emma as Indira, the indigo butterfly from Indigo Satellite.

Princess Bryanna was accompanied by not only Bixby, her bumblebee planner from Crimson Satellite, but Queen Bee flew in with Bryanna's tiara as well.

Ming's quiet demeanor kept her girls still until their announcement. "Ming, Adjutant of all the Orbs of Ziv with her princesses," Chippy said.

The crowd hushed as she slippered into the ball room. Princess Karah, carrying a bunch of violets, walked softly beside her escorts. Herman, the hermit crab, clicked his pincers, while Crawford, the crawdad, scurried back and forth beside the slow moving crab.

Princess Leah, radiant in her white gown with its scarlet sash, came in with McGee Macaw on her shoulder. McGee flapped his wings just once to keep his balance.

The last princesses to join the happy throng were Princess Jessica who came in her plastic bubble as an aqua angel fish and Caileigh who was an aqua Adelie penguin.

In the next Ziv second the Vliganite singers from the various satellites flew in. "Tum, tum, tiddley tee. Tee, tee, tiddley tum," they sang.

From a far corner the Bucci and the K-Katz struck up their band. Notes from a sedate Ziva dance filled the room. General Nicky led Princess Andrea onto the dance floor. They were soon surrounded by the many guests from all the Lands of Ziv. All were eager to dance to the Ziva.

"May I have this dance?" a boy said behind Princess Andrea. Drake held out a tiny golden cup of chilled peppermint tea.

The princess royal still had the taste of peppermint tea on her lips when she found herself back home in her own room. "I had a wonderful time on Crimson Satellite. Will it soon be time for me to visit Aqua Orb? Cousin Jessica told me how much fun she and Cousin Caileigh have there," she said to her pink-and-white teddy bear who was sitting on her dresser.

Love, Grandma Schoe

Andrea Swims in Aqua Orb

SLIPPING OUT OF BED ANDREA pulled on an aqua colored warm-up suit. She walked barefoot out of her room and quietly crept out to the porch to watch the full moon, as it rose over the pond Grandpa had built in the back yard.

Already the full moon was rising in a darkening evening sky. Later tonight it would be high overhead. Andrea stepped onto the lawn and twizzled and twizzled in its mysterious glow. She felt more alive than ever before.

A bit dizzy from twirling around she sank to the grass. Her fingers traced the shape of a cat stitched on the front of her aqua tracksuit.

"Meow," said the cat and jumped onto her lap. Her coat was white with orange and black patches. A black shape came out of the shadows. It rubbed its soft fur against Andrea's cheek and sat beside her.

"Hi Pix! Hi Sundri! Why are you here? You should be on my Orange Moon having a party," Andrea said.

"We've been invited to the biggest party in the land of Ziv," said Pix. She rubbed her cheek along Andrea's arm.

"We wouldn't miss it for a thing," Sundri said and standing on her back feet twirled around once.

Andrea turned toward the sound of crickets chirping down by the pond. The full moon was reflected in the pond, but instead of golden it was watery.

Her adjutant of all of the Orbs of Ziv appeared by the pond. Looking ethereal in a blue-green gown tied with a violet sash she reached into the pond, and cupping her hands under the moon reflected there, lifted it before the Princess Andrea.

"I am Ming, Adjutant of all Three Orbs of the Land of Eau de Phyn. Prepare for your journey to Aqua Orb!" Ming said.

Sundri leapt into the bubble and disappeared. "Toodles!" said Pix and leapt into the floating orb right behind Sundri. Andrea felt herself following them into a watery world. She floated into a bubble that was just bigger than a tennis ball.

The young princess took a breath. Water filled her mouth and swept out of gills on the side of her head. Her tracksuit had become aqua-colored bumpy skin. Her eyes, set just above her gills, looked to both sides.

An aqua angel fish swam into a bubble beside her. "Hi! I'm Jessica. This is how I move around when I'm out of the water," she said. Her mouth moved against the side of the bubble as she talked.

Andrea was sure she couldn't hear what the fish was saying but she knew anyway. The princess of all of Ziv bounced up and down in her bubble.

"I remember you! You were the aqua sunfish at my gala. You were floating around in a plastic bubble just like this," she said.

"Well it gets hard and soft as we want it to. You're an angel fish now and can swim out of the bubble whenever you choose," Jessica said to her princess.

"The bubble is for when we want to be out of the water then," Andrea said.

"Yes, of course, it is. Come on. I want to show you the home cousin Caileigh and I have in this wonderful watery world of Aqua Orb," Jessica answered.

Andrea floated out of her bubble. With her teeth she caught one end of a cord that Jessica held in her mouth and carefully held the seaweed as she swam.

Jessica tugged on the other end. "I can't be losing you down here. We've dozens and dozens of family who look exactly like us," she said.

The body of the princess royal felt very flat. She tried to move what felt like her feet and found that her toes had become a fluffy tail fin. When she wriggled her right arm it moved the delicate fin that stretched below her tail fins. Her left arm was a fin that floated gracefully in the water over her back.

It was weird to have her feet move back and forth. *They should move up and down like swim fins,* she thought.

"You're a fish not a dolphin. We can try dolphin later if you like. It's fun to shape-shift here in Aqua Orb," Jessica said she read Andrea's her mind.

Andrea sent a thought to princess Jessica. "Aren't you afraid of getting stuck here? I know I would be," Andrea said.

Jessica began a dive as she talked. "Never! This is Ziv remember! I just say 'Ziva, Quiva, Liva,' to come here, and I reverse it when I want to go home," she said.

"Peachy-keen! I thought rainbows would be scarce down here," the princess royal of all the Lands of Ziv said.

"Of course not," the princess of Aqua Orb said. She swam into the edge of a school of angelfish.

They were all swimming in the same direction, and Andrea was soon surrounded by a myriad of creatures exactly like herself. She felt as if she had lost her identity. She had been absorbed by togetherness and was grateful for the cord that held her to Jessica.

A very pretty angelfish swam up to Jessica. Her mouth was moving as if she were talking, but Andrea realized that it was just the way she was breathing. Still her thoughts penetrated the dense fog that had become Andrea's mind.

"Hi! Who do you have here?" she said.

"This angel fish is Andrea, Princess of all the Lands of the Eau de Phyn. She is our guest," Jessica said.

The whole school of fish changed direction. They surrounded Andrea just as if they could pick each other out from the rest of the school.

"Welcome!" said a large angel fish. Her greeting was mouthed by dozens and dozens of little fish voices. All were doing the wave. Andrea waved her delicate fins to everyone, as she and Jessica swam away.

Andrea forgot to watch were she was going. She bumped into a fish about the size of a teacup. Bright orange with three white stripes he backed away from her toward a bed of sea anemones.

"Watch it, Princess. I could have been a shark for all you know," the fish said. He darted around her while Andrea read the thoughts he sent her.

Jessica turned toward them. "Cut out the clowning, Ernie! You know nothing here would harm our princess," she said.

"Good thing she's not a clown fish. I'm looking for a new anemone bed," Ernie said. He darted to the nearest multi- colored sea anemone and began his dance. Gently he touched the animal's tentacles with each part of his body.

Princess Andrea watched in amazement. "Won't he get stung?" she said.

"No. His skin is coated with mucus. The anemone's sting keeps Ernie safe from predators. It's a win-win situation for both of them. When parasites attack the anemones, Ernie picks them off. I learned that in school in Outland," Jessica said.

Andrea swam very carefully to avoid getting caught in the lance-shaped leaves. She noticed that the dark green leaves grew in a rosette shape around their base root.

Another angel fish swam up. "Catch me!" she said and darted into a clump of waving fern. Andrea tried to find her new friend among the ferns. When they swam through an underwater forest of stems, Jessica was right behind her.

"What's up there? It looks like a thick mat," Andrea said to her cousin.

"You'll be surprised. I think we have guests," Jessica said.

A gray shape swam up to the angel fish. Propelled by a paddle-like tail he moved very slowly. Andrea noticed walrus like bristles on his mouth and the white patch on his wrinkled chest.

"Good morning, Mr. Manatee. "Enjoying a lily-pad breakfast in the upper air?" Jessica said.

The big animal spoke very slowly. "Aliens. Don't go up there! It's dangerous," he said.

Another manatee swam up through the long stems followed by her small pup. "I've never seen such creatures in our water home. There are two of them, and they have long legs and a long tail. One looks like the shadows on the bottom of the water. The other is like patches of sunlight in the dark shadows," she said.

"They just have to be Sundri and Pix! They are cats from my Orange Moon," Andrea said.

"Aliens. Come to take our food. Best stay away," Mrs. Manatee said to her pup. She led him in the direction of a different lily pad for lunch.

Andrea surfaced beside the lily pad where the aliens were said to be. Pix and Sundri were touching noses with a cat she had never seen before.

As the two princesses watched from the water the cats put their heads together. It seemed they were deep in a serious conversation.

Excited Pix and Sundri twitched their tails. They looked at each other and nodded to the ginger colored cat beside them.

"I've heard of these Rex cats with their short hair. This one has very long legs and tail with no hair on her ears at all," Jessica said from inside her bubble.

Andrea looked into the cat's bright eyes. They looked like drops of water set in her narrow face. The young princess blinked in the sunlight. When she looked again the ginger colored cat had disappeared.

In her excitement Andrea jumped up and down in the water. The slight splash she made on the lily pad attracted Pix' attention.

"I want to talk to those cats. How can I make them hear me?" Andrea said to Jessica, as they swam around the edge of the pad of dark green leaves.

Jessica paused for a minute. "You'll have to swim out of your bubble and leap onto the lily pad I think. Just make sure you change into your person-self when you land. It looks as if that calico might make short work of a flying angel-fish," she said.

Both cats stared at Andrea as she landed. They sat down and watched as her legs stopped swishing back and forth. When she pulled her arm down from over her back it tingled. Her aqua tracksuit soon became warm and dry.

"We have to talk," she said.

Andrea was bowled over by the two cats who leapt from the lily pad into her arms. They rubbed themselves all over her face. "Princess! We thought we had lost you! We were sure you'd never make the party," Pix said.

"Where is the party? Am I invited?" Jessica said as she landed and became her princess self.

"Sure thing! It wouldn't be a party without you. Your invitation should arrive any Ziv minute. The flying fish were rerouted past a thunderstorm," Pix said.

"Everyone is coming. Mrs. Butterball from Golden Globe is already there, and Stasia from Orange Moon is floating around on her purple cushion. Stasia is one cool cat. She is getting everything organized for The Rex," Sundri said.

"I've never met a Rex before, but she's the greatest. She knows so much about everything," said Pix.

"Her eyes! They're so different from ours. They look like misty blue pools," Sundri said. Her golden eyes opened wide as she talked.

Sundri and Pix looked at each other. "Should we tell her?" the cats said to each other.

Andrea, princess of all the Orbs of the Land of Eau de Phyn, clapped her hands. "Now. Right now!" she said.

"She's a Qu," said Pix.

"She's from Quziv," said Sundri.

"Quziv is the next world," Pix said. She waved her tail.

"It's The Rex's party," Sundri said to the princesses. She sat down, licked her paws, and washed her face.

The ginger colored cat reappeared and sauntered over to where Pix and Sundri sat. The long slender cat turned and looked Andrea in the eyes. She stretched out to her full length on the lily pad.

"I'm Ginger Snap co-ruler with my brother Kabir of Star System Qu. You have to find your own way to Quziv, Princess," she said.

With one twitch of Ginger Snap's very long tail all three cats disappeared. Andrea shook her head. She blinked her eyes and blinked again.

Jessica bounced up and down on the lily pad. "Who are Mrs. Butterball and Stasia? How come they are already at the party?" she said.

The princess of all of Ziv hesitated for a moment. "Stasia is a cat from Orange Moon. Cats seem to know about a different world. Mrs. Butterball is a chipmunk from Golden Globe. I don't know why she would be there already, and I have to find my own way," Andrea said.

"I think maybe it's because she knows she is a chipmunk and not someone else," Jessica said slowly.

"Are you saying that because I am Princess of Ziv I don't know who Andrea is?" the young princess said and stared into the watery depths.

A very large snout poked out of the water. Mr. Manatee took a big bite of the lily pad. "Someone called Caileigh sent a message from the other side. 'Long time. Princess Jessica has been missed,'" Mr. Manatee said and chewed thoughtfully on the bite of pad.

Andrea sat upright. Her eyes opened wide. "Other side! Does he mean the other world?" she said.

"Of course not we're close to Big Island. Cousin Caileigh is an Adelie penguin who lives on the other side of the island," Jessica said.

"I remember her. She danced with me at the gala on Crimson Satellite. She was the only one in a tuxedo," Andrea said and laughed.

Jessica stood up and walked to the edge of the lily pad. "Can you swim? I mean without being a fish," she said.

"Dogpaddle," Andrea said. She dove into the water behind the already swimming princess of Aqua Orb. She came up spitting out a mouthful of water.

Turning onto her back she rested on the water for a minute to catch her breath. The dome of Aqua Orb was a perfect mirror image of the water below. They were close to the rocky island Jessica had told her was home to some unusual plants and animals. Andrea turned over in the water and dogpaddled furiously to the shore. She lay face down on the sand for a few minutes before climbing onto the rocks.

Andrea looked up and down the beach. There was nobody anywhere in sight. She picked up a handful of aqua colored sand, and let it drift through her fingers.

Am I going to have to cross this island all by myself, she wondered. The princess wriggled her bare toes in the sand.

A lone seabird flew low over Andrea. "Fear! Fear!" he said.

He's right. I am afraid, but I must be brave. I have to find out who I really am inside of myself or I can't go to the party, Andrea thought. Taking a deep breath she began to climb the rocks by the beach.

When she reached the first ledge, Andrea put her hand on a sheer rock face to lean against it. Her hand brushed against the squiggly body of an insect which was about two inches long. "Yuck!" Andrea said and wiped her hand on her tracksuit.

The insect was crawling out of a crack in the rock face leg- side up. About twenty legs stuck out of one side of the insect's body. Both body and legs of the creature were the sickly pale shade of one living in the dark.

"Watch it! You nearly squashed me," it said.

"I thought the princess of Ziv would have at least twenty legs instead of the four you look to have," a voice said from near her feet.

Andrea moved her two legs as fast as she could away from the sheer rock face. She bumped into the bare twisted trunk of a lone tree. The gray waving branches at the top looked like the top of a carrot. Suddenly one branch swooped down and wrapped itself around the startled princess. When it straightened up, Andrea was hanging far above the rocky ground. She started to cry.

"Stop that! Your tears are salty. They will ruin my gorgeous skin. Who are you anyway? We've never had a 'two-legs' here before," the tree said.

The princess royal of Aqua Orb brushed her tears away. "I am a girl named Andrea, and I think you're horrid," she said.

"Well stop scuffing your roots on the rock. I've barely room to wriggle my way down through it to reach water," the tree said and shook the branch holding her.

Andrea looked around for something to help her get down. A soft squiggly thing was sliding over the bare rock toward the tree. The creature looked like a pink brain cactus.

"Hold on! I'm coming," the creature said.

Still frightened the young princess looked for its mouth. She could see none though the creature twisted and turned as it moved. The creature stopped at the root of the tree.

"I think you should let the girl down," she said.

"Why? She doesn't belong here," the tree said and shook it's top again.

The pink squiggly thing tipped on one side and looked up to the waving branches of the tree.

"She'll be sick. You don't want that sticky mess around your roots," she said the tree.

The top leaned over and set Andrea on the ground. "No! Never! Off with you! Or I'll pick you up again," the tree said.

Happy to be set free Andrea ran away from the twisted tree. She hoped Jessica would be at the edge of the water she could see at the far side of the rocky island.

Andrea sat down on a smooth rock to rest. The sea looked calm, but no penguins dotted the rocky shore. She put her head in her hands and wondered what to do next. A soft squishy sound made her jump.

"Hello brave girl. You did well back there," the pink creature said.

"I'm not really. I was really scared, and I couldn't have gotten down without your help. Thank you," Andrea said.

The creature slid closer to Andrea. "You knew that if you had called your adjutants they would have been there in a Ziv thought," she said.

Andrea shook her head. "Yes, but I'm not really a princess, or I wouldn't be so scared," she said.

The pink squiggly creature pulled herself up to her full height. "Remember what your cousin Diana told you before you went to Midnight Globe. Your grandma is a queen in Ziv, and you are a princess," she said.

"Our grandmothers are always Queens of Ziv, so I guess we're always princesses," Andrea said very softly.

At that moment an aqua colored penguin pulled itself out of the water onto the rocky ledge. "Thanks for your help, but I must get to Caileigh before she dives again," Andrea said.

The princess watched carefully where she stepped as she walked to the shore. When she looked up again Caileigh was gone.

What Andrea had thought was an aqua colored rock stood up. Hoping it was Jessica she began to run. When she tripped over a stick that poked up in front of her, she landed flat on her stomach.

"Ouch," she said and stared at the strange looking stick.

The stick pulled itself over to her. "Sorry Princess. I didn't see you coming," he said.

Andrea looked into the two eyes of a creature that was about two feet long, but to her surprise was only about as big around as her wrist. From button nose to stubby tail its rough hair looked like brown bark.

It moved over the rocks by making a loop in its back like an inch worm. First, it slid its front part forward. Next when it pulled its backmost feet to its foremost feet, the creature's back raised up.

Andrea sat up and stared at the little animal. "Why do you walk that way?" she said.

"Because it's fun. Wanna try it? You could be me if you wanted to," he said.

"No thank you. It was nice meeting you, but Jessica and I have to get to a party," Andrea said. She couldn't believe she was talking to a walking stick.

"Party," the creature said. His back half nearly tripped on his front half as he raced beside the princess. He and Andrea slid down to the edge of the rock jutting over the water. When they stopped they were just above Jessica.

The stick-like creature stood on his back end and looked at the princess of Aqua Orb. "May I come?" he said.

"We'll send someone for you, Howard," Jessica said. She grabbed Andrea's hand and helped her down onto the ledge.

Caileigh Penguin surfaced and pulled herself onto the rock beside them. "Bye, bye," she said and dove into the deep water again.

"Be a penguin!" Jessica said and dove into the water after Caileigh. Andrea took a deep breath and dove into the water behind the Princesses of Aqua Orb.

Andrea plunged down through the cold water for about as long as she could hold her breath. Suddenly she was being pulled up into a hole she thought must be under Big Island.

Her small body twisted and turned as it went through a slippery tunnel. Sensing the surface just ahead of her she swam fast and leapt out of the water onto her white tummy. Using her tummy for a toboggan she slid across the wet rock of a huge cavern.

Beside her a dazzling waterfall splashed the rocks, as it fell into a deep pool with the sound of thunder. The other side of the cavern was too dark for her to see anything.

"Wow! Wasn't that some ride!" a voice beside her said.

Andrea turned to see a bark-colored penguin sliding all over the slippery rocks on his belly. The creature's bright brown eyes stared into hers.

"Howard? You're supposed to be a stick not a penguin. Did you follow us?" Andrea said and looked for Jessica. The aqua angel fish was nowhere in sight.

"Sure thing Princess. I knew if you could do it I could do it. After all this is Ziv," Howard said and tried to stand up. To Andrea's amazement his front half had short flippers.

"Somehow I don't think we're in Ziv now. It doesn't feel right. We're not quite penguins but we're not ourselves either," the princess said.

Howard flopped down beside Andrea. "So where are we? And where is the party?" he said.

A ginger colored cat, with very long legs and tail, strode out of the blackness. "Welcome, Princess of all the Lands of Ziv. Welcome to you as well, Howard the Stick. You are in the Cavern of Peaceful Dreams. Beyond this is Quziv," she said.

Andrea stood up on her flat penguin-feet. "Thank you. Should I say, 'Your Highness' or do you have another title?" she said.

"At this time I choose to be merely a Rex from Outland. You may call me Ginger Snap. I am an alien, and when an alien essence blends with a human soul the entity chooses a life form that suits his or her new self. That is why I'm a Rex cat. I like it this way," the cat said and stretched out to her full length.

Howard stood up and shuffled over to the cat. "May I ask where the party is and how do I get there?" he said.

The Rex sat down and stroked her short whiskers. "You're a party crasher or you wouldn't be here. Just walk through the darkness to the light you see away over there. You will be welcomed," she said.

Andrea took a step to follow Howard, but the Rex stopped her. "You were brought this way to prepare you for your place at the party. You will no longer be Princess of Ziv only. When you walk through that door you and each of your entire court will be a future princess of Quziv. That is if one of you is chosen."

Andrea shuffled her feet. "Didn't you notice that I'm almost a penguin? I'm an aqua penguin instead of a black-and-white one," she said.

"Most of the guests at the party will be aliens. The princesses of Ziv who will be there might be frightened by their appearance, so they will be in costume as well," the long-legged cat said.

Andrea giggled. "I get it. I'm already in costume and so are Jessica and Caileigh," she said.

"Jessica has decided to be an angelfish. She is floating around in her bubble now. Her cousin Caileigh is already there," Ginger Snap said. Her words faded as she disappeared into the darkness.

In her penguin body, Andrea shuffled slowly towards the light at the far side of the cavern. She wondered if she could possibly be chosen Princess of Quziv. *Even if I am chosen am I worthy,* she thought as she looked down as her penguin feet. In taking her eyes from the light she got turned around.

In the near darkness she fell into a pool of water that was fed by the cascading falls. A shape loomed up in front of her and in the dim light she saw a gigantic star fish. Fear, more terrifying than she had ever felt, crept over her. Her body began to shrink. The strange creature waved one of his long arms toward her, and she felt his eye on its tip staring at her.

Sure she was about to be sucked into his huge stomach she cried out. "I am Andrea," she said, but she could say no more. As the terrifying creature shriveled, the light in the distance became a five-point star leading her from the dark cavern to the Rex's Quziv party.

Andrea walked from the darkness into a light-filled party room. She was still blinking her eyes when Sundri and Pix pounced on her.

"Princess! Great costume but I'd know you anywhere!" Pix said.

Sundri rubbed against the aqua penguin that was Andrea. "I've been watching over you from the shadows. Now it's time to party," she said and disappeared into the crowd of creatures from all the Zivoids of the Land of Be Alive.

A smiling girl, whose blue-green gown brushed her scarlet slippers, held a tiny cup of chilled tea for Andrea to take a sip. "To your health, Princess," Ming said.

M-m-m mint, Andrea thought. She rubbed her flipper over the golden dragon on the side of the cup.

A tiny figure on a golden key stuck to the golden dragon. In a Quziv moment Princess Diana was standing beside Andrea. "Some costume, Cousin! I'd never have known you," she said and in her navy-and-pink tutu twizzled into the crowd.

Princess Lauren from Orange Moon stopped. She looked at the strange color of the penguin. "What's with the aqua penguin bit, Cousin? One look into your eyes and I knew it was you," she said.

A boy, dressed as a general with a row of medals on his khaki jacket, tapped Andrea on the shoulder. "May I have this dance, Sis," he said.

"I'm very glad to see you Nick, but we'll have to do the Shuffle," Andrea said and laughed. Taking her brother's arm with her flipper she shuffled with him from the party room to the stadium.

Standing guard at the entrance were Donald and Drake. Both adjutants bowed to Andrea and Nick as they passed.

The guests were chattering about the princess to be chosen as Princess Elect of the Lands of Quziv. Each of the many princesses, both from Ziv and aliens from Quziv, hoped it would be she.

Gabi, her adjutant of all the globes of Ziv, shuffled with Andrea to their seats. Gabi's gold bracelets jangled on her black arms, and gold hoops dangled from her ears.

"The program is about to start," Gabi said, as she sat down beside her princess.

Andrea, who was still a very short penguin, stood quietly watching to see who would be chosen. *I am just one of many princesses here. There is no reason I should be chosen,* she thought.

A sleek black panther appeared beside Andrea. It touched its nose to hers and crouched down. "You are the chosen one. Slide onto my back and I will carry you to the throne," she said. The panther with Andrea on her back leapt into the air. She landed on a dais in the center of the stadium.

The awkward aqua penguin that had been Andrea was changed. She was now standing tall and straight in a gown of royal purple. A diadem set with coral and pearls adorned her dark- brown hair.

The Rex Cats came forward. "I am Kabir co-regent with Ginger Snap of the Star System Qu. We declare you now and forever Princess Elect of all the Lands of Quziv. You have earned it. Your next assignment, however, will be in Ziva. Your guide will be the Meme just as the ancients had," the larger of the two cats said and fastened a red cord around her neck.

"She who can rule herself can rule the world," Ginger Snap said beside him. They bowed to the princess, to the crowd, and disappeared.

All twelve princesses of Ziv rushed from their seats to greet her. They were followed by a crowd of creatures from the worlds of Ziv. Chippy from Golden Globe climbed over everyone. He held his microphone in front of Andrea. "How are you feeling right now?" he said.

Andrea burst into tears. "I may be a princess, but I'm still a young girl. I love everyone here but I want to go back to my home in Outland. Liva, Quiva, Ziva," she said quietly and waved goodbye to all her princesses and the crowd of alien princesses.

The next thing she knew she was back at Grandma and Grandpa's home in Outland. The full moon was shining in her bedroom window. *It sort of looks watery tonight,* she thought as she went to sleep.

Love, Grandma Schoe

Printed in the United States
By Bookmasters